Sale 7/6

2/6

Memoirs of a New Man

Memoirs of a New Man

A NOVEL BY

WILLIAM COOPER

LONDON

MACMILLAN

MELBOURNE · TORONTO

1966

MACMILLAN AND COMPANY LIMITED
Little Essex Street London WC 2
also Bombay Calcutta Madras Melbourne

THE MACMILLAN COMPANY OF CANADA LIMITED
70 Bond Street Toronto 2

ST MARTIN'S PRESS INC
175 Fifth Avenue New York NY 10010

PRINTED IN GREAT BRITAIN

Contents

PART THREE

Part One

A*

CHAPTER ONE

Meet the Family

The 4.45 from Paddington got into Oxford punctually as usual. While I made for the station exit I didn't look among the crowd for any other dons I knew, all returning from a day's business in London, because I was hoping to find my eighteen-year-old daughter, Rosalind, waiting for me with the car outside. It was a beastly dark cold night and I somehow felt sure she'd be there. I was very fond of her.

I emerged into the station yard, which was peculiarly raw and icy — we were just in the New Year — and a gust of sleet sprayed my spectacle lenses.

'Jack!' I heard my name called.

It was Roz. I was happy. I waited for some taxis to bear away the other dons, all returning from a day's business in London, and then I crossed to the line of parked cars.

Rosalind swung open the door for me and I got in. Before the light went off I noticed she was wearing a new jacket, made of black leather. 'Oh?' I said.

'Do you like it?' She turned the ignition key.

'I think it looks very In.' (The year was 1962.)

'I thought *you*'d like it,' she said, not above buttering up her father. She paused. 'Alice is a bit doubtful . . .'

She started the engine. Alice is her mother's name. She mimicked Alice's over-accentuated drawl. '*Dar*ling, are you *sure* it's quite *you*? . . .'

Disloyally to Alice, whom I had loved dearly for half a lifetime, I laughed. Then I said:

'I might only have *my* doubts if I thought it signified you're going to do a ton on the back of somebody's motor-bike.'

It was one of those remarks, diagnosed nowadays as symptoms of age/youth tension, that I could never resist making — and which Roz in return usually stone-walled. This time she said:

'Actually it would be too long for riding on the back of a motor-bike in. It's seven-eighths.'

I was always delighted by the fractional designation of women's coat-lengths.

'What would be the right length for riding on the back of a motor-bike in?' I asked. 'Seven-elevenths? Eight-thirteenths? . . .'

Silence. A smiling stone-wall.

We were waiting at the traffic lights at the corner of Worcester Street. Tiny flakes of drizzly snow were accumulating on the windscreen. I looked at Roz while she watched for the lights to change. She was a pretty girl. I suppose most fathers think their daughters are pretty. She had large, blue-grey eyes and a firm, smiling mouth. Since she left school six months ago she had done up her hair, which was darkish and fine-textured, in a ring-doughnut on top of her head. Alice and I thought the style was possibly more appropriate to a Zulu lady.

The car moved forward. I suddenly had a frightening idea. My speech about doing a ton on the back of somebody's motor-bike was merely meant to provoke, so far as I knew when I made it — it had no reference to reality.

Or *had* it a reference to reality? That was the frightening thought. It suddenly occurred to me that she actually might have done a hundred miles an hour. On the back of a motor-bike ridden by a young man called Michael Bowen.

In the previous autumn I had been out to California, taking Rosalind with me. I had several aims in view. One, the reason for taking Rosalind, was to fix up for her to go to Stanford University in the autumn of the present year.

Two, the official reason for the trip, was to give a short series of seminars at Berkeley. And three, the unofficial reason, was to have a look at Bowen, who was doing research at Berkeley, and see what I thought of him personally as a prospective Fellow of Clarendon. He was an Australian who had never worked in England.

Roz had met Bowen and they had been out together a few times. She called him Mike. He owned a high-powered motor-cycle on which he scorched up and down the precipitously winding roads behind the Berkeley campus.

We stopped at the Carfax traffic lights. Roz wiped the inside of the windscreen with the palm of her glove. Her smile had melted away. She merely looked alert as a driver — she drove very well I may say.

I supposed I should not gain anything but disquiet from questioning her about Bowen. The evening before we left Berkeley he had asked my permission to take her down to Oakland, to the quayside restaurant called The Sea Wolf, famed as having been a haunt of Jack London. He assured me it was respectable. He needn't have. It always piqued me to think of Jack London Square being prettily laid out with grass and flower-beds and ornamental trees, and the ships tied up to the wharf having been converted into expensive restaurants. Talk about *The Call of The Wild!* The only thing Jack London would have recognised now was the railroad across the back of the square, where huge snorting locomotives still trundled freight cars at night to the market. The rest was *The Call of The Chic!*

I asked Bowen if he had read any Jack London. To my surprise he said he had. I was won. I said Roz could go with him. And then I asked how they were going to get there. He was wearing his black leather jacket. I ought to have known.

Sitting beside Roz in the car now, I cowered at the thought of it. The experience of cowering at the thought of one's offspring travelling too fast — I was not worried about their getting a ticket for it — was, I concluded, one of the con-

comitants of present-day parental love. Then I made myself
cower still more by thinking they had probably gone into
some of the dives on Broadway before speeding home. Even
though it's one of my tenets of belief that an Australian can
always hold his liquor, I couldn't bear to think about it
any more. I opened up conversation again. I said:

'I saw Stanley Forbes in the train.' Stanley was the President of Clarendon — he was Lord Forbes.

Roz said lightly: 'It *is* a commuters' special, isn't it?'

'Stanley was talking about Michael Bowen,' I said. 'Have
you heard from him recently?'

'From Mike? Yes. I had a letter last week.'

'How is he?'

'He's getting a bit anxious over not hearing from you
about the Fellowship.'

'God damn it! Is there any one of these young men, even
the best of them, who doesn't claim to be anxious about
what he's going to do next?'

'I should relax, if I were you,' said Roz.

I was reacting with more emotion than the occasion might
have been thought to warrant because, although I regarded
it as a foregone conclusion that the College would elect
Bowen, we had to go through the performance of hearing
claims for a rival candidate, an Oxford man, who also was
pretty good. That was what Stanley Forbes had come into
my compartment to discuss with me.

I said: 'Oh, all right, then . . .'

Roz explained. 'He's anxious because Berkeley are trying
to make him say he'll stay another year there.'

'That's what I meant,' I said. 'He's so good that he's safe,
whatever happens. He must know that.'

'I think he does know that.' Roz smiled to herself. 'Perhaps anxious wasn't the right word. Not the right word for
what he is all the time.' She thought it over. 'I think there's
something restless about him.'

'Ah, I don't doubt that!' I laughed, and embarked on
one of my favourite generalised observations. 'Theoreticians

are the gypsies of the scientific world. They're not tied to some huge machine or some elaborate piece of equipment. As soon as they hear of an experiment that excites them, they just pick up their beds and walk there, do their calculations — for just as long as it jointly interests them and the people who're doing the experiments — and then . . . off again.'

'*You* don't do that.'

I felt like saying 'That's not because I wouldn't like to!' But actually I said:

'I'm not that sort of theoretician. I started out as an ordinary practical metallurgist, and slowly turned myself by the sweat of my brow into a theoretician. I didn't spring fully-armed from Heisenberg's head, the way these boys do.'

'Also Mike hasn't got a wife and children,' Rosalind said, 'yet.'

We stopped outside our house, which was one of an early-nineteenth-century terrace built straight up from the pavement. It looked pleasing in a domestic way, with nicely disposed and proportioned sash-windows and a pretty fanlight over the front door. The door was painted a golden ochrous colour. Alice had mixed the paint herself, going to great lengths to find a shade that would not look hideously distorted at night by sodium vapour street-lamps.

As she switched off the engine, Rosalind said: 'Alice has got a stinking cold and has gone to bed. I'm going to cook the dinner.' She laughed. 'I'm going to do spaghetti with a new kind of sauce.'

It was too late to say I would dine in college. As we got out of the car into the icy sleet, I said: 'I bet you wish that jacket were *one* and seven-eighths.' And then I said: 'How much did you pay for it?'

'Never mind. I paid for it myself.'

'Yourself? What with?'

'Money.'

'Where from?'

'I won it.'

'How?' I said How? but I knew.

In a falsely light tone, Rosalind said:

'Oh, on a dog.'

I picked my brief-case off the back seat and stumped into the house. I was saying to myself, furiously: 'That's her mother's example!'

I have already said that I loved Alice dearly. Our marriage had been the success of our lives. But Alice's addiction to betting on horses was something that had irritated me without perceptible diminution for nearly thirty years. And now Roz was starting — on dogs. *Dogs!* Horse-racing sounded to me corrupt enough; dog-racing corrupt beyond belief. Though why, when I was no gambler at all, I should get so heated by the comparison, you may well ask.

I opened the front door, and was greeted —

'Yikes! . . . It's *you!* I didn't know you were going to come before I went to bed.'

My son George's small daughter, Julia, was living with us. I bent down and embraced her lavishly. If most fathers think their daughters are pretty, I guess all of them think their granddaughters are adorable.

'I'm afraid I let her stay up,' said Rosalind, who had come in behind me. 'Come on, Julie, time for bed.'

'I've been watching Fun Fare,' Julia said to me.

'How was it?' I asked, taking off my overcoat.

'Smashing.'

'Yikes!' I said. (I had once been very puzzled by the use of Yikes! as an exclamation. It struck me as peculiarly unnatural, compared with Oh! and Ah! and suchlike. I had been puzzled till I saw it written in balloons issuing from the mouths of characters in Julia's comics. All was then clear: it was another unnerving example of the power of the written word to become the spoken word.)

'Fred Earnshaw did a new trick,' Julia went on. 'He had this sort of thing like a table, and Dorothy Leggett came in, and *she* said —'

Roz interrupted: 'Come on, Julie. That's enough.'

Julia looked at me appealingly. She had liquid grey eyes
and flaxen hair flopping over her brows. 'I was just telling
him . . .'

I told her I had better go up and see Alice.

'She's got a cold. She says it's a stinking cold. Why does
she say it's stinking? . . .'

Rosalind took her away. She was surprisingly good at
handling her. I went up to Alice's room.

There was a faint lily-of-the-valleyish smell, which came
from the scent Alice used. The room was warm, and lit from
a lamp beside the bed. Alice was sitting up with a book in
one hand and a tumbler in the other. As I got nearer I
noticed the lily-of-the-valleyish smell was spiked by the scent
of old malt.

'Don't get my *cold*, darling! . . .'

'Too late.'

I sat down in an armchair. Alice drank some of her
whisky.

'Roz'll be bringing *you* one, in a *moment* . . .' Her
drawl, with its over-emphasis on stressed words, was a relic
of her aristocratic upbringing. It was half-meant to be
amusing now. 'This has got hot *water* in it, anyway. It *isn't*
criminal to put water in this whisky if it's *medicine*, is it?
I mean, it *isn't*, is it, darling?'

I lay back in the chair. Alice had made the room comfortable as well as attractive visually. The colours were
maize and white and a sort of silvery fawn. (There was no
gilt: she had a rule — '*No* gilt in the bedroom, dear.') She
was wearing a pretty blue bed-jacket, and I thought . . .
oh well, we'd been married getting on for thirty years and I
thought she looked beautiful.

Wait! I can explain it. Bone structure. That was the
explanation. Bone structure. No man in his senses can
think a woman looks as beautiful at fifty-something as she
did at twenty-something, even Garbo. But if some beauty
is to remain, some relic, it may lie in the lightness and the
contours of the bone beneath the complexion.

Alice's forehead was broad and light, her eyebrows nearly straight, her eyes a sparkling hazel. Her cold, I thought, had brought an additional sparkle to her eyes, as it had also brought a reddish tinge to her thin shapely nostrils.

'Tell me what you think of Roz's leather coat before she comes in,' she said.

'The coat's all right. But I deplore the way she got it.'

'*I* didn't tell her to put anything on the creature. I only sent her down to the *grocer's*. But you know what *he* is . . .'

'On a dog, of all things! I suppose one's just got to get used to one's children choosing the lowest when they see it. Julia's enthralled by the commercials on I.T.V.' I sat up. 'I wish Roz'd bring that drink.'

Alice stretched out her arm with the glass. 'You look as if you'd had a wearing day. Was the Power Board awful?'

I began: 'Not entirely —' The telephone rang. Alice answered it.

'That was Joan,' she said, when the conversation ended. Joan was another don's wife: a difference between them, as such, was that Joan was extremely rich. She was also extremely anxious to climb. 'She just rang me,' Alice said, 'to tell me her Rothko's come.'

'Rothko. Pooh, soft-edged stuff!' It was meant to sound as if I thought soft-edged was effeminate compared with hard-edged. 'I don't know how far she thinks that's going to take her.'

'I don't know how you can say that,' said Alice. 'Even if anyone says Rothko's not *In* for London any more, I can tell you he's still In for Oxford. People will come *miles* to see it. It will take Joan *quite* a long way.'

I burst into laughter.

Alice changed her tune. 'Anyway, darling, even *you* agreed that Rothkos look terribly nice in public places, like airport *lounges* . . .' Her eyes sparkled as she quoted our favourite Rothko press-review: 'Colour that brings you to your *knees* . . .'

'Perhaps when Joan's got hers installed, she'll find herself calling her sitting-room the lounge. And when she has parties none of us will be able to stand up.'

Alice said: 'Joan's sitting-room looks jolly dee, I can tell you, with or without her Rothko.'

I was checked. Alice did consulting—for money—in interior decoration, and Joan was one of her clients. It was a subject for argument whether Joan consulted her because she was a talented decorator or because she was a Lady.

The door opened and Roz came in carrying a drink for me and one for herself. Mine, I could see, was straight. Hers, I could also see, was not as dilute as it would have been if I'd made it for her. The shadow of her Zulu topknot bobbed up and down on the ceiling as she walked across the room.

'Sorry I've been so long. I've been fighting Julie.' She looked at us. 'What are you both laughing at?'

I said: 'Joan.'

Roz settled herself in another chair: 'Joan's got a lot of dough.'

I said: 'It sounds as if one trip to the U.S.A. has gone to your head, my girl.'

Roz's eyes flashed. 'Well, Joan's in a position to laugh at *us*, isn't she?'

I said: 'If the rich think they're in a position to laugh at the poor, so much the worse for *them*!'

Roz shrugged her shoulders calmly.

I put my nose into my glass and sniffed the whisky. When I glanced up I saw Alice give me a smile.

After a few moments' quietness, Alice said: 'Tell us about your day in London! You don't seem in terribly high *spirits* . . .'

'It wasn't a high-spirit-making day.' I paused. 'I spent most of the afternoon with Bill. There's going to be a row in the N.P.B.' (The letters stood for National Power Board.) 'The balloon's due to go up any moment now.'

'How *agitating* for you, darling. Will Bill Taylor be involved?'

'Involved's putting it mildly!' Bill Taylor was Deputy Chairman of the Board — we were old friends.

'What's it going to be about?' said Roz.

I glanced at her. She was looking at me over the top of her glass. She was quite clever as well as pretty. I said:

'Are you really interested to know?'

'Of course I am. We always are.' She looked at Alice. 'You know we always are.' Her cheeks had gone pinker. 'If you can tell us, tell us!'

Although I always enquired first if they were interested to know, I always tried to tell them. I wanted them not to feel cut off from my work, which was to me the most important thing in my life. Although neither of them knew any science, I argued that when I talked to them about it the effect of their hearing the words float by, even if the words didn't mean much to them, would induce a sort of familiarity, a not-feeling-cut-offness.

On this occasion, though, the point I was going to arrive at would offer them no difficulties in comprehension, far from it.

I duly explained how, just over a couple of years ago, when Stanley Forbes was Chairman of the National Power Board, the Board had decided to go in for a costly metallurgical investigation of a particular metal which was not at that time used in industry, although quite a lot was known about it in the lab. It had some particularly useful properties at high temperatures — useful especially to the Nuclear Division, for which Bill Taylor was then board member. The decision had been pushed through largely by Bill, with Stanley Forbes's support.

I explained why everybody wanted to operate power-generating engines, be they reactors or boilers or anything else, at higher and higher temperatures — the efficiency of a heat-engine is higher the higher the working temperature. Ergo . . .

'I *think* I can understand that,' said Alice.

The metal in question had not been tried out in industry

because it was very difficult to work in the metallurgical sense. The costly investigation had been into finding out methods for working it. And methods *had* been found out . . .

I paused. And then delivered the point that everybody could comprehend.

'But they'd overlooked the elementary fact that when the metal cools down from the high temperatures to normal temperatures, it happens to be peculiarly susceptible to brittle fracture. So they can't use it after all.'

Alice said: 'How extraordinary!'

I said: 'It's not so much extraordinary as fantastic. Because it's so simple. They've spent millions on something — '

'How *many* millions?' Alice interrupted.

It was typical of her to pull me up with a factual question. Alice is a bit of a civil servant by nature. I said crossly:

'First of all, it's the order of magnitude that's important. Secondly, it'd be practically impossible to disentangle the cost of this particular thing. All sorts of people have been doing work on it — firms, such as Matthewson's for example, as well as the Power Board's research and development labs. I suppose it must have been two millions, but I may be wrong.' I paused. 'What's fantastic is that it should have been spent, ever.'

Alice asked me where I came into it.

Giving Roz a glance, I said sarcastically: 'They didn't need to bring in a high-powered academic to ask the 64,000-dollar question. Just an ordinary practical metallurgist would have done — a metallurgical lab-assistant . . .'

I expected Roz to point out that a metallurgical lab-assistant was exactly what I had started life as. But she was quiet, and I replied to Alice's question directly.

'At present I'm on the side-lines. But when the repercussions get going I shall have a job not to get drawn in. Through supporting Bill Taylor, if nothing else.' I drank some whisky. 'And you can take it from me there *will* be repercussions. Not half!' I thought about them. 'Unless we're lucky, they'll be really *something*.'

Alice murmured: 'Oh dear! . . .' She'd heard me talk often enough about Bill's enemies in the N.P.B.

I said: 'You can take it that a lot of people, outside the National Power Board as well as inside, are going to take a high line.' I glanced at Roz. 'Whether they've any right to is a different matter. As usual with any high line, most of the people taking it don't have any special right to it.' I paused. 'One of the highest of lines will be taken by non-technical people. You can imagine it — "This is what happens when we let the technical people have their heads." '

'Why not?' said Roz.

'The irony of the situation is that when "the technical people" originally put up their case for this investigation, it could only have been challenged by other technical people. The *non*-technical people, who'll talk so big now, could only have gone along, sheep-like, with those of the technical people who made the most noise.'

I grinned at them, and added: 'Therefore everybody ought to be technical.'

'Don't be beastly,' said Alice. 'You know it's too late for us to try.'

A new idea struck me. 'You know,' I said enthusiastically, 'I bet this sort of thing happens sometimes in Russia.'

'Why bring in Russia?' said Roz.

'Because I like comparative thought,' I said. 'Also, to be more frank, because I was imagining the more dramatic changes there'd be in Russia if this particular mistake had been made there. We should find Norman Standsfield' — the Power Board's present Chairman — 'turning up next as Secretary of the Turnip Marketing Board. And Bill Taylor as superintendent of a 15-megawatt power-station in East Fife.'

'But Bill *would* work his way up again, wouldn't he?' said Alice.

Roz said: 'Shall I freshen your drink?' I shook my head.

'Do you really think Norman and Bill will be penalised?'
Alice went on.

'Not in the Russian manner, if that's what you mean. As
the decision was made while Stanley Forbes was Chairman
of the Board, Norman Standsfield's in the clear, anyway.
And the Minister is not likely to demand the immediate
sacking of Bill Taylor — that's not the way the system
works.' I looked at my empty glass. 'From an external point
of view, in spite of the high line taken by all and sundry,
the Board can carry it off if they don't insist on doing anything foolish. Not that I can guarantee that they won't do
that . . .'

'Oh, darling,' said Alice reproachfully.

'It's from an internal point of view that ructions are
bound to ensue. Bound to, when every board member is
already engaged in private warfare with every other board
member . . .'

I looked at my empty glass again. And I said to Roz:

'I think I will have my drink freshened, after all.'

She took my glass from me and went out of the room.

I went and sat on the bed beside Alice.

'You really will get my cold,' she said.

Suddenly the telephone rang again. Alice answered it.
She handed me the receiver. 'It's for you. Bill Taylor.'

I took it from her. 'Here we go,' I said, before I held it
to my ear.

CHAPTER TWO

The Prima Donna Type?

The next day but one saw the three of us, Norman Stands-field, Bill Taylor and me, riding in Norman's car — his official car, that is — round Hyde Park Corner. At the National Power Board the balloon had gone up. But we were riding in Norman's car, which was a large black affair, beautifully polished all over, with lots of room at the back, calmly, quietly. We were on our way to a memorial service. The official solemnity of the occasion demanded a mora-torium on acrimonious discussion.

(Later in the day there was going to be a meeting at Power Centre of full-time board members. As a part-time board member I had been bidden by the Chairman to attend. I saw no limits to the acrimony ahead.)

It was a bright cold morning, and we were warm and comfortable inside the car, which was commodious in the style of an earlier period — the choice of Stanley Forbes when he was Chairman of the Board. I was always a bit surprised that when Norman moved from the Treasury to succeed Stanley he had not had it changed. It would have been in order for Norman to say he wanted a car that looked more in keeping with the times and with the job. And if Norman Standsfield actually had said that, his reputation for imperiousness and touchiness would have ensured his getting it double quick. He was that sort of man. Bill Taylor had the phrase to describe him —

Before I record Bill's phrase I must repeat that he was

an old friend, that in my eyes he was full of excellencies of every kind. (I shall be expatiating on them in a little while.) But if there was a cliché around, especially one which involved the misuse of a quasi-technical expression — e.g. 'fall-out', used to mean not dust from the skies that would kill us all, but an incidental *bonus* of some sort — Bill would unerringly come out with it as if he'd freshly minted it himself.

'Norman Standsfield is' — he looked me in the eye — 'The Prima Donna Type.'

'I see what you mean,' I said.

So, I must try and describe Norman myself.

Norman Standsfield was extremely tall. Tall-headed, rosy-cheeked, blue-eyed, with silvery grey hair clipped short. When he came into a room, looking distractedly busy, one got the impression that he was thin and stooping and slightly hunted. Yet if one happened to catch sight of him as he strode solitarily down a corridor, one was struck by the breadth of his shoulders and his triangular athletic outline. He was really strong. And he was always on the go. At that present moment, sitting in his car, sitting diagonally into his corner as if he were keeping himself physically apart from us, he was on the go sniffing a benzedrine inhaler twice in alternation up each nostril — and probably thinking about who was persecuting him or whom he intended to persecute.

Brilliantly clever, a man of vivid emotions, — even his enemies must have conceded that — Norman was in my private opinion commanded by a battery of neuroses whose variegation was unique. I was fascinated by him. Everybody said he hadn't got a friend in the world. . . . I felt that he ought to have. I felt that *I* should have liked to be friend.

My emotions were not shared by Bill Taylor.

The sunshine began to make the car warmer and I undid the buttons of my overcoat. The engine whirred smoothly. Somehow this car, with its sumptuous acres of faintly-smelling leather, and its slice of plate-glass which rose at the touch of a button to cut one off from the driver, always took me straight back to my boyhood. I saw three or four similar cars lined up outside a small house in one of the side-streets of a smoky Midlands town. It was the sort of car the people I came from hired for funerals. The only time in their lives when they achieved a ride in this secluded grandeur was when one of them was dead: while here was I. . . . In point of fact, though, I was riding in it this time to a memorial service.

The Memorial Service for Lord Matthewson. It was an official occasion, yet I was feeling personal regret. Old Alfred Matthewson, there'll never be another like him, I was thinking — not a specially original thought for someone on the way to a memorial service: but there *wouldn't* be another like him. The way the world was run nowadays didn't permit of a man's raising such a monument to himself as the firm of Matthewson's. And when I had started life as one of the firm's employees, it happened that Alfred Matthewson had done a lot for me.

The car suddenly jerked. 'What's happened *now*? . . .' I heard Norman say.

If I have given the impression that while riding in his big black car round Hyde Park Corner we were making any speed, it was an error. For a couple of hundred yards in any direction from where we were now sitting stationary, the ground was laid waste in the cause of building the underpass for traffic between Knightsbridge and Piccadilly Circus. The January sunshine lit up the most impressive earthworks in London — not to mention colossal white signs naming the executors of this benefaction, CUBITTS FITZPATRICK SHAND.

We were marooned in a conglomeration of halted traffic. I turned to look at Norman. I was sitting on a folding seat that came up from the floor. Norman was sitting at the back of the car, separated by an upholstered armrest about two feet wide from Bill Taylor.

'Nothing's happened now,' said Bill.

'This driver's a fool!' said Norman.

I switched round to make sure that the slice of plate-glass had cut us off from the driver completely.

Then I recalled that when Norman moved in from the Civil Service he had brought our present driver with him, on the grounds that the man was a better driver than he was likely to find in the National Power Board — thus ensuring that he gave offence, right from the start, to all the drivers in the transport pool of the N.P.B.

'Oh really?' I said to Norman. '*He* thinks *you* are absolutely wonderful. He once told me so.' I rubbed it in. 'Apparently you make a wonderful companion on a long trip.'

Immediately, Norman's cheeks went rosier. A brighter light glowed in his blue eyes.

I thought: Good gracious, what a man! He was abnormally moved by the driver's loyalty, but he hadn't bothered in the least about the man's overhearing his vituperative comment.

It was the old story, and I took care not to catch Bill Taylor's eye. What Norman Standsfield seemed to want, to demand above all else from the people around him, was loyalty, personal loyalty to himself. Yet the way he went about handling them made it all but impossible for them to *be* loyal to him.

It was only a matter of time, I thought, before Bill unerringly came out with 'The Führer Type'.

Meanwhile Norman was fussing with his watch, which he kept on a thin chain elegantly festooned across his waistcoat — he was dressed in the sort of black jacket and grey striped trousers that he had worn most of the time when he was a civil servant.

'I shall be furious if we're late.'

Bill looked at his wrist-watch. 'I would say our estimated time of arrival will be spot-on.'

Norman's expression changed into a charming smile, a really sunlit smile. He bowed to Bill. 'I'm sure you'll be shown to be *right*,' he said.

Bill glanced at me and I glanced at him.

It's here that I must expatiate on Bill's excellencies. You'll see why in a moment.

Bill was an engineer, an exceptionally good engineer. Ever since I'd first met him he'd fascinated me with what, for want of a better word, I called creativeness. (Incidentally, he too happened to have spent some years at Matthewson's, later than me.) Bill constantly generated ideas, for experiments, designs, projects, all of which bore his own idiosyncratic imprint. Brilliantly fresh ideas. That usually *worked.*

There'd been a pretty colossal example of Bill Taylor's creativeness in the last eighteen months. He had produced a brilliantly fresh idea for modifying the design of the Board's latest power-generating nuclear reactor, the consequence being that the cost of building it (still to generate the same amount of power) was cut by thirty per cent. The cost was getting on for twenty million pounds. That's what I, at least, mean by an idea that *works.*

This particular *coup* had then stirred Bill to get really interested in the N.P.B.'s policy for capital investment, with the inevitable consequence of his producing what I'd no doubt was a brilliantly fresh idea for modifying the Board's line in that field of its endeavour. I didn't understand the subject well enough to have any views myself. 'Adventurous as usual' was the view I heard from pundits in the field who were not actually inimical to Bill. He was still cogitating about it.

And now, I can surprise you — I'd taken him to see a show of sculpture in metal: he'd promptly borrowed a welding-set from one of the Board's engineering workshops and taken to sculpture in metal in his workshop at home — with startling results. He'd made some fantastic objects out of sheet iron that made one think of butterflies.

That's enough expatiation: I'm getting too far from explaining the glances we exchanged in the car, which depended on technology, not art. I wanted to say something about Bill as an engineer; and to remind you that as Deputy Chairman of the Board he had Norman as his Chairman — Norman, who, as you may have inferred from my saying he came in from the Treasury, was neither engineer nor scientist. Bill and I exchanged our glances when Norman told him he would be shown to be right, because we were thinking of many well-known occasions, where technical matters were being argued, when Norman Standsfield had told Bill that he would be shown to be *wrong*. With a smile the reverse of sunlit. In public.

I turned hastily away to discourage Bill from saying anything.

In the traffic there was a bus standing beside us. Several of the people in it glanced down at the car and then looked inside to see who the bigwigs were. When they saw we were nobody really recognisable, such as members of the Royal House or stars on television, they promptly glanced up again. One of them was a pretty woman of about thirty-five. Bill said:

'What about that, Jack?'

I swivelled round to him.

'If only we were sitting in that bus instead of here,' he said, 'we could be looking at her.' He paused. 'Even if we weren't able to do anything about it.'

Of course he might have meant, very properly I must say, that we should have been inhibited by the dignity of our position in society from making passes at the lady. Which might not have gone unheeded from Bill. He was a handsome little man, square-shouldered, very active and vigorous: he was square-faced, too, with a short military-looking haircut, a very small moustache, and large light-grey eyes. But I was afraid that was not what he meant.

I noticed Norman opening a small tin from which you shake through a hole those beastly little black bead-like lozenges that are supposed to clear your throat for public speaking.

Bill, like many very active vigorous men of his age, was

given to complaining nowadays about his decline in virility. He was a few years younger than me — he was just over fifty, against my fifty-five — and though I sympathised with his failing, as an old friend should, I wished he wouldn't mention it so often.

'Even if,' he repeated balefully, 'we were unable to do anything about it.'

Norman leaned forward and offered him the tin. 'Have one of these!'

'What are *these* supposed to be for?'

I burst into laughter. 'Not what you might think!'

'The trouble with you,' Bill said truculently, 'and with you too, Norman' — Norman's glance flicked away — 'is that you never have any fun. I don't have any fun, either.' He summed it up in more official language. 'No fun is had by any of us.'

We didn't reply and he glared at us accusingly. 'There's something wrong. I don't necessarily mean there's anything wrong physically.' He gave a comic thump on his chest. 'At least there isn't with me.'

True, I thought. His taut muscularity often made me feel self-conscious about my own shamblingness. (I took refuge in the fact that I was a head taller than him.)

'*Sober rectitude!* That's what it is. Just look at us! We're' — he looked at us — 'Pillars of the Establishment. And got down by sober rectitude.' His crisply resonant voice twanged on the word 'sober' with a Hampshire accent. 'Anyway, I don't know why I'm spending my time talking to you two chaps about it.' He now summed us up. 'You have a very poor appreciation of the problems.'

The car moved again. I must say my thoughts were more concerned with the problems they'd declared their moratorium on discussing; and incidentally I wondered at the capacity of officials for apparently dissociating themselves, while they took part in a public performance, from their major preoccupations.

We had got as far as Piccadilly. The smell of Norman's

throat lozenge became noticeable to me — and to Bill. He said:

'My God, Norman, the memorial oration isn't going to be made by you, is it?'

'I wasn't asked.' Norman smiled amusedly to himself. 'Perhaps it was thought that I lacked the appropriate expertise.'

'I would think,' said Bill, 'it was the necessary practice you were thought to lack. Men like Old Alfred Matthewson don't die every day.'

Norman said thoughtfully: 'I suppose I've had more practice in making memorial orations over the living.'

Over the living — over men he'd got rid of, had had sacked. Witticism though it was, it made me start. Bill took it in his stride, although in my opinion it ought to have made him start too.

Bill was Deputy Chairman: on several occasions, I knew, he'd been as good as promised the Chairmanship when Norman retired from it. (You'll notice I was careful to say as good as promised: I didn't say promised in writing.) Now Bill knew, as did everyone else, that Norman would not be in a position to ensure that he got the job. On the other hand Norman could go a long way, if he felt so disposed, to ensure that Bill didn't get it.

The Chairmanship carried a salary of over £10,000 a year, which in 1962 was pretty good for a near-Governmental job. (For Norman it was nothing like good enough in comparison with the salary of the man who'd been moved in from industry at £24,000 to reorganise the country's railway system — 'The British public can't help,' Norman cried, 'but think he's worth *two and a half Norman Standsfields!*')

But more important than the salary the Chairmanship carried was the power. The National Power Board was the country's largest nationalised industry — far too large, some people thought. Where power was concerned, the factor of two and a half was in Norman's favour. It was power at the heart of the technological world, at the heart of the country's economy. And Norman knew it.

Bill was going on. 'As a matter of fact a smashing oration could be made by me. This is true. I *knew* Old Matthewson. You, Norman, not being a bloody engineer, or even bloody technical, just couldn't have the knowledge of him. Oh yes, I know you were together on committees, playing Administrators' ping-pong across the conference table. But, my dear chap, you just couldn't have the sort of knowledge of him that I had, or that Jack here had.' His voice was loud. 'Alfred Matthewson was the last great engineering tycoon. The last, great, paternalistic, engineering tycoon! . . .'

As he uttered the word 'tycoon' his tone filled with awe and praise. As a matter of fact I'd heard him refer to himself as a tycoon, and I was certain Norman thought of himself as one.

Not surprisingly we were all silenced.

For my own part, I was silenced by a different emotion. It happened to be in a paternalistic way that Alfred Matthewson had done a lot for me. Matthewson's was a firm of heavy engineers and I'd started in the metallurgical lab when I was sixteen. The fact that I was being exceptionally bright in evening classes at the local Tech. had brought me to the Old man's notice; and he had promptly created a scholarship — in memory of his only son, who had been killed in a motor accident — so that I could take a full-time B.Sc. in metallurgy at Birmingham University. That act had liberated me into my subsequent career. I had gone on to Cambridge, to do a degree in physics, then a Ph.D., and then post-doctorate research.

I had never returned to Matthewson's. In 1947 the Old Man had asked me if I would like to be head of the firm's research and development. Alas! I'd had to tell him it was not the sort of thing I was looking for.

But I'd not allowed my connection with the firm to lapse. My job at the Ministry of Aircraft Production during the war had brought me into official dealings with Matthewson's; and in my university jobs since the war I'd tried to fit in the contracts Matthewson's offered me for extramural research.

'The last, great, paternalistic, engineering tycoon . . .'

Norman gave me a malicious look. He'd heard me express a different sentiment before now. Though tycoons might have a great name for giving away their gains, I'd always said it must be through greed that they'd gotten them. As for Free Enterprise, I could always stop the show, especially in the U.S.A., by remarking that under Free Enterprise the strong were free to get richer and the poor were free to go to the wall. And I meant it, too.

I heard Bill switch straight from romantic abandon to sarcasm. 'Who'd have thought I had a belief in Father-Figures?"

In the sweetest of tones Norman said:

'It's interesting to hear you speak in that way, Bill. Just considering it in general terms, I would say the organisation of engineering society — of which I'm only a member, though perhaps one of its leading members, by courtesy! — no longer lent itself to paternalism. Or the organisation of industrial society as a whole. Of course you may correct me on this one.'

Bill was going to say something, but Norman went on.

'I would think it was people like ourselves, Bill, whose work puts paternalism once and for all out of court.'

Bill thought. Norman's eyes suddenly gleamed: he looked at Bill with vivid intensity —

'I'm sure *my* Image is not that of a father-figure!'

'My dear chap, of course it isn't! Because fathers are creators. You, Norman, are a Bureaucrat.' The antithesis was plain. 'Nowadays I'm becoming a bureaucrat, too. It's years since I got the chance to create anything. As for Jack' — he gave me a less than flattering glance — 'I don't know how much of his research *he* does for himself, these days. . . . But Old Alfred Matthewson went on being creative right to the end!'

B

Earlier in the day he'd been telling me that for the last eighteen months the Old Man had been getting quite gaga, but at this moment it was the spirit of the speech that mattered. Bill was giving one of his periodic displays of not giving a damn for the Norman Standsfields.

I thought they were regrettable and ill-advised at any time. In the present state of the game, dotty.

I could understand the speech's genesis, though. Norman, as I've already remarked, was not an engineer, not a scientist, not a technological man at all — at Oxford he'd read Modern Greats (coming out top of his year, of course); and after that he'd been all his life in the Civil Service.

Bill Taylor thought Norman Standsfield's general attitude to the life and society of his times, despite his present job, was rooted in the part of the culture in which he'd been educated. When he was in really uninhibited form Bill declared that Norman

  (i) regretted the Industrial Revolution;
 (ii) was opposed to the Technological Culture; and
(iii) at the bottom of his heart not only disliked but *scorned* all Scientists and Engineers.

Bill was an engineer. By my lights he was a scientist as well: in a man like Bill I couldn't distinguish between the two. But in the present state of the game he was an engineer and scientist combined at whose door, that same day, Norman, a non-technological person, was going to lay an egregious technological lapse.

Abused as a bureaucrat, Norman suddenly drew back into his corner of the car, *pour mieux sauter* in retaliation, I thought. My first instinct was to try and find a composing remark, if such existed. But I knew it was only to me that it mattered. Their kind of head-banging exchange was part of the normal expression of their man-of-action temperaments. So I acted on my second instinct, which was to keep quiet.

To my surprise Norman restrained himself at the last

moment. Bill, having shown he didn't give a damn for the Norman Standsfields, and having got away with it, said nothing more.

After that we rode till nearly the end of the journey in silence. And what a silence! . . .

At last Norman said:

'We're nearly there. Has either of you got a sheet of writing paper?'

Bill felt in his pockets and I did the same in mine. We were both wearing soberly rectitudinous dark clothes. Bill as usual looked spruce: he had nothing in his pockets. I as usual was doing my best to look spruce, but had to accept Roz's opinion — not shared by Alice, I'm glad to say — that I didn't get very far with it: I was able to produce a largish notebook from one pocket and a small one from the other.

'Oh, the bigger one,' said Norman. 'May I tear a page out of it, Jack?'

I tore a page out for him, and with curiosity Bill and I watched him write on it:

SIR NORMAN STANDSFIELD K.C.B.
(NATIONAL POWER BOARD)
SIR WILLIAM TAYLOR K.B.E.
(NATIONAL POWER BOARD)
PROFESSOR J. T. CARTERET KT. F.R.S.
(UNIVERSITY OF OXFORD)

The car had drawn up at the church; the driver was opening the door of the car; we got out. Norman was holding the sheet of paper. 'What in God's name is he going to do with it?' I said to Bill under my breath.

The three of us went up the grey stone steps side by side. At the top there were two ushers handing out programmes of the memorial service. When we came to them Norman, holding out the sheet of paper in his hand, accelerated so as to precede us.

As one of the ushers handed a programme of the service for Lord Matthewson to Norman, Norman imperiously handed the list of our names to *him*! Bill and I looked at each other in astonishment.

'The prima donna type,' I said. 'He's making sure they'll get the billing right!'

Bill looked at me with contempt — which I suppose was not undeserved, in the circumstances.

'The trouble is,' he said savagely, 'we've got that prima donna singing in the wrong bloody opera!'

We went into the church.

CHAPTER THREE

A Spot of Verfremdungseffekt

The attenders at the memorial service were a superior lot, and Norman's action was explicable: the names of the most superior, those representing the most notable official bodies, would appear in *The Times* next morning. Norman was taking appropriate action to insure against mistakes in the list.

Inside the church we all nodded in this direction and that as we noticed men we knew — nodded in a reverent way. But when the service began I found it difficult to keep my thoughts on it. The presence of Bill and Norman beside me was a reminder of the moratorium which had only a few more hours to go. And anyway a church service, like a long symphony, always inclines my thoughts to wander.

Some of the things I thought about can very well come into this chapter I'm writing now. Bill Taylor would call it 'filling you in with the background, giving special attention' — in view of the background's never being as exciting as the foreground — 'to the highlights.'

Meditating about the ructions to come at the National Power Board sent me back to contemplating the N.P.B. *de novo*. The ructions were the upshot of an egregious technical lapse. But they were going to be inflamed with acrimony, and with enmity, which were already long in existence. I remarked to Alice that all the board members were engaged in private warfare with each other: that was less, much less, than the half of it. The National Power

Board was riven from top to bottom — and, come to that, from side to side — by factions.

All large organisations have their factions, especially at the top, where the jobs with the power are. The N.P.B. seemed to me more riven by factions than most organisations. In fact there were moments when the N.P.B. seemed to me more devoted to internal infighting than it was to providing the country with Power.

But impatience is no help in describing any state of affairs, let alone one which is difficult enough to describe at all without drastically over-simplifying it. I will try to be patient — and I shall drastically over-simplify.

The National Power Board had been formed by merging parts of three large industries which still remained more or less intact. They were called *Divisions*. (It was one of Bill's bitter gibes that whoever christened them Divisions was nearer to the truth than he dreamed.) One was called *Coal & Oil*; another *Nuclear*; and the third *Generation*. Each was represented on the Board itself by its own board member. It's obvious that each was designed, practically by the Deity, to be a massive, ready-made faction.

But the N.P.B. was riven again, especially in the upper reaches, by the swarming of three factions referring to each other as *The Administrators*, *The Scientists*, and *The Engineers*. It was a sort of polarisation on Two Cultures lines, with the technological culture in its wisdom seeing fit to present a divided front. Incidentally I assure you they really did refer not only to each other but to themselves by these titles. Any day of the week in the N.P.B. you could hear such remarks as:

'You can't reason with The Scientists.' (Administrator)
'We could get on better without The Administrators.' (Scientist)
'Of course I'm only an Engineer.' (Engineer)

The Administrators were what they said they were. Brought in to administer the Power Board, they were generally men from the non-technological part of society. A lot of them, like the present Chairman himself, had come in from the Civil Service.

The Scientists were men whose job was original scientific investigation — no matter if it was into things as diverse as fundamental physics, engineering design, or operational research. The bulk of them, it is true, worked in laboratories: they were in Research and Development — in the jargon of the trade, R. & D.

The Engineers were mainly concerned with day-to-day operations — running a mine, say; manufacturing atomic fuel elements; operating a power-generating system. It was largely the managerial element in their work which bound them together.

The existence of the three Divisions in the Board split it twice from top to bottom. As each Division had its quota of administrators, scientists and engineers, their faction-forming split it again twice from side to side.

There's the picture drastically over-simplified. If you now try to imagine it with the sharp lines smudged, the pattern shifting, a single personality showing up first in one place and then in another, you'll be moving a step nearer to the truth. But you still may not know what the factions were doing.

The N.P.B.'s factions were of course struggling, alone or in seeming alliance, for power, for position. But power and position to be used for what?

A very good question. It leads me back to where I started. Sometimes they were to be used, clearly in the eyes of the faction that got them, for enabling the Board more efficiently to do its job of providing the country with Power.

Other times they were not, definitely not. Other times the N.P.B. would have been enabled to do its job a damned sight more efficiently by cutting out its factional struggles — even the factions could have got on with their own jobs more efficiently. But no. . . . Once factions have come into existence, struggling with each other seems to become a way of life in itself. Like Montagues and Capulets, they feel obliged to engage each other on all occasions, whether there's anything to be gained or not.

I see I'm working myself up into a state about it, so it's time to change the subject. (I'll come back to it later.) I'll change to a minor subject which is more fun. Norman, Bill and I, all sitting there in the church in a row, all our names down on Norman's list in a row . . . all three of us were Knights. We'd all got our K.s.

My own name had Kt. after it and no Sir in front, let me explain in case you don't happen to know the protocol, because I'd only appeared a few days ago in the New Year Honours List as a Knight Bachelor and hadn't yet received the accolade. I had not yet gone through the ceremony which the scout who was employed to look after my room in College referred to as 'the dubbing' — invariably making me think first of the grease I used to smear on my football boots when I was a boy.

'Any news of the dubbing, sir?' he asked out of temporarily frustrated sychophancy. He was dying to call me Sir Jack, especially when discussing me, no doubt otherwise to my discredit, with his fellow scouts.

Everything was correct, as you might expect, on Norman's list: the Orders of Knighthood to which we had been called were correctly indicated. Some passage or other in the church service inexplicably stirred me to a flight of fancy in which I was explaining the Orders of Knighthood to an American. (In my experience Americans combined being unduly fascinated by such matters with being startlingly inhibited from comprehending them.)

'Well, you see, K.C.B. stands for Knight Commander of the Bath, and K.B.E. for Knight Commander of the British Empire. The Bath and The British Empire are two Orders of Knighthood, and The Bath takes precedence over The British Empire. It's like one going in to dinner in front of the other. The Bath goes in before the British Empire. You see?'

If the American asked what about me, I should have to

admit that Knights Bachelor came last. Everybody went in to dinner in front of us.

But perhaps the idea of us all going into dinner was not serious-minded enough for an American. Suppose I put it that for me to become a K.B.E. like Bill would be a move up the ladder. For Bill to become a K.C.B. like Norman would be a move up the ladder. And for Norman to become What? Like whom? . . . Why, a Lord! Like his predecessor as Chairman of the National Power Board, Stanley Forbes.

Incidentally I hope that our all having K.s won't lead any American to think he is at the beginning of a book about English Lords and Ladies. Or even, for that matter, about English ladies and gentlemen.

Lords and Ladies there can be no argument about. Norman, Bill and I could scarcely have been further from being noble by birth. If we had got our K.s *by* anything, I suppose one might say it was by effort. But that has a disagreeably immodest sound. So let me close for saying that we had got our K.s by virtue of the Honours System.

As for being in the ladies-and-gentlemen category, we were non-starters. The evidence of accent and school gave no help at all even to judges who were out to do their best for us. I have already disclosed that Bill spoke with a Hampshire twang, incorporating peculiarly degraded 'ow' sounds. Norman Standsfield had begun with a Cumberland accent, and I with a Birmingham accent: since then we had worked on them to the extent that they *normally* passed for non-regional — which means they passed for non-regional to people who weren't listening for them.

All three of us had been to grammar schools and not to boarding-schools. Norman had actually been to a grammar school. Bill and I had been to what in those days were called merely secondary schools, though they later moved up the scale of nomenclature and now more grandly styled themselves grammar schools — thus forcing us to a delicate choice when we filled up our entries under Educ. in *Who's Who*.

After school we had made our way to the university,

B*

Norman to Oxford, Bill to London, and I to Birmingham and then Cambridge — though I'd finished up anomalously at Oxford in the end.

Here we were, then: three lower-class boys who had moved up in the world, three men who might have been cited by sociologists to illustrate the high degree of mobility endemic to present-day society. Truly we were examples of a certain kind of mobility in society; but not the kind one might have assumed from reading the sociological feature-columns in the daily newspapers, which gave one to understand that the Education Acts of the last few decades had made it a pushover for a clever boy to climb up the social strata.

Norman, Bill and I had climbed all right — and hadn't stopped, either! — but it was in the part of society whose grades are determined by power in running the country, and certainly not in the part of society whose grades are determined by birth. In fact those two parts of society seemed to me distinctly different, and also to be becoming more, rather than less, separated from each other. (I except the Conservative Cabinet of the day, where running the country appeared to be a bonus on the regular perquisites of birth.)

As Norman Standsfield, Bill Taylor and I climbed the grades of 'power in running the country' society, we still found ourselves among men with similar social origins to our own. At the top of the Civil Service, for instance, the majority of the bosses, of whom Norman had been one, were grammar-school boys. It was rare for us to come across anyone from comparable grades of 'birth' society. The only Lords whom Norman and Bill regularly came across were either men such as Alfred Matthewson and Stanley Forbes, who were Lords through effort; or else Lords who actually came from the aristocracy but crossed our paths because they had decided — usually because they were younger sons — to compete in 'running the country' society. (My own case was only marginally different as a result of being mar-

ried to Alice, who came from the aristocracy, where 'came'
is a polite word for 'reneged'.)

That brings me to the end of my change of subject. Incidentally it occurs to me that you may be surprised to find
me favouring you, in the middle of telling a story, with
pages of extended comment about society, education, rank,
power and God knows what-all. I call it *my* Alienation
Effect. My idea is that there lurks in a lot of novel-readers
enough of the old Brechtian to approve being *verfremdet*
every now and then. (Let me assure anyone who fears I
may be going to make a thorough Brechtian job of it that I
don't intend, for example, to interleave the chapters of this
book with pull-out pages printed with the words of popular
songs.) In other words I really believe a lot of readers don't
mind being invited every now and then to sit back from
the story and think.

But what about readers who want to experience total
immersion in a book? Happily they're catered for still, by
the dear old *'avant-garde'* — please don't point out that
they've fallen about thirty years behind! — who still turn
out their streams-of-consciousness, Existentialist fluxes and
suchlike, all of which can be relied on not to trouble their
readers for an instant with invitations to sit back from it
all and think.

So much for that. Being in a more equable state, I can
finish writing down my meditations on the National Power
Board. I'd got as far as filling you in with the background:
now for the highlights.

Each of the factions had its leader. It goes without saying
that Norman Standsfield, the Chairman, was the doyen of
The Administrators.

Bill Taylor was the doyen of The Scientists. I have remarked that he was an engineer by training; all his inborn
tastes, and most of his gifts, had swerved him away from
the managerial side of engineering towards what I've called
original scientific investigation. (Remember that most of
the original investigation that the N.P.B., being a large

industry, went in for was in *applied* science.) Before he became Deputy Chairman, Bill had been the board member for the Nuclear Division, which was the Division that did the most research and development. Needless to say the bright boys in that Division's R. & D. scorned him as a research scientist. But they lined up behind him — he was wholeheartedly on their side: he *believed* in them.

And The Engineers. Their leader was Herbert Hobbs, the board member for Coal & Oil. Herbert Hobbs, fat, wily, crypto-Trades Union leader, given to crocodile tears and labyrinthine manoeuvres . . . universally known throughout C. & O. Division — and proud of it! — as Uncle Bert.

Bert Hobbs was Bill Taylor's arch-enemy.

'I don't *see* it,' said Bill, when I told him.

Bert Hobbs took his time. Bert Hobbs aimed at his target deviously. He was apparently under-educated. He was apparently humble. He hated Bill.

'I don't *see* it, Jack.'

I must say I felt inclined to ask him what on earth he thought those great big beautiful grey orbs of his were for.

On the Board itself there were two other men. One was the board member for Finance and Administration: like Norman he came from 'Whitehall', as the Scientists and Engineers paranoiacally called it, so he was a born member of The Administrators.

And Generation Division had its board member, an engineer. There's quite a lot to be said about him — I'll say it later.

I feel I've now said enough, what with background and highlights, to make it clear that in the N.P.B. any lapse, any blunder, any mistake was red meat to the factional maw.

As the lapse which had just come to light was made while Bill Taylor was Member for Nuclear Division — that being the Division which instigated the costly investigation — it was red meat for Generation Division and Coal & Oil Division. And as the investigation was a Scientists' project — Stanley Forbes, the then Chairman, was also the then leader of The Scientists — it was red meat for The Adminis-trators and the Engineers.

You can see why I was perturbed on Bill's behalf, and on the N.P.B.'s behalf too. Though I've written the story as if it amused me, the laughter was really on the wrong side of my face. So far as the National Power Board was concerned, I could have looked for it, unwieldy though it was, to be held together in adversity by everybody in it having a feel-ing for an organisation that was greater than the one to which he immediately belonged. Not so. Instead of being held together by *esprit de corps*, it was split in pieces by group-loyalties. I could understand it, I suppose; but that didn't stop me regretting it. After all, the N.P.B. was not totally unrepresentative of the world at large. There were times when, looking at factional struggles in the world at large, I concluded that group-loyalty is the enemy of progress in mankind.

As for Bill, I had a feeling that he was in for a lot of trouble, over a long stretch of time. This afternoon's meet-ing might produce head-on collisions, rows, shouts about resignation; but I didn't for a moment believe it would. When I came to tell Alice about it, she'd expect me to fore-cast logically what would happen and when. I couldn't do that. I might be able to report a few sharp, superficial bangs: but the repercussions that I'd told her were going to be *something*, though they'd definitely be starting, would as yet be rumbles well below the frequencies we could hear.

I jumped in my pew: the organ had started to play the closing hymn.

After the service the three of us walked to the Club for lunch. Norman's office had reserved a table and he went straight to the dining-room to see about it. Bill and I went to the lavatory.

Bill was momentarily preoccupied with Norman's having handed the usher a list of our names.

'I couldn't have done it,' he said.

'Oh.'

'When *I*'m Chairman, I shan't do things like that.'

'No.'

'I suppose you think I will.'

I realised that he'd turned his head and was looking up at me for an answer. I said: 'Not if you say you won't.'

We stepped across to the row of wash-basins. We began to wash our hands.

'The trouble with Norman,' said Bill, 'is that he's' — he hit on the word triumphantly — 'Insecure.'

I washed my hands with vigour.

'You wouldn't think he would be, but he is. What's the reason for it, Jack?' (The question was rhetorical.) 'I suppose that realising he was never going to get the top job of all in the Civil Service shook him to his fundament for ever.'

By the top job of all he meant one of the two Joint Secretaryships of the Treasury — the one which I personally thought was the less exciting of the two, being mainly a matter, so far as I could see, of running the Civil Service and the Honours System. Honorific beyond belief, of course, but not specially exciting. Its holder was Head of the Civil Service and might expect to become a Lord; but he didn't get the scope for plunging into running the country that the other Joint Secretary got, or even some of the Second and Third Secretaries.

All the same it was the top job; and the idea of Norman Standsfield's ever having it seemed to me nonsense. I thought Bill had got it all wrong.

'Perhaps,' I said.

'Don't sound so damned judicious!'

'Well,' I said, tugging vainly at one of those mechanical roller-towels which are supposed to dispense a fresh length to each new person, 'if you want to know what I really think, I can't believe Norman Standsfield was ever sufficiently unrealistic to think he was in line for it. Even granted that some of the men who get top jobs are more crashingly eccentric than people at large seem to imagine. Norman simply must have known that *he* was a bit too much of a good thing.'

Even as I said it I wanted to take it back. Nobody ever thinks he's too much of a good thing for the job he wants.

'You think he saw,' said Bill, 'the Red Light?'

I said: 'I don't know about that. But I'd have you a bet Norman saw he'd either got to stay where he was in the Civil Service or move up by moving out.'

'He'd reached,' said Bill, now tugging at his roller-towel, 'his Ceiling.'

'If you care to put it that way.' I noticed that his towel had dispensed him a fresh length immediately.

'So,' he said, drying his hands, 'Norman had the alternative of staying where he was, or moving up by moving into outer darkness.'

'Whether the N.P.B. is outer darkness is for you to say, Bill.'

I wasn't going to encourage him; but I admitted to myself that anyone round about the top of the Treasury usually gave the impression that he thought anywhere else, so far as being at the centre of running the country was concerned, was if not actually outer darkness at very most an area of diminished light.

As for Norman Standsfield, there had been long-standing rumours that the Treasury were looking for an opportunity to unload him elsewhere. The chairmanship of the Power Board fell vacant when Stanley Forbes was translated to Oxford, so the N.P.B. for better or worse got Norman. (Norman claimed that as a civil servant he'd always had a special interest in Power.)

'You can't pretend Norman doesn't regard us as outer darkness, Jack.' Bill straightened his tie. In the mirror I saw his expression. 'And at regular intervals he makes sure we know it.'

I was definitely not going to encourage him. 'Let's go,' I said.

The room on the ground floor in which we usually had a

glass of sherry was occupied by workmen doing alterations, so we went straight to the dining-room, where we found Norman standing beside the table reserved in our names. What names! Not that there weren't plenty more Knights in the same room. At the thought of it I couldn't help recalling one of my favourite snatches of overheard conversation: 'As me and another Knight was walking down Victoria Street. . . .'

Norman looked very tall, slightly stooping imperiously. He launched his opening remark with beautifully stylised fluency and sweetness.

'I can't imagine how a club like this can tolerate a head waiter — if that's what he calls himself — who's unctuous, insolent, *and* facetious.'

I glanced at him again, as it were in a double-take. With the afternoon's performance to come, he was at the top — there was no doubt about it — of his form.

Letter from the College of Heralds

Back to Oxford again by the 4.45.

You'll want to know straight away what had happened at the meeting.

The Chairman had isolated two questions to be answered immediately. The first, the major one, was: What do we do about the investigation now? The second, the minor, was: What do we tell the Press about it?

To the first question there was only one answer: We wind it up straight away! Thus had the Board unanimously decided.

To the second there had been two answers, as there always are to What do we tell the Press? — roughly speaking, the truth or not the truth. That decision had been postponed as too knotty to be settled on the spot.

On the whole the proceedings had been conducted on the plane of reason. There had been a fair number of acrimonious head-banging exchanges; but, as I'd expected, there had been no violent or abusive attacks on Bill Taylor. The repercussions that were to come showed no signs at all of being near the threshold of audibility. Perhaps they never would. Perhaps there'd never be any repercussions! . . .

I felt as if the skies had lightened. I took out of my brief-case the proofs of a text-book I'd written, and settled down to some hard work, some real work.

I was so absorbed that I don't know how long had passed — it must have been more than half the journey — when

I was interrupted by the sound of the door into the corridor opening and somebody coming in.

'Ah, there you are, Jack!' A friendly, mellow voice.

It was Stanley Forbes, of course.

I had seen him in the distance at the memorial service and again at the Club, so I might have guessed he'd be on the same train. He slipped into the empty middle seat beside me. I put down my proofs.

The first thing I must say about Stanley Forbes is that although he was about sixty-eight, he looked easily ten years younger; and that he was strikingly good-looking, chiefly because of his colouring. He was of medium height, strongly but not heavily built. His features were sufficiently regular to qualify him for being above average good-looking; but they were transformed into what, if he were a woman instead of a man, I could call beauty, by their colour. In fact his eyes actually were beautiful, and that's that. By the age of sixty-eight most men's irises have faded, but Forbes's remained a vivid periwinkle blue. His complexion was uniformly fine and pink; and his hair purely silver. His nose was the only thing against him — it was rather long and it distinctly turned up at the end.

Stanley Forbes's face always looked to me as if it were illumined by some inner radiance. And why not? He was a Lord: he was President of the most interesting college in Oxford: he was a scientist of international reputation. The inner radiance that floods a man's spirit at the top of a successful climb? Could be.

'I thought it would be useful to have a few words with you now,' he said, 'in case I don't get a chance to take you aside before the Fellowship election meeting.' His tone was amiable, intimate.

I glanced at him. I couldn't help liking him.

I think I ought to tell you that there were quite a lot of people who didn't like him, and in due course I will explain why. I was substantially in agreement with their case against him; yet I couldn't help being warmed by his manner, which was friendly, amiable, intimate and (in a non-pejorative sense) smooth.

'I take it you've made up your mind who you want,' he said.

'Yes,' I said. Michael Bowen was the man for me.

Forbes smiled. 'You usually have. You're pleasingly decisive.' At that he was probably thinking I was a pain in the neck, but he enhanced the compliment by sighting me gently along his upturned nose. His eyes looked very blue.

I said: 'I should be content with either of them, Stanley. But for my money, Bowen's the one. He's got edge, and flair — alpha quality for certain. And if he has luck he may turn out alpha plus.' I paused. 'But I should be content . . .'

It was the College's idea to elect a young Fellow in somewhere near my own line of research, so I felt it behoved me to be generous about any of the candidates they put up.

'I agree with you,' said Stanley.

If you think that meant when the Election Committee met, Lord Forbes, presiding over it, was going to express rousing, unequivocal support for M. J. Bowen over R. Mac-Robert, you are mistaken.

Stanley said: 'There's a good deal of support for Mac-Robert in the College. I suppose his being an Oxford man, who's always worked in Oxford — '

'But not much support on the Election Committee itself, so far as I know, is there?'

'I don't think so,' said Stanley. 'I suppose that will make it easier. He turned to me with a smile. 'I suppose it's my duty to spend the next few days on canvassing opinion, if only for the looks of it.'

I nodded my head ambiguously.

We were silent for a few moments. The train rattled on. I looked through the window, into the darkness of the countryside.

'I see I've disturbed your work,' he said.

'Not at all.'

He showed no signs of going. Actually I wondered why

he'd ever come, as we'd held the same conversation in the same train only two nights ago.

He said: 'I suppose you've been to a meeting at the Power Board since the Memorial Service.'

'Yes.' I guessed that he knew what the meeting had been about, and I wondered if he was hanging round now to try and find out what had happened.

He sighted me again along his upturned nose. 'You'd be surprised how far away my own Power Board days seem to me now, Jack.'

I must say I thought that was very nice, seeing that the meeting had been about a lapse made when *he* was Chairman.

'Yes, very far away,' he said.

I considered that he'd established that point. I looked forward to the happy day when I might have the knack, where my past mistakes were concerned, of looking upon myself in a previous job as somebody else.

Stanley said: 'What sort of a Chairman of the Board is Norman Standsfield making?'

'Oh, you know . . .' I wagged my head.

'I think he was a very bad appointment.'

I thought that was pretty nice, too, since I assumed that Stanley had been at least a party to the choice of Norman.

'Of course,' Stanley said, 'you're in the advantageous position of being only a part-time member.'

'If that's what it is — being on the side-lines all the time.'

'I've often wondered,' Stanley said, 'why you accepted it.'

I laughed and replied: 'Alice thought it would be good for me!'

Stanley turned his glowing pink face fully towards me.

'My dear Jack, I think it *is* good for you!'

He gave me his most intimate smile, and stood up to leave.

I settled down again to my proof-reading.

For the sake of the record, I should like to say that the answers I'd given him about myself were substantially true.

I had been asked just over a year ago if I would be a part-time member of the Board — nominally as a metallurgist, though I should no longer have called myself that, exactly: I had begun life as a metallurgist, but then I'd moved over to physics on the way to getting into the theory of metals. (Had I been asked to invent a name for my line now, I should have chosen some such title as Materials Design.)

Before that, while Stanley Forbes was Chairman, I had been a consultant to the Board. *Not* — let me establish my alibi! — on the subject of Stanley's and Bill's lapse. That was the investigation of a metal about which as much as needed to be known from an academic point of view was known already. What the Board consulted me about was what you might call 'future metals', in particular the combinations of metals and ceramics known as cermets.

I was truthful when I said Alice was responsible for my accepting. I was not as keen as all that because I had pretty well everything I wanted in Oxford. I'm called the Dr. Gurney's Professor of Natural Philosophy, and the Dr. Gurney's Chair happens to be a chair without a department, than which I can imagine nothing more satisfactory, after seven years of being the head of a department at Derby University, a department milling with undergraduates and grinding with administrative chores. The Dr. Gurney's Chair is a chair without a department, and, what's more, without a retiring age. Actually it's so anomalous that I don't see it being allowed to survive beyond my time — in fact I was surprised that it was allowed, in the light of the contribution to Natural Philosophy made by the previous incumbent, to get as far as me.

The previous incumbent of the chair was an ancient palaeontologist whose main occupation, so far as anyone could see, was sunbathing in the nude at Parson's Pleasure. Behind a low canvas wind-shield he was observed occasionally to be reading a copy of the *Journal of the Palaeontologists' Association*, or even examining a fossil through a magnifying-glass. His buttocks were said to look like old leather.

'You do better than *that*, darling,' said Alice when I happened to tell her about him. 'I mean, don't you? . . .'

Modesty apart, I considered that I did. I had a small lab, situated in the new Engineering Science building, where I worked with a few hand-picked post-graduate and post-doctorate students. I don't know whether it was being spurred by them or having some leisure for the first time in my life — perhaps it was both — but I seemed to have come into a fruitful phase of research again, at the age of fifty-five. Happy man!

I ought never to have told Alice about the lotus-eating palaeontologist. I'm sure the true source of her enthusiasm for my accepting part-time board membership of the N.P.B. was a desire to make certain of my being kept up to scratch. She rationalised it, which made it seem even funnier to me, though not to her. (One of the things about rationalising is that you simply have to do it humourlessly — any spark of laughter, and you're lost!)

'You *know* you'll *enjoy* it,' Alice had said, artfully appealing to the worse side of my nature to begin with.

I said I got enough certain enjoyment out of life already without gambling on comedy to be found at N.P.B. board meetings.

She tried another tack — the second, I had better warn you, of about fifteen tacks — which boiled down to the idea that as a part-time member I should have more weight to chuck about at Courtenay Bagpuize — the jewel in the Power Board's crown of research and development establishments, situated about fifteen miles outside Oxford.

But the fact of the matter was that I didn't really need much from Courtenay. I was interested in the materials side of their experimental programme, and sometimes they were willing to do experiments that I thought might produce exciting results. But my main need was for their computing service, and for those I paid my money like any other customer. And as a matter of fact, I was meaning to use the Courtenay computing service less rather than more — I meant to whittle down routine calculations and concentrate on a few crucial ones. Just as I had never been able to see why, because a mountain was there, you had to climb it, I had never been able to see why, because an I.B.M. 7090 was there, you had to think of calculations to do on it — unless you had been rash enough to tie up your capital in it. (Thus I display the fact that I'm like to be cast out of the company of decent men from Everest to Poughkeepsie.)

Alice said next: 'What about Bill Taylor?'

I said: 'What about Bill Taylor?'

'Won't you be able to do more for him?'

'You mean, to make sure he gets the chairmanship?' I looked at her. 'The short answer to that, my dear, is No.'

'But what about the *long* answer? . . .'

I thought about it for a moment. I am a great believer in *mana*, that is to say the influence of one's bodily presence. Everybody knows that if you want something you're more likely to get it if you're physically on the spot. Conversely, people are much happier about stopping you getting what you want if you're physically somewhere else. I said:

'If Norman Standsfield does feel inclined to do Bill down, he'll feel just a shade more uncomfortable about doing it if I'm around. But it wouldn't in the least stop him.'

'Well, I do think you ought to do all you can.' Which was generous of Alice, since Bill, as a man, was not her cup of tea.

I was prepared for Alice's fifteen arguments for keeping me from intellectual and moral decline as Dr. Gurney's Professor, but I was not prepared for the argument launched by Roz.

'I suppose,' she said, 'it will make it a bit more likely you'll get a Knighthood or something, won't it?'

Now I have to say that despite my apparent insouciance about generalities, I belong to a generation that's still pretty souciant when it comes to cases. It was all very well for me to talk lightly about K.s for other people. But it was quite a different matter for Roz to talk about my getting one.

'I shouldn't think so,' I said, meaning to end the conversation there.

'But don't you really? . . .'

Roz inherits, I'm afraid, some of her mother's nagging persistence.

'No, I don't.'

'I bet if somebody else did it, you'd say that was his reason.' Her cheeks went a little pinker and her eyes opened wider. She spoke with force, not even looking at Alice for support.

I had intimations that as time went on I was not going to find Roz easy to cope with. I hadn't found George, my son, easy to cope with either, but he was different from Roz. George had, in the language of the day, 'opted out' from my sort of cosmos — for his profession he'd taken up acting, of all things.

Roz, according to my intimations, meant to meet me on my own ground. I said to her:

'I might say it was his *reason*, but that wouldn't be conceding that I thought there was any *sense* in it.'

I enjoyed getting into this sort of debate with Roz. She took a moment to work out the meaning of the remark.

'I see,' she said.

I sought to promote her education. 'It's maddening that the word 'reason' has two uses. When someone gives a reason for doing something, it doesn't follow that it's reasonable. People's reasons for doing things often range from the baseless to the senseless.'

'You expect too much of people.'

I took a moment to work that out.

Then Alice carried on with what she deemed to be the good work. I could never make her see that the total argument for doing something was not the sum of the component arguments for doing it; in fact that if she produced

fifteen reasons, it was probably because she hadn't got one
really good one.

Part-time board membership would keep me, Alice argued
next, in touch. 'In touch' was a phrase everybody used
without specifying what it was that you had to be in touch
with. They used it in a pro sense; being in touch was most
desirable, I can tell you. Alice's friend Joan, for instance,
was always 'in touch' — she seemed to be directly plugged
in to the *Zeitgeist*.

In the end I gave in. I didn't need the job. (Incidentally,
I didn't get paid much for it.) I didn't specially want it.
But I accepted, almost for the hell of doing something for
the first time in my life because I didn't have to — you
might perhaps say it was the nearest I'd ever come to an
acte gratuit. And the nearest, let me tell you, I was ever
going to come.

When the recent New Year Honours List came out, Alice
and Roz naturally saw with their own eyes that they'd
always been right.

Now you understand my reply to Stanley Forbes: 'Alice
thought it would be good for me.'

The train stopped. Looking out into the darkness, I saw
that it was the usual stop beside the cemetery. (For the
benefit of elderly dons who learn railway time-tables off by
heart, I must say I know that the 4.45 from Paddington no
longer runs, let alone makes its usual unscheduled stop
beside the cemetery — though I realise that with Bradshaw
no longer published, alas!, they mayn't even care any more.)

Somebody coming along the corridor stopped at the door
of the compartment. It was Stanley Forbes again. He put
his head round the door.

'In two or three days time, will you drop in and have a
glass of sherry with me? By then I should have something
I shall want to chat with you about.'

'Of course.'

He went on down the corridor. In a minute or two the
train started again, and we drew into Oxford Station.

This time Alice met me with the car. 'It's such a horrible night,' she said; 'someone *had* to come and collect you.' Her cold was supposed to be better. 'What happened at the meeting?'

I told her.

'Oh,' she said. 'Then it wasn't so bad — I mean, each time there *isn't* a row means one occasion *less* when there might have been one, if you see what I mean. . .'

I laughed, and there was a pause. 'What's the news at home?' I said.

'There's a letter for you from the College of Heralds. According to the postmark you should have got it *days* ago . . .'

'What does it say?'

'I haven't opened it. I expect Garter'll want you to sign the *book*, and all *that*.' She was busy negotiating the Carfax.

I smiled and said nothing. I have to admit I was amused to see Alice's reaction to my being elevated to a rank that would have been several notches below her father's notice, that was in fact several notches below her own. I remarked, when saying earlier on that I had married someone who came from the aristocracy, that 'came' was a polite word for 'reneged'. I had a theory about Alice's so-called 'reneging'.

Certainly Alice, when first I met her, couldn't have looked more like a renegade from her class. She was in Berlin, and I met her there when I went over to the Technische Hochschule during my first Cambridge Long Vac. What was she doing there? Well, what I assumed she was doing there was being a member of the Communist Party.

It was the summer of 1933, four months after the Reichstag had gone up in flames and the Nazi Party got the opening they — and the Communists, too, for that matter — had been knowing would come up. Alice was not the only dissident youthful member of the English aristocracy to be around the place at the time, indulging his or her dissidence in the shape of political activity.

I was scarcely interested in politics at all. To tell the

truth, I was scarcely thinking about anything at that time outside quantum mechanics. You could have cited it as a typical example of a scientist's 'naïveté and inhumanity' that politics only came to my notice through the disappearance, from the complex of Technische Hochschule cum University cum Max Planck Institute, of its greatest figures. Planck himself had gone away in 1928: Einstein went the year I was there. Von Laue was the only major physicist left: Ewald, the theoretician, was still there. I deplored the situation passionately, of course. Yet I consoled myself that the atmosphere of greatness still lingered, greatness and rigour — one still couldn't get away, there, with what's called sloppy thinking.

And later on I consoled myself with the historical fact that it had fallen to me to realise that quantum mechanics gave some absolute values to constants needed in my calculations — sooner or later it was bound to fall to somebody, and in other circumstances it might have been somebody else.

So much for my admission of 'naïveté and inhumanity'. I believe they were only transient, for one thing. For another, the phrase, the accusation, was Alice's. There she was, beautiful and clever — her broad square brow was deliciously clear and her hazel eyes sparkled and dazzled — telling me I was a stinker. We fell in love, practically at first blow.

'So I'm naïf and inhuman!' I said. 'What the hell do you expect, when I've never thought about it? Tell me the problems and I'll get the right answers!'

Alice looked at me with a glance that was fierce and darting.

I wanted to marry her.

The upshot of our arguments was that we came to similar answers. It turned out that she was not a member of the Communist Party, though she says that for a time she was 'pretty near it', whatever that may mean. It didn't matter to me, in those days, one way or the other. What rapidly came to matter to me was that several of her rebellious upper-class friends turned Nazi — as, let it be remembered, did large numbers of German Communists. Alice never showed any signs of doing that.

I saw her as a renegade from her class, and that seemed to me perfectly reasonable — what a class to renege from! I remember snidely pointing out to her that she and her fellow-aristocrats were either joining the Communist Party or the National Socialist Party because they were looking for an authority their class couldn't give them. (I'm not so sure, now, that I was right.) And Alice accepted that she was a renegade from her class. She had all the reasons for being it that went straight home with me. And so they seemed enough for me — at the time.

They wouldn't seem enough for me now, I think. Nor, for that matter, would they for Alice. She reneged from her class thirty years ago, and she has mellowed a good deal since. We married and I have found out a lot more about her; and she has found out a lot more about herself.

We married in 1934. She was still in Berlin, and I have to admit that learning more quantum mechanics was not the sole reason for my spending a second Long Vac at the Technische Hochschule. I knew I was going to ask her to marry me. What I didn't know was that she would accept me. I was astonished by it. I should have been inclined to keep on asking her 'Do you really mean it?' if she hadn't got in first with the same question. First, second, and so on to last . . . That was when I first met Alice's nagging persistence.

We got married three weeks later.

And what conclusions have I come to in getting on for thirty years? What is my theory about her? I can put it simply — possibly too simply, but I'll risk that as a start. When she was young Alice sincerely hated her class, or at least hated some of the cardinal things about it. But more than she hated her class, she hated her father. All right — I'm willing to substitute love/hate, but that doesn't alter anything. Between Alice and her father there was a violent emotion, mutual, which made their getting-on with each other impossible. They simply had to cast each other off.

There was what a lot of people found an acceptable cause for the conflict. Alice was her father's first child, and her mother died in giving her birth. Her father was abandonedly in love with her mother and felt he had been robbed of her by his child. I can tell you a lot of people found that an acceptable cause for Alice's behaviour. And they claimed that it was strengthened by the child who had robbed Alice's father of her mother being a daughter, not a son who could inherit.

Alice's father got married again, to a woman who was exceptionally sweet-natured and who gave him an heir. But his feelings towards Alice never changed. It was a strange story, apparently the opposite of the one in all the fairy-stories: Alice found herself with a kind and loving step-mother and a cruel father.

Alice's father died about a year after Alice and I were married. He refused to meet me — as he refused to meet Alice, I didn't feel unduly discriminated against. Her step-mother thought he was beginning to come round to the extent of being willing to see our son George, who had just been born; but he died before that happened. Alice's half-brother inherited everything, of course, excepting a small sum of money which was left to George, a sum which George spent on going to the Royal Academy of Dramatic Art, of all places.

So there you have the story: the facts remain, the inter-pretation may change. Nominally Alice had reneged from her class; it was my private opinion that what she had reneged from was her father. She had married me — a pretty irrevocable step on the road of reneging. On the other hand she had not given up the right to be addressed as Lady Alice.

I was more than amused, then, to see Alice's reaction to my being elevated to a rank that would have been several notches below her father's notice. The higher the Lord the bigger the snob, is my general observation from life. The proposition that high Lords and Ladies are really too grand to care about titles is so much humbug. The higher they are the more, rather than the less, they think of titles. And the same goes for people who are very rich. The richer they are the more, rather than the less, they think of money!

My letter from the College of Heralds was waiting for me on a table just inside the front door. I opened it straight away, before we took off our overcoats — I held it so that Alice and I could read it together.

'You were right about them wanting me to go and sign the book.' I grinned. She was beginning to take off her coat.

'What happens when I go and do that?' I said.

'Oh, they'll want to know if you want to have a coat of arms. Or if you want them to find out if there's one in your family already.' I thought she was on home ground, whether she had reneged from it or not. 'You *know*,' she went on: 'They'll want to know if you want them to make a search through their records.'

'And that will cost how much?'

'Oh, I don't know how much it costs nowadays. I should think . . . some hundreds of pounds, darling.'

I glanced at her suddenly — 'You seem to know a lot about it. How come?'

Alice said: 'Oh, a cousin of Mummy's used to work for Garter. Actually a second cousin, once removed. He was terribly dim, but quite nice. Kind of *obliging*, you know . . .'

Before I had time to say anything else she began to help me out of my overcoat. 'Come on, darling, you must be dying for a drink.'

We went up to the sitting-room.

'Some Scotch,' I said. 'With a bit of ice in it.'

Alice gave it to me. She made a drink for herself. I was sitting on a sofa and she came and sat beside me. I kissed the side of her neck — and noticed the delightful lily-of-the-valleyish scent.

She handed the letter to me. She was waiting for me to say what I was going to do. I was surprised she didn't ask me.

'I hadn't thought about the College of Heralds operating as a business concern,' I said. 'What becomes of the profits, I wonder? Who owns it?'

'Are you going to help them to make a profit?'

'Certainly not.'

I drank some whisky. I was amused. I liked the idea of people paying for a coat of arms. I didn't intend to disburse a penny.

Alice drank some of her drink. Then she put her hand lightly on mine. We were quiet for a little while. I forgot that her reaction hadn't been quite what I might have expected.

The room seemed warm and cosy. It went across the front of the house and was smaller than it might have been because Alice had cut a bit off the back of it — 'One *does* want to get away from that eternal *L*-shape, doesn't one?' All the lampshades were white, so it had a radiant look. It had also a cluttered look. Alice was fond of furniture made of light-coloured woods, fruitwood, satinwood, maple, amboyna. (With it she had put curtains and covers in clear blues.) Over the fireplace there was a picture Alice had got on the cheap because its owner, and everyone else, was not quite sure it was a Gainsborough. (But we did have an authentic Klee.)

I looked down at Alice's hand — it was long-fingered. I had been expecting her to say: 'But *why* aren't you going to do it,' and so on. On and on. I said:

'I think the letter's rather fun.'

Alice said: 'Poor Cousin Bertie's dead, now . . .'

I said: 'I don't want a coat of arms. Nobody in my family's ever had one and I'm damned if I'll make a start. We've got our tradition, you know.'

'It's quite a good *name* . . .'

'What is?'

'Carteret . . . George the Third appointed a Carteret to be Governor of New Jersey.' She laughed. 'I think he was the *last* one before the Revolution, *actually*.'

I suddenly had a visual recollection — a signboard, CARTERET, beside the road on the way to Princeton. Followed by an even more vivid olefactory recollection of the New Jersey turnpike, like the highway in Dante's Inferno, raised above a plain covered with belching chemical factories — the smelliest road in the U.S.A. I said:

'In my opinion, our name is an illiterate's spelling of Cartwright — after our trade.'

'What would you do if you discovered you had got a coat of arms in your family?'

'I'm not going to discover it. I'm not going to part with some hundred of pounds, assuming we'd got it — or any other sum of money.'

She was silent. Suddenly, at last, I was suspicious.

'You don't mean to say,' I said, '*you*'re thinking of letting them make a search?'

Alice did not reply.

I shook her fingers.

She looked at me. Her eyes were darting with triumph and fun. 'I *have*. I mean, I *did* . . .'

'When?'

'Just after we were married.'

I was speechless.

'Of course I didn't pay all that money,' she said. 'I got Cousin Bertie just to do a little — '

'Look-see.' I couldn't resist introducing the term used by our chief security officer at the N.P.B. for the same kind of operation on a different kind of record.

Alice looked at me with surprise.

I said: 'Did they trace my family?'

'Well . . .' — she kept me waiting — 'not with Cousin Bertie's little . . .'

'Look-see.'

We stared at each other. I leaned towards her — and the door of the room burst open and in came Julia, wearing her dressing-gown and carrying the little soft toy cat she took to bed with her.

She surveyed us, her fair hair flopping, neatly combed, over her forehead, her large grey eyes wide open.

'You two do kiss a lot,' she said.

Alice and I glanced at each other. 'Well, fancy that!' I said.

Julia came and stood between us and Alice stroked her hair.

'You two kiss more than Daddy and Mummy.'

Alice and I glanced at each other again, this time differently. I put my arms round the child and hugged her.

Julia kissed each of us in turn.

'If I wake up in the night, can I come in and see you?'

'Of course.' It was the answer I gave every night.

She heard Roz coming up the stairs for her and went out of the room.

At first Alice and I did not speak. The reason Julia was living with us was that George was making a film in Hollywood and Katie, her mother, was doing a season at Stratford on Avon. George was due back in the spring, and Katie came over to Oxford most weekends. There was nothing going wrong. Or was there? . . . Julia used to come into our room once or twice a week.

I drank some more of my drink. Alice drank some of hers. My letter from Garter King-at-Arms had fallen on to the floor. Alice picked it up and handed it to me. I dropped it on the nearest table.

Alice said quietly: 'A cloud's gone in front of the sun, hasn't it?'

CHAPTER FIVE

The President in His Lodgings . . .

I got my summons to sherry with Stanley Forbes.

I presumed that the Fellowship election must be bringing the College up to the boil. When I was young, making my way from the depths of the metallurgical lab at Matthewson's to the plateau of Birmingham University and then to the heights of Cambridge, I had imagined the men who ran the affairs of the world, whom I then thought of as the Great Ones, conducted their operations with God-like temperacy. In Matthewson's we imagined Old Alfred creating the firm's policy in the manner of God the Father — not either of the Other Two, of course. And when I was first elected to a Fellowship of a Cambridge college in 1935, it really came very naturally to me to call the Master 'Master! . . .'

Even when seeing it, I had a job to reconcile myself to believing the *in*temperacy with which men of power often ran their affairs. Things were always coming up to the boil. God-like the Great Ones might be; but temperate, no. None of them. Even the most God-like in my experience, old Matthewson, had only to get going about his difficulties in creating the policy of the firm to start referring to his enemies as 'Snakes in the Grass' — thus showing the reverse, to my way of thinking, of temperacy.

Less, far less than I'd ever imagined, does temperacy go with action. So perhaps there was nothing surprising about intemperacy making its appearance when a college had got to choose between two candidates for a Fellowship.

I had better spend a few moments describing the college set-up. Clarendon was Oxford University's contemporary gesture towards Science. It was founded to educate scientists only, that is to say all the undergraduates were reading scientific subjects. Two were even reading engineering. (As it had been traditional for the Oxford School of Engineering to be spectacularly tiny, we were clearly doing well.)

It will be seen at once that Clarendon had a Cambridge counterpart. If I may put not too fine a literary point on it, reverting to the language of the engineering apprentices during my time at Matthewson's — and who could expect of them, in their social environment, too fine a literary point on anything? — Clarendon College was a Chinese copy of Churchill College.

Although the undergraduates of Clarendon were all scientists, the Fellows were not. The governing body had decided that although the undergraduates were destined to find their vocation in only one of The Two Cultures, they should be educated to have some conversance with the other. Among the Fellows, then, we had a sociologist, a political scientist, a philosopher, an Eng. Lit. man, and an Oxford novelist who came in to give the boys a course in Creative Writing.

According to my own lights, the college was, or could have been, an admirable institution, in fact the pattern for a whole university — come to that, for several whole universities. I may say that the science Fellows were very bright. They were mostly quite young. I, together with two or three others, was exceptional in being over forty, let alone over fifty. At our head was Stanley Forbes, getting on for seventy; but it wasn't his age that was his trouble.

On the evening in question Stanley had invited me to drop in at his Lodgings before we dined in Hall. The chiming clocks of Oxford were part-way through their diurnal performance of indicating in series that it was seven o'clock when I walked through the first quadrangle of the college. Up to now there were two quads completed, a third nearly completed, and a fourth still to come.

The interesting thing was that the quadrangles were irregular in shape, that is to say although they were four-sided, none of the sides was the same length, while the buildings that flanked them were of different heights. The architectural design, the work of a New York firm called Skootz, Merridge & Potherill, was the winner in a competition that had been thrown open internationally. It was justified theoretically, we were given to understand, by the principle of Organic Aggregation. That is as may be.

The Gibbs building at King's College in Cambridge elevated one's spirit with a style, elegant and formal, to live up to. The first quad at Clarendon College tended to let one's spirit alone. Yet although it struck most people as architecturally quite new, it still seemed as if it had been there a long time. And now that I was getting used to it, it struck me as frankly, not to say oddly, homey — although that may be because Skootz, Merridge & Potherill had gone in for red brick; and red brick to me, coming from the Midlands, means home.

The President's Lodgings were on the far side of the first quad. The door was opened for me by his wife, Doris. It was a handsome glass door, through which I could see her crossing first the living-room and then the entrance-hall on her way towards me. Apart from the glass in the front door the Lodgings had scarcely any windows looking on the quad: its opposite aspect, however, was on a small private garden, from which it was separated by scarcely anything *but* glass.

Doris opened the door. 'How kind of you to come. I know He wants to see you.'

She looked up at me with large, singularly opaque blue eyes. She was a short woman, short in the leg and protuberant in the rear. Her hair was grey and wavy, her complexion a beige colour. She always referred to her husband as **He** or **Him**.

I went into the hall and took off my overcoat. 'It's nice and warm in here.'

Doris took the coat from me. 'This under-floor heating's all very well. But it's very hard on the feet.' She looked up at me and her eyes glared. 'It makes them swell.'

'Perhaps you could wear a slightly larger pair of shoes indoors,' I said, shamefully feeling that I was taking advantage of her — she was humourless.

'And charge them up to Skootz, Merridge and Potherill!' she said fiercely. 'Not that we should ever see the money this side of the grave.'

I shook my head, showing myself to be aware of a scandalous state of affairs which arose thus. Whenever a college held a competition for the architectural design of a building it was usual, the moment the winner was decided by the building committee, for a dissenting caucus to appear in the governing body, refusing to accept the committee's verdict and proposing that a totally fresh design should be called for from an architect outside the competition.

That was what had been in the offing at Clarendon. But as a result of masterly action by some of the building committee, in unauthorisedly cabling the winner straight away, the dissenting caucus's guns had been spiked. S. M. & P. had got the contract.

The next dissenting moves, then, were to demand alterations to the existing design. In this context dissent was so general that it needed no caucus to promote it. Letters from the college went flying across the Atlantic like doves from the Ark. But no matter how often Skootz, Merridge & Potherill were otherwise instructed, the replies came by sea — often, as it appeared from the length of the delay, via Cape Horn and the Cape of Good Hope.

'Oh, you never know,' I said.

Doris gave me a look that scarcely hid the contempt she felt for any man who could make that remark.

'I do know,' she retorted. Then she lifted her head, listening. 'I hear Him coming down,' she said. 'He's heard you.'

Doris led me across the hall into the living-room. The wooden floor was highly polished: in the middle of it was a large rectangle of first-quality Wilton — in a shade that Alice said used to be called '*rust*, dear'. There were standard lamps, comfortable Edwardian-looking armchairs and sofas, and a glass-fronted cupboard containing a Rockingham tea-service. All along the window wall the curtains, made of green brocade, were drawn.

'My dear fellow!' Stanley came up and put his hand cordially on my shoulder.

'Sherry?' said Doris to him.

'I think so, don't you, Jack?' He smiled at me. 'Let's sit down!'

We sat down opposite each other. In the lamplight Stanley's pink complexion looked particularly radiant, his silver hair particularly wavy and sleek. Who could have thought he was nearly sixty-eight? (Answer: All those people who were waiting for him to take himself off the official scene!)

'Let's get down to business straight away,' he said. 'I'm sure you won't mind that, will you, Jack?' He went on. 'You'll want to know what my findings have been, and I want to hear your views on them.' He paused. 'We're not going to have an easy passage, of course.' He shook his head. 'Colleges aren't made for easy passages — I knew that before I came here. One might have thought it would put me off coming. . . . Ha, it didn't! Now I've made my bed I must lie on it.'

My interpretation of this rigmarole didn't much please me. However, I said, smiling at him:

'One might say the same for me.'

'Yes, but you're still in science. And I'm not. I'm an administrator now.'

'And a very skilful administrator, at that,' said I, thinking

I was hanged if I'd be less smooth than him. I wondered what the people who were waiting for him to take himself off the official scene would have thought of my answer. I imagined contemptuous grimaces.

Stanley gave me a smile that made me feel delightfully intimate. I have to say again that I couldn't help liking him. (And after all, I was not being as amiable as all that, myself.)

At that moment Doris came in carrying a small silver tray on which there was a decanter of sherry, two glasses, and a plate of cheese-straws. Doris was an excellent cook. The cheese-straws were still warm, delicious.

'I'll leave you with Him,' she said to me, and went away again.

'I've canvassed about ninety per cent of College opinion,' Stanley said.

While he drank some sherry I said: 'And it's divided?'

'Exactly.' His tone was melodious, untroubled. That's how an administrator's tone always ought to be, I thought.

'Each of the two candidates,' he went on, 'has established his own individual claim. Of course they're both good scientists — we shouldn't dream of offering you a man who isn't. And we all know what high standards you have, Jack. Quite rightly so, if I may say so. I'm very glad for the sake of the College that you have.' He paused for breath, as well he might. 'And they're both good teachers — I'm sure that goes without saying, although I haven't had the pleasure of meeting any of Bowen's pupils — a little difficulty that some of them in the College feel, the Dean, for instance . . .'

(The Dean was our full-time administrator, a former botanist whose greatest claim to fame in the college was a remark made after a British Council trip to Peking: 'We thought Mao was a nice old gentleman. It was extraordinary to think he had blood on his hands!')

'Oh yes, the Dean,' I said.

'Bowen, I think we can be sure, has established himself as the better scientist of the two. I know that's your opinion.'

'And yours,' I said. Being melodious and untroubled, there was no reason why he shouldn't get everything that was coming to him.

'We're all bound to attach a lot of weight to what you say, Jack.'

'Yes?'

'And MacRobert seems to have definitely established himself as the better teacher. He's been in Oxford all the time, so he's had the best experience.' (Stanley himslf happened to be an Oxford man.)

'I see,' I said. I damn well did see.

'I think one can take it the division of opinion is explicable, even understandable.' He paused. 'We shall just have to walk delicately, that's all.' He looked at me seriously. 'I think we shall have to give special attention to Presentation.'

Bill Taylor and his colleagues at the N.P.B. would have known instantly what the last sentence meant and would have seen its importance. Presentation was one of the In words of the moment. It went with Image, Communication, and various kindred terms that sounded as if they emanated from the advertising industry. Whenever I heard two people serious-mindedly handing them to and fro I was struck by the beauteous power they seemed to possess of conferring confidence on both donor and recipient.

'Yes,' I said, and put it into more official language. 'Special attention will have to be given to Presentation.' I was irritated.

'But I don't think you need worry about the result,' Stanley wound up, with what an innocent person might have taken as decision.

I repeated what I had said to him on the train: 'On the Election Committee, if not in the College, there's a healthy majority for Bowen.'

Stanley quietly drank some sherry. He appeared to have finished saying what he had to say. This was what he had called me in for. Christ!

Stanley drank his sherry slowly and with relish, like a man who feels he has done a good day's work.

I drank some sherry, too. And I contemplated Stanley Forbes, Lord Forbes.

The time has come for me to say more about him, to say why he was disliked by some people and why others had no use for him, despite his scientific distinction and his charm of personality.

Stanley Forbes was a scientist who had turned from science to affairs. Now a scientist who turns from science to affairs, having been successful at one and then having had some success at the other, tends to be regarded by men of affairs as an interloper, and by scientists as having betrayed Science.

By the young Fellows of Clarendon, Stanley was regarded as an Establishment man. They considered he'd sold his soul to the Establishment in return for the worldly rewards that the Establishment has made it its business to confer. They might have pardoned him to a very limited extent if he'd continued, as they put it, to stick up for them and to stick up for Science. They considered that he had not continued. And they happened to be right — but not in their own terms.

Stanley's manner was that of a man-pleaser: he made it easy for one to imagine him going along, smoothly and judgematically, with whoever was in power. Yet he was not really a man-pleaser now. And in the past he had been the reverse.

In the early 1930s, when Stanley was a scientist, a physical chemist, his research had roused violent controversy. He and his group of pupils had comprised the smallest of minorities to start with; and he had been unshakable, uncompromising. There were no signs of a weakness for going along with whoever was in power. And he was right. His work stood. Why, then, did he get no credit now?

One reason was that his work during the thirties now sounded unfortunately — and unjustifiably — antiquated.

c*

Because it was so seminal a whole corpus of research had grown out of it, as it were burying it in the past. Stanley was the victim of a phenomenon which is universal — the burying of innovation. If you want examples of it outside science they're just as easy to find. In the case of techniques, for instance, it has become really difficult to see exactly what an innovator Liszt was, when you now hear his innovations coming from night-club pianists; or what an innovator James Joyce was, when you now read his innovations in brewer's advertisements. As for innovatory concepts, you have only to consider the Bohr-Rutherford model of the hydrogen atom in terms of one electron and one proton. Magnificently crucial though it was, it can't help seeming, nowadays, when physicists think of there being thirty-three elementary particles — or ninety-two, depending on how you look at it — just the faintest bit old hat.

Stanley Forbes as a scientist had produced ideas ahead of his time. A reaction mechanism he'd elucidated in the late twenties was the basis for one of the most important advances in chemical engineering since the war. But now he was by choice an operator in the world of affairs, a big wheel, a Lord.

'You can write him off as a scientist,' said the young Fellows, and did so.

Meanwhile, the fact of the matter was — although they didn't seem to know it — that there was something wrong with him as an operator in the world of affairs.

When the National Power Board was formed, Stanley Forbes had been one of its progenitors. He was supposed to have had the ear of the Prime Minister at the time. Uncharitable people had said he was so enthusiastic about its being formed because he wanted the chairmanship for himself. Just so. He got the chairmanship. The interesting revelation came later.

Somehow Forbes's grip on the N.P.B., his first big job of its kind, turned out to be curiously nerveless. He'd got the N.P.B.: he was supposedly master of it: yet he seemed quite

incapable of first of all pulling it together. He sat there, with
the power in his hands.

It was odd but not unheard-of. The clue to Stanley Forbes
was not that he was a bought member of the Establishment,
nor that he was a man-pleaser. It was something different
and more profound. Stanley Forbes was a man who wanted
power, who went after power; but when he got it, he didn't
want to do anything with it.

Men like Norman Standsfield, Bill Taylor, Herbert
Hobbs, wanted power and went after it — and by God they
knew what they wanted to do with it! Not so Stanley Forbes.
It was not even that he didn't *know* what to do with it —
there are power-seeking men of that kind. Stanley simply
did not *want* to do anything *with* it.

It hadn't taken men like Norman Standsfield or Bill
Taylor long to realise that Stanley's hand was nerveless, and
they thought little of him. His retirement to Oxford was
encouraged. Of course he was incorporated in the Establishment: but the men who drove the Establishment along
its appointed course knew perfectly well that he was not
one of them. He still sat on important committees, set up
to advise the Government on scientific policy, manpower,
defence, and so on. It would have been interesting to know
if any of them had ever set its course by Stanley's will.
(Actually, as I sat on some of them myself, I can tell you
the answer was No.)

So that was the case against Stanley Forbes. As I sat watching him drinking his sherry, I tried to tot up the chances
of his pulling Clarendon together. Or even of using his
weight to see that M. J. Bowen was elected.

Somewhere in the room a small clock gave a ping, indicating quarter past seven. From another room came the call
of Doris's voice.

'Stanley, Dear! . . . Don't forget you'll need your hat
and your gloves as well as your coat!'

Stanley finished his glass of sherry. I did the same.

'I'm so glad you came, Jack. These get-togethers are very

useful. They're one of the things that college life makes easy to come by. Official life would benefit from them . . .'

He stood up, pulled down his waistcoat and straightened his tie. As he started to walk he caught one foot against the other.

'We've plenty of time,' he said.

...and Two Cultures in the College

Outside the Lodgings the night seemed to have got colder, and in the black wintry sky above the heads of Stanley Forbes and me as we strolled in to Hall the stars were as brilliant as inspiration.

Bowen had established himself in the minds of my colleagues as the better scientist, MacRobert as the better teacher. I could very well see what was going on. I was not seeing it for the first time, either. If we appointed Mac-Robert, then in the sense that mattered most we were appointing second-best. Nobody has ever said university people are freer than anyone else from envy and jealousy. First-best tends to make one feel second-best unless one's pretty sure of oneself. In choosing second-best one closes for a certain comfort, a freedom from having anyone around the place who shakes one's self-esteem.

Without making myself out to be either saintly by nature of Calvanist by indoctrination, I thought it was a certain comfort that academic society, academic society above all, ought not to allow itself. About Mike Bowen, I asked myself the question: Assuming he might turn out to be as bright as I said he would, how much did I really like the idea of having him around the place, under my nose all the time? A very good question. (One observes 'That's a very good question' when one either can't face giving the answer or else doesn't know it — the asker doesn't get his answer, but he gets congratulation, which may please him better.) Whatever the answer to my own very good question was, I still meant to get Mike Bowen into the College.

My self-confidence was based on 'what I had actually achieved, essentially on a piece of work that had a permanent place in the story of my particular subject. However good Mike Bowen might be going to be, I had already chalked up a score for myself that couldn't be rubbed out. Whenever I thought about it I felt solid ground under my feet.

I'd had the original idea for it while I was doing my Ph.D. and most of the research was projected, if not completely worked out, during the years of my Cambridge Fellowship — brought to an end by World War II, of course.

I was the first person who happened to get into words the idea that some metals were harder and tougher than others because they contained submicroscopic precipitates, and to bring enough *theoretical* ability to bear on understanding rates of precipitation to make something of it. I'm not being specially unkind if I say that theoretical ability in the subject was not too common in those days. I'd deliberately tried to make the most of mine — that's why I spent the Long Vacs of my Ph.D. years in the Berlin Technische Hochschule and the year 1936-7 there full-time. After that I really did know something about applying quantum mechanics to the thermodynamics of precipitation.

I worked up my idea about submicroscopic precipitates theoretically. But I was conditioned as a practical metallurgist not to forget that what interested everybody else was the mechanical properties of metals. So I looked at mechanical properties and microscopic structure in some precipitating alloys; and then extrapolated back, to the gentler heat-treatments metallurgists went in for which led to precipitation on a scale *too small* for them to observe experimentally. (The mechanical properties kept me on the right lines.)

In due course the electron microscope came along and enabled the metallurgists actually to observe particles on the submicroscopic scale. And I was shown to have been right. Solid ground came up under my feet.

And that piece of work, overlaid though it might now be by other people's research, and by my own too, was really the origin of most of the work I'd done since. For example, at the present time I was doing calculations for the N.P.B. on cermets, which are metals with particles of ceramics precipitated throughout them.

But private enthusiasm — plus a bit of *Verfremdungseffekt* — is taking me too far off-course. I had to say what the solid ground under my feet was that enabled me to support the prospect of Mike Bowen's passing through my lab like a comet. And anyway I've got to get back to where I was in the story — strolling with Stanley Forbes to the dining-hall.

As Stanley and I were going through the doorway I bumped into our theoretical nuclear physicist, an excellent young man called Reg Popper. He was just what everyone expects a theoretical physicist to look like: scrawny, spectacled, fuzzy-haired and generally farouche; he was aged about twenty-nine, married, father of a couple of children. With him was a young man I'd seen before. Reg said:

'D'you know my g-g-guest, Harry Sinkins? Another theoretician. This is him. Prof. Carteret.'

The friend held out his hand which I shook. He was just *not* what everyone expects a theoretical physicist to look like; round-faced, sleek and athletic, with a handsome flashing smile.

I said to Reg playfully: 'Descended from Mrs. Sinkins, I presume?'

Reg took the allusion —

'He hasn't gone in for g-g-gardening yet, Prof. He's still a bachelor.'

'Mrs. Sinkins is that species of pink,' I explained to his friend, 'that you see growing in everybody's garden. White and straggly and out of hand.'

'My d-d-dad was very partial to it,' said Reg. 'He was a

park-attendant.' Through his thick spectacle lenses I caught a peculiarly bright-eyed glance. He was just the sort of man who'd have made it his business to find out what *my* father was. I thought I'd take the wind out of his sails.

'Oh,' I said. 'My dad was a foundry-man.' I turned to the young Sinkins. 'What was yours?'

'A merchant . . .' He blushed.

I remembered now that he'd recently joined the theoretical group at Courtenay Bagpuize — that's where I'd seen him.

We were strolling inside. 'Are you going to eat with us?' Reg asked me.

I said Thank you.

'We're going to talk sh-sh-shop,' he said menacingly. 'We're going to think up the experiments *we*'d like them to do' — with a collusive grin at Sinkins — 'if anybody ever builds a 1,000 GeV accelerator.'

There was some talk about building one on the West Coast. I said: 'I can listen. I might even learn something.'

Popper looked as if he thought that was hardly likely.

We joined the crowd of Fellows filing from the ante-room into the dining-hall. Actually we remained in file when we got inside.

The dining-hall was done by Alice in the manner called contemporary with stunning effect, not to mention stunning expense. The walls were a chalky white. Lights shaded by jewel-coloured glasses hung in irregular clusters above long teak dining-tables, laid with Swedish-looking (actually Royal College of Art-designed) table silver. The curtains — which somehow asked to be called drapes, non-U Americanism though that might be — had also been designed for us, printed in big heraldic devices, white on a dark mulberry colour. As yet the College had acquired only two pictures. One, given to us by Alice's friend Joan, was a huge American action-painting that had resulted in what looked, in the manner of a giant Rohrschach test, like two enormous black sea-birds colliding in mid-sky. The other, equally huge and dramatic, was an Australian painting of stark Anzac soldiers playing in the waves at Gallipoli — it was only on loan till the painter's death, when it was destined for the Tate. (A portrait of Stanley Forbes was in the process of being painted for us.)

We remained in file because the hall, despite its dramatic splendour, was really a help-yourself cafeteria. Out of a bizarre egalitarianism the Fellows, as well as the undergraduates, were made to serve themselves; and what's more, to eat, except on grand and festive occasions, the same food.

I queued up with Popper and Sinkins. They looked at me, waiting for me to say something. I said:

'Well, what's the In-est thing in nuclear physics? Still Regge poles?'

Popper said Yes. He knew perfectly well that although I could ask about Regge poles, I couldn't understand them.

'Has he heard,' said Sinkins to him, 'about Chew's bootstraps programme?'

I shook my head.

'Actually,' said Sinkins to me, 'none of us really knows how useful Regge poles are going to be, yet.'

'Are you including Regge in that?' I said. I'd heard part of the story, which as I understood it was that Regge, an Italian mathematician, had published some mildly incomprehensible work a few years back; only just recently it had been enthusiastically taken up, on a different line, by a lot of other people. Without any evidence I secretly hoped he would turn out to be a very obtuse man who disapproved of them and dissociated himself from their activities; or, perhaps better still for the human comedy, he would insist on proving to them, as mathematicians are always ready to prove at the drop of a hat to theoretical physicists, that their approximations couldn't be justified.

We had reached the servery: we collected our food and carried it back to what egalitarianism had failed to deprive of being called the High Table.

We found there weren't three empty places next to each other — there must have been more than twenty Fellows sitting down already. We had got to separate. Reg Popper turned to me.

'I had something to say to you, Prof.' His tone was lower than the one he had been using earlier — but not much lower. He nodded his head in the direction of our President.

'Make *h-h-him*,' he said, 'squash this bloody silly party that's campaigning against Bowen!'

I said to myself 'Hell!' and made for the nearest empty place. The man who was sitting in it hastily moved over, leaving his own place for me —

'Now you can sit between Alec and me, Jack,' he said.

His name was Brian Challoner. He was our sociologist. I liked him. He was tall and thin and sharp-eyed, and he always seemed to be quivering with nervous apprehension. Given also that he was tiny-nosed and had his hair razor-cut into a furry sort of cap, I could see why Alice said that when he came to our parties she was always expecting him to run up the curtains like a hamster and disappear from sight.

Alec, with whom he often sat in Hall, was Alec Benda. He wrote historical novels and was the Fellow who'd been appointed to give the course in Creative Writing.

I sat down. 'What's going on?'

Challoner started. He looked hunted. He said: 'The usual phenomenon of controversy getting under way.'

Although Brian Challoner might look as if he were going to run up the curtains out of sight, he always spoke firmly and definitely — with a just-perceptible American accent, relic of his once having held a Commonwealth Fellowship.

'After all,' he added, his sharp little eyes sparkling with sarcasm, 'a college is a microcosm. Here we see being fought out some of the major issues that preoccupy society in general. For example, what are we supposed to be here for? In our microcosmic way, are we here to teach or to prosecute research? That is the issue!'

'Oh, *is* it?' I said.

'Isn't it *terrifying*,' said Alec Benda. 'And so *boring* . . .'

Benda spoke in rapid bursts, over-emphasising stressed words as Alice did — but not, I may say, as the result of an aristocratic upbringing.

'You'd have thought,' he went on, 'we'd all have settled it — who's to say rightly or wrongly? — *years* ago. *But* years ago! I mean this teaching versus research bit. The Tudor England idea of the university versus the Hohenzollern Germany idea. You *know* . . .' He had large brown eyes with heavy halfmoon-shaped lids, and a head that was amazingly bald for a man under forty. (Alec Benda always referred to himself as being under forty.) His voice was high-pitched and fluting — it had caught the attention at this particular moment of the men on either side of us. So he went on.

'I'm for Tudor England! You scientists can *have* your Hohenzollern Germany, Technische Hochschule and all that — living for *research*. . . . I'm for what I can *understand*.' He gave a sweeping actor's glance round all those of his neighbours who he thought might be within earshot. 'I can understand teaching. But research in science — I know I shouldn't say it here — is *abracadabra* to me!'

I said: 'Does that mean you want MacRobert?'

He blinked his half-moon eyelids — to show that he knew I knew he wasn't as silly as the act he put on. 'Well, even if you are cross about it, I think I *am* for MacRobert.'

I was more than usually 'cross' with him, because I held myself to some extent responsible for him. It was I who'd campaigned with great energy for the College's having a Fellow in Creative Writing as an alternative to having one in Eng. Lit. 'Get the boys to pick up their pens and write things!' was my slogan — instead of teaching them to spend their time analysing puns in *Ulysses* or hunting up symbols in *Howard's End*.

I turned to Brian Challoner: 'What about you?'

He gave me a nervous glance. 'I've got my research, Jack,

just as much as you have. Or Bowen. And Alec's scarcely done any teaching before —'

'Not at all!' Benda interrupted. 'I did a whole semester at Cedar Rapids!'

'But if this place doesn't get a reputation for teaching undergraduates science' — Brian looked away, down the table — 'we're just not going to get undergraduates.'

I didn't agree, of course. If Clarendon had the brightest scientists in Oxford, we should get the undergraduates — lining up to get in, whether or not they had to put up with some incomprehensible lectures or eccentric tutorials. And the argument happened to be nonsense in this case, anyway, because Bowen would make a perfectly adequate teacher.

I saw which side he was going to be on. I said: 'I see. . . .'

Momentarily he looked ashamed of himself. Then he said:

'If you want to catch up on how things are going — all the scientists who are any good want Bowen. All the non-scientists want MacRobert.'

'And you can guess,' said Benda, maliciously, 'who's the strongest man for MacRobert.'

I could guess. It must be the Eng. Lit. man, whom we had got after all as a result of Stanley's nerveless hand in the College. He was my *bête noire*. Among other things he was a worshipper of D. H. Lawrence, from which you could infer automatically that he was about as *against* the Industrial Revolution as you could be — hardly the best person to appoint as a teacher of scientists and engineers, you might think. Furthermore he cultivated a jeering manner which he seemed to imagine made him both funny and attractive. (It was his idea of a joke to call me Lord Alice behind my back.)

'The division,' said Brian Challoner, turning back to me, 'is pretty easily predictable on theoretical lines.'

I thought it was too predictable to be borne. I said:

'What about the rest?'

'They're sitting on the fence.'

'Which gives them the best view of *both* sides of the question,' said Benda. 'Let's face it!'

'People who sit on the fence,' I said, 'always come down on the cosy, unfrightening side.'

I looked round the table. Intelligent men, some of them very clever men, few of them devoid of goodwill. The scientists were for the researcher: the non-scientists were for the teacher, i.e. for keeping out the better scientist. It was so predictable theoretically that there was something almost creepy about it. It boded ill for the future.

'I don't know why *you*'re worried,' said Alec Benda, interrupting my thoughts. 'The Election Committee's *packed* . . .'

I was angry. 'The Election Committee's constituted perfectly legally.' I stopped. I didn't want to quarrel, even though his remark seemed to me intemperate to the point of absurdity.

I turned away from him. At the end of the table Stanley Forbes caught my attention, looking radiantly pink and silver, our President, carefully sighting along his upturned nose the Dean, our administrator, who was nodding his head seriously — both no doubt viewing the question from the vantage point of the fence.

Two more discouraging thoughts crossed my mind. One was to wonder if it was a mistake to introduce non-scientist Fellows into the college. The other was to recall that plenty of people in Oxford had really believed it was a mistake to found a college for scientists and engineers in the first place.

I took to private self-consolation: 'We shall elect Mike Bowen, anyway . . .'

But it wasn't much use. We could elect Mike Bowen. And then, what?

CHAPTER SEVEN

Power and Money!

Things were simmering at the National Power Board. When I was reporting the last meeting I went to, I said the major item had been settled unanimously; because, though it might be red meat to the factional maw, it gave no cause for reasonable men to argue — and for once the members had all been reasonable. The minor item was a different matter: the Chairman had postponed it to another meeting.

I had a telephone call from Norman Standsfield's office, asking me to go to it. 'To attend,' one of his private secretaries said, with the polite, faintly casual authority private secretaries always seem to acquire, 'for one item on the agenda at 11.55 a.m. I'll let you have the relevant papers.'

I didn't disturb him with comments — I knew what it was all about. On the other hand I didn't see that my attendance was in the least necessary. It must be Norman's own idea.

I arrived at Power Centre ten minutes early as a consequence of having travelled from Paddington to Victoria by Underground instead of by taxi. It was a brand-new tall building. The board-room was on the next to top floor, and from its windows, and from the windows of the ante-room into which I was shown by a messenger to wait, there was a magnificent view across the roofs of Pimlico to the river. The morning was a dark yellowish-grey, and the clouds hung over Battersea full of snow. The other tall buildings, with their strip-lights shining in all the rooms, floated in the haze like delicately-lit crates.

In the ante-room I found the Power Board's chief security officer, waiting to be called in to the item on the agenda which preceded mine. He was looking glum — temporarily at being kept waiting so long, permanently at not having much of a job nowadays. He'd once been in the Weapons line, but had taken the wrong turning when the Power Board was set up and everything to do with The Bomb was hived off to what was then the War Office. The poor fellow, his secrets nowadays were only commercial. What a come-down!

'Hello!' he said, trying to make out that he was cheerful.

I may say I hadn't the faintest sympathy for him in his come-down. People in counter-espionage, I thought, just like people in espionage, seriously over-estimated the importance of what they were doing and seriously under-estimated their own detestableness while doing it. The two wings of the spying-classes — I sometimes had a job to see the essential distinction between them. Living on each other, made for each other, sneaks all, each lot seemed closer to the other than either seemed to the rest of us. Judged by the frequency with which one of them was discovered spying and counter-spying for both sides simultaneously, they obviously had a job to see the essential distinction themselves.

It's true I might have had some patience if the secrets they communicated to each other had been of more than trivial importance. So far as technical secrets were concerned, everybody knew that whenever the technical people from both sides were allowed to get together, they learnt there was scarcely anything they hadn't all discovered off their own bat already. Science gets the same answers everywhere — that's what Science is!

But on went the compulsive sneaks, spying and counter-spying, encouraged by thriller-writers and the popular Press, who combined a defective sense of proportion with a

vested interest in puffing them up. The reason so many
spies got themselves discovered, I suspected, was because
they finally couldn't bear any longer our not knowing all
those terribly clever things they were doing behind our
backs; and as for counter-spies — memoirs, memoirs,
memoirs. . . .

Our chief security officer was not notable, however, for
inflated ego. He gave the impression of being a humble,
humdrum sort of fellow, a retired colonel. In fact like most
of his kind at that level he struck one as not quite clever
enough for his job — although that might, I agree, have
been part of the game. (The only members of his wing of
the spying-classes who ever struck one as being clever enough
for their jobs were the really high bosses; and one couldn't
congratulate *them* on being clever enough because it wasn't
done to let on that one knew what their trade was.)

Our man looked at his watch.

'I've been kept waiting for three-quarters of an hour,' he
said.

I wondered about my own chances of getting in
punctually.

'I don't know why Sir Norman asked me to come,' he said.

It wasn't any use expecting me to answer for Norman.

He looked at me hyper-shrewdly. 'Sometimes I think he
does this sort of thing on purpose . . .'

I shook my head. I could imagine only too well the
sadistic gleam in Norman's eye if he were reminded that
this poor chap was waiting outside his door.

'I don't think,' he went on, with a faint smile as he tried
out my opinion, 'he cares much for our chaps.'

'Who do you mean?' I asked, hoping to lead him into
some further circumlocutory designation of his fellow-spies,
preferably beginning with Our Friends, e.g. Our Friends
over the Way, Our Friends on the Other Side of the Water,
Our Friends in the Box, Our Friends — who knows? — up
the Pole.

The board-room door opened. 'Come in, Jack!'

I went in.

The table at which the members sat was long and so narrow that it gave the impression, as one came into the room, that they were all sitting two-by-two up the length of it, with the Chairman, as Mr. Noah, sitting at the top.

Today the table looked much barer than usual. Not all the full-time members were present: two were missing. I was surprised. Or was I? Everyone knew the Chairman was capable, when faced with a disagreement between the members out of which he could make no capital himself, of changing from the regular day for a full-time members' meeting to a day when some of them couldn't come.

As I went through the door Norman stood up, elegantly giraffe-like, to greet me. At the table were sitting Bill Taylor plus two other members; Amos Wilson, of Generation Division, and Herbert Hobbs, Coal & Oil's Uncle Bert. That was all.

'Do come in, Jack!' Norman bowed to me. 'It was so good of you to come.'

I saw at once that he was in manic spirits. I glanced at the other three men and observed the desultory air which had characterised them at the start of other meetings of theirs that I'd been to — I imagined acrimony and enmity driven underground by boredom.

'I'm sure your bringing to us a different expertise will prove most valuable,' Norman went on. 'Come here and sit beside *me*!'

For this flummery he raised his voice to a higher, sweeter pitch than ever. 'I fear it's too late to offer you coffee, my dear Jack. . . . Have one of these!'

He held out a cylindrical packet of boiled sweets called Life Savers.

I thought if I took one I should be unable to talk. Norman was not so deterred.

We were all sitting now. The meeting resumed.

'At this stage a long exposé of the situation is not necessary,' Norman said, merrily crunching the sweet. 'But a brief recap is in order.'

The meeting had indeed resumed: he'd resumed National Power Board language. Goodbye, then, to the vigour of the active voice and the personal form — and a glum hail to the broken-backed flatness of the passive voice and the impersonal form! Instead of 'We tried to find out' I was going to get 'An investigation was performed'. One got the impression that they'd been taught to regard 'We tried to find out' as an unwarranted and deplorable manifestation of ego — pronounced 'eego'.)

'There would appear to be two propositions for what the Press should be told,' Norman began. 'The first is that the investigation is being discontinued by the Board for *economic* reasons. This to to say, it isn't foreseen that it will be profitable enough in the future to justify further expenditure on it.' He paused. 'The second is that it is being discontinued for *technical* reasons. This is to admit that a course which was open to technical criticism was taken initially.'

Before anyone could say anything, he added: 'It was agreed by you all at the last meeting that this is essentially a minor matter, in any case.' He glanced round at us, his blue eyes gleaming and his teeth crunching the Life Saver. 'There'll be a limit on the time for it.' And he looked across at the clock on the wall as if it were a stop-watch that he was just setting.

I reflected that he had brought me all the way from Oxford.

'Personally I hope,' he went on, 'that no one is proposing to speak at inordinate length about the Board's Image. All *that* can be taken as said at the last meeting.' He stopped smiling for a moment. 'The Board has its Image, and it is a good one. What has to be resolved by us now is how best to preserve it.' He bowed to us all.

'If it can't be *improved*.' Bill Taylor was leaning back in his chair, but looking none the less active and energetic.

His thatch of grey hair looked springy and his moustache was clipped to the last millimetre.

'Improved if possible, I'm sure, Bill.' Norman bowed specially to him. Norman was always bowing — it was a mannerism: he held his head on one side and swooped backwards and forwards from the waist as if by clockwork.

'But for the moment the fact to be faced, Bill, is that there's a crack, if I may say so, in our Image. Or could it be more aptly expressed as' — he gave Bill a honeyed, piercing look — 'a brittle fracture?'

There was a short guffaw from my neighbour, and then a pause.

My neighbour was Amos Wilson. (He was Sir Amos.) Of all the members he was the one who didn't give a damn for anything. I remarked earlier that there was quite a lot to be said about him. Some of it can be said very shortly to start with. Amos Wilson was a very clever man in a non-academic way, a very good engineer, independent-minded, realistic, and sometimes unusually far-sighted. In my opinion he was the man who ought to have been speaking for the Engineers instead of Herbert Hobbs.

But Amos Wilson didn't give a damn. It was a pity, but there was no use pretending he did — and his position in the Power Board was strong enough for him to get away with it. Whatever happened in the N.P.B., the Division he was sitting on top of (*a*) turned out the final product, and (*b*) made a hefty profit on it. From a professional point of view he was entirely sure of himself. And from another point of view, too, I thought. He was more than pleased with his title in the N.P.B. of Member for Generation — he had a pretty secretary without whom he never spent a night away from home, so who was to say him nay?

He was a tough, hard-baked, former power-station man; tall and lean, with a long face and small sly-looking eyes set rather too high up and too close together. And when he grinned his mouth went down at the corners wolfishly.

The pause went on, Bill Taylor's gaze at Norman remaining absolutely unwavering.

'This being so,' Norman concluded, 'there is something to be repaired.'

'Or papered over,' said Amos Wilson, in his Cockney accent.

'This is what the first proposition amounts to,' said Bill.

'Not at all!' Norman's rosy cheeks went rosier. 'Unless you show insistence in calling it so.' Acrimony was beginning to stir.

Bill sat forward and said nothing. He obviously did 'show insistence'. (In their determination to take the force out of their native tongue they seemed to cultivate the habit of replacing any verb with punch in it by a dim auxiliary verb plus a noun.)

The silence gave me time for second thoughts about acrimony stirring: I guessed that enmity had begun to stir as well. Sides, as they might have put it, had clearly been taken. And on my over-simplified view of the Board's affairs, the basis of the side-taking was clear.

The Administrators wanted to give the Press the so-called economic reason: The Scientists, the technical. The Administrators wanted to give a reason from the part of affairs that was in their own hands — even at the cost of getting all the blame. The Scientists wanted to do exactly the same.

What didn't appear to come into either of their calculations, as I've already remarked, was the little matter of telling the truth or untruth.

Norman continued to address himself to Bill.

'I would prefer you *not* to show insistence, my dear Bill, because it happens to be the proposition favoured by myself!' He went on very quickly, now looking at the others. 'And I must express my refusal to be attacked on the grounds that giving an economic reason is disingenuous.'

Suddenly I wondered if truth and untruth might be going to come into it after all. Extraordinary! Truth and untruth were going to come into it, definitely. And they were going to choose untruth, of course.

'It isn't for me to say, ever, that the Press should be told as little as possible,' Norman said. 'But in the circumstances it isn't disingenuous to tell them what will draw least attention to us, subject us to the least unfavourable criticism. This is a matter of Presentation.'

They all bowed their heads. 'This is true,' Herbert Hobbs breathed, as if to himself but audibly to everyone else. Norman went on.

'Economic reasons are reasons that are understood by everybody, and expected by everybody.' He looked away and his eyes gleamed again — with what could scarcely be called *in*genuousness. 'The Press are used to them. They hear them every day of their lives . . .' He gave us all a mischievous smile. 'And I won't conceal from you that at the Treasury I had the opportunity to develop my own personal expertise in presenting them.'

There was another guffaw from Amos Wilson. I glanced at Herbert Hobbs. He was breathing heavily — he was always breathing heavily, anyway.

Bill Taylor spoke.

'This is what you're saying, if I have the correct understanding of it. An economic reason should be given, because this distracts attention from the real reason, which is a technical reason. This is what your Presentation means. It hides the fact that a damned great technical mistake has been made.' His voice loudened. 'To this I am opposed!'

It sounded as if Hobbs were going to speak, but Bill went on.

'A technical mistake has been made. O.K. Use presentation to play it down as much as you like — but don't use it to cover it with something that's non-technical! This is *wrong*. And I'll give you two reasons why it's wrong. First: it's bad for the scientists and engineers who made the mistake, treating them as if they can't stand on their own feet and have to be carried by the rest of you. By this their morale is weakened, not strengthened. Second: it keeps up the public Image of technology as something infallible, which never makes mistakes. This is a false Image, which only makes matters worse for technical people when the public sees through it.'

Bill and the Chairman glared at each other.

'If I may speak,' came a breathy, pacifying voice, 'as an old hand in this game . . .'

Herbert Hobbs, everybody's Uncle Bert, with his honest Yorkshire accent. We all turned to look at him.

Bert Hobbs was a big fat man, with a cascade of chins, small protruding hazel eyes and a high rectangular forehead. He was not old — he was only in his middle fifties. His temperament was fluid on the surface and stable at the core. He was cunning, highly emotional and very clever. *Uncle* indeed! I called him a crypto-Trades Union leader because he practised the way of presenting himself that Trades Union leaders nowadays seem to find it essential to practise — as being solely the mouthpiece for a group which has been wronged; as being totally free, both personally and group-wise, from the taint of being on the make. When Uncle Bert spoke, we were to understand he spoke solely for all those unappreciated lads out in his Division who trusted him to speak for them. An old hand at the game! . . . His total preoccupation in life was with his own personal empire.

'This you may certainly do,' said Norman, bowing to him. 'As an old hand!' I presumed he saw a chance of getting Bill Taylor and Bert Hobbs embroiled with each other. 'A very old hand, if I may say so.'

Hobbs remained equable. He was the last man to be rattled by the Chairman's insolence.

'It shall never be said by me,' he began, 'that in my Division there's never been a wrong technical decision.'

Norman said privately to me: 'Do have a Life Saver!' He held out the packet again.

'But we've always found,' Hobbs went on, 'that it paid

to keep it to ourselves.' He nodded his head in approval, presumably of himself.

I did not risk a glance at Bill Taylor.

'Found it paid?' said Amos Wilson. 'Paid in what sense?' It was a reference to the fact that although Hobbs's Division made a profit, his, Amos Wilson's, made a much greater profit. (Nuclear Division, needless to say, ran at a loss: as soon as they developed at great cost a reactor that was profitable, they had to hand it over to Generation Division to run!)

It was typical of Amos Wilson not to do something more useful than stick pins in Bert Hobbs — such as weigh in alongside Bill, which would have been the most useful thing of all.

'If a mistake's been made by any of my technical lads,' Hobbs said, 'it's my belief that the best thing I can do for them is to cover them from attacks from the outside while they put it right.'

Bill Taylor didn't think Bert Hobbs's 'technical lads' did anything technical worth speaking about, anyway. He said shortly:

'It's not a matter of putting anything right, Hobbs. A major investigation has been written off, not put right. So what are we going to say about it here and now? This is the question.'

Hobbs went on gently and easily. 'There's no need to wash our dirty linen in public, is there?'

'When we're always washing it in private,' said Amos Wilson with a leer.

'Do you imagine,' said Bill, 'the Press won't notice the stink of it?'

There was a momentary pause — the metaphor was exhausted.

'Come on, chaps,' said Amos. 'Time to make up your minds. All this we've gone over enough times already. You know what my view is, don't you?' He looked round at us all, his small eyes — too close together — flickering with an expression of extraordinary knowingness. 'It doesn't matter a tinker's cuss *which* we say! Provided we give the Press the impression we're taking them into our confidence. This is what matters. Make them feel we're taking them into our confidence, and we can tell them anything we please!'

'Thank you, Amos,' said Norman, very quickly, with a furious smile. 'This makes your position delightfully clear.' He shook out another Life Saver and put it in his mouth. His cheeks, I noticed, were now bright red.

He turned to me — with a politeness that couldn't have been exceeded. 'And now we must have *your* view, my dear Jack. Let us hear what someone has to say from the point of view of a quite different expertise!'

I said what my view was, and I could only hope I sounded reasonable and interested, since I can't pretend I felt it mattered in the least or was even appropriate. My main emotion was stupefaction at them all sitting there — at a very considerable cost to the State — making a full-scale meal out of practically nothing. Though I knew it wasn't unusual. (According to Bill they'd spent most of their time at a previous meeting of full-time members in dispute over the assignment of parking spaces.)

'Yes, yes. Thank you!' Norman did his swooping bow several times rapidly — it looked as if the spring of the clockwork had been wound up tighter. He turned to Hobbs: 'And now Herbert?'

Bert Hobbs drew in his breath slowly, meanwhile eyeing Amos Wilson. He said:

'Wilson says that it doesn't matter which course we decide on. This I am not in agreement with. I think it matters a great deal, Mr. Chairman.'

He waited for the gravity of the remark to tell.

'It's a serious matter,' he went on. 'My thought is about' — his tone became hushed — 'the money. It's a lot of money to have thrown away.'

'Thrown away, my arse!' Bill Taylor burst out. 'It's been worth the money for The Technical Fall-Out!'

There was a silence. They all recognised the good of Technical Fall-Out. He went on.

'The investigation isn't going to be of the use to us that we thought it was going to be. The end-results are negative.' He paused. 'But the things we've picked up on the way are positive. This you seem to be forgetting. I'm thinking of' — he paused for emphasis — 'the Expertises!'

I considered the implied accusation was unjust. Judged by the frequency with which I heard the word, they were always thinking about *expertise*, new or old, the word being used *not* to mean (as you might think from having seen it properly inscribed in the land of its origin over the doorways of men whose profession was examining, judging for authenticity, and valuing *objets d'art*) 'connoisseurship'; but as an alternative for another of their most-favoured expressions, 'technical know-how'.

'And this,' Bill went on again, 'is only the technical fall-out as it affects *us*. For industry as a whole its value will be correspondingly greater — since it will be distributed over a wider area and will therefore have correspondingly increased potentialities.' He paused. 'I could tell you here and now of three major lines of technical advance currently being pursued in industry that will benefit critically.' His little moustache lengthened as he grinned wryly. 'And if I were given so much as a night's thought, I could invent three more.'

I didn't doubt that he could.

'Yes, Bill, yes.' Norman broke his flow.

'I was just saying,' said Herbert Hobbs, easily and determinedly, 'it's a lot of money . . .' (I wondered at his not having said 'brass'.) 'All the same, I think the responsibility for what's happened should be taken by us technical people.'

I glanced at Bill — and found him glancing at me. *Us* technical people! . . .

'Frankly, gentlemen, *I don't!*' Norman's voice was raised. The whole of his face had now turned red, with a

D

purplish kind of sheen. His eyes looked brilliantly blue.

'Oh, no, I didn't mean all the responsibility, Mr. Chairman,' said Hobbs. 'This wasn't my thought. There's got to be co-operation. My thought was of making it clear to the Press, and the public behind them — again, it comes down to presentation — that we have to keep our eye on the Money and the Science. And when one of them pulls a bit too much —'

'Yes!' Norman interrupted finally. He was twisting his fingers with impatience. '*My* thought is this! It's high time a speech was made by *me*. About money and science. About technical advances and what we spend on them — and what, if anything, we get out of them. Or even what other industries' — he bowed venomously at Bill — 'may get out of them!' He paused. 'I should like to think we were a charitable institution. All praise and no anxiety. Unfortunately we're not. We're something quite different. And in case we're inclined to forget it, it's my duty to remind you of it. It's my duty to remind you of what we are and what we're here for. We're a nationalised *industry*. As such we're not here to make technical advances. We're not even here to make Power!' He paused for the shock to take effect. 'We're here, my friends, to make *Money*!'

Nobody said anything.

Norman went on: 'As for the minor matter before us here, today — nothing has been said to convince me I was wrong in my initial belief. Therefore my proposal is to take the responsibility entirely on my own shoulders. I shall inform the Minister.'

That was that. The room seemed oddly quiet, as well it might. Suddenly, irrelevantly, I thought of Stanley Forbes — oh! the difference. . . .

'Thank you, my dear Jack, for coming along today.' Norman was bowing to me. I pulled myself together. 'I hope you don't feel,' he was saying, 'you've wasted your time.'

The other men round the table began to rustle their

papers, getting ready for the next item on the agenda. Their desultory air was returning, that air under which each of them, I now thought, must be ruminating steadfastly and independently upon how to 'do' Norman Standsfield, their Chairman.

CHAPTER EIGHT

A Scenario

I left the board-room in the mood to make a rousing speech about being *for* or *against* the Industrial Revolution. The only recipient for it in view was the chief security officer, still sitting glumly in the ante-room. Despicable though his trade was, I hadn't the heart to inflict a speech on him.

Herbert Hobbs had asked me to wait and have lunch with him after the meeting was over, so I went along the corridor to the spare room set aside for part-time members. It was a comfortable room, whose furnishing, like that of the board-room, exemplified the taste — thus providing a constant source of surprise to Alice, in view of the fact that the building had been designed by a very classy firm of architects — of the local head of Office Services. His taste happened to be agreeable, but I can tell you the Power Board hadn't the faintest knowledge of that when they appointed him. For all they knew he might have got everything from Everybody-Knows-Who's — chairs with cabriole legs and standard lamps with pompoms round the shades.

I went across to the window and looked out at the urban scene. The sky had darkened and the snow seemed about to burst through the bottom of it like feathers through the bottom of an over-stuffed pillow. The other tall buildings now floated entirely above the lowering haze, shining cellularly, looking curiously at ease in their surroundings. I, on the other hand, was simmering in mine.

'We're not here to make technical advances. We're not even here to make Power. We're here to make *Money!*'

How in God's name, I wanted to know, does an industrialised society survive in a competitive world other than by its technical advances?

I was all the more simmering because I knew there was another answer, the answer that came from non-technical people. We can survive, they said, by using our wits for shrewd investment in other countries' technical advances. Let other countries squander their resources of intelligence and energy in being technical: *we* will opt out of that, and make our living smartly like gentlemen on the Stock Exchange out of their technical successes — and leave them to pay for their own technical mistakes!

That answer was anathema to me. Of course I'm an interested party. I could be, and wanted to be, one of the people taking part in making technical advances. But beyond that I had confidence in my fellow scientists and technological men: they had already proved that England is good at making advances in science and technology. (Who, I'd like to know, actually pioneered the Industrial Revolution?) And being good at it, we could make money out of it — that's what competing in an industrialised capitalist world means. Since the Industrial Revolution happened, making technical advances and making money have been two aspects of the same thing.

In most of the large industrial concerns I'd had anything to do with there was a school of thought among the board members, usually emanating from the accountant caucus, which proposed that the firm should give up research and development and take to manufacturing its products under licence from some other firm, usually American, which did do research and development. The argument was, of course, a financial one — we're here to make money.

Very nice too. Of course under this arrangement you needed scientists still. They were indispensable — as your servants, but not as your masters, or even as one of *you*.

. . . 'On tap,' as the old Whitehall saying about scientists goes, 'but not on top.' They were indispensable to advise you in your shrewd investment in the technical advances they'd give their eyes to be doing, and possibly doing better, themselves — and which, as a matter of fact, they couldn't possibly comprehend in the instinctive way you needed unless some of them actually were doing. Very nice too!

I turned away from the window. The first flakes of snow were falling. The delicately illuminated egg-boxes looked like something on a nineteenth-century Japanese print. There was probably up to an hour to go before Herbert Hobbs would come out of the meeting — unless Norman ended the whole thing with a decision to settle all the items of the agenda himself.

I sat down in one of the armchairs chosen by the head of Office Services and opened my brief-case. There was an hour in which to get on with some real work. One of my research students had just got the answers to some of our sums from the computer group at Courtenay Bagpuize. To me, not a mathematician — and also, according to Reg Popper, 'a typical member of the old school' — it was always interesting to see how near the rigorous answers one got from the I.B.M. 7090 were to those one originally had got for oneself on the back of an envelope.

I was so immersed that I was startled when the door opened and Hobbs came in, followed by Bill Taylor.

'It's all right,' Bert said good-humouredly to Bill. 'It's me who's taking him out to lunch today.'

Bill gave me a light-eyed glance and then, with a decisive athletic step, went out again.

Bert said: 'I've told Binney' — his chauffeur — 'to take us to a restaurant. If we go to the Club we shall see people we know.' He smiled breathily. 'And get a poor lunch.'

It may have sounded as if the choice of restaurant were to be Binney's, but that was not the case. Herbert Hobbs did not carry his fine *embonpoint* for nothing. We made for a restaurant in Jermyn Street. As the car whirred slowly through the thin slush round Hyde Park Corner, he said:

'I don't know what you thought of our meeting.'

'Up to standard,' I said.

'I really meant what you thought of *us*.' He was glancing at me out of the corner of his eye.

'The Chairman didn't give you much of a chance.' I grinned. 'Or me, for that matter.' I laughed. 'The lash fell on us all alike, wouldn't you say?'

'He certainly holds the whip-hand, does our Norman.'

'And he certainly enjoys using it!' I spoke lightly.

'Do you think,' said Herbert Hobbs slowly, 'that's what he enjoys *most*?'

I was startled, although I'd heard him do this sort of thing before. Where anyone else might have made an oblique, allusive remark, he asked a direct over-simple question, humbly, as if for information. I'd never forgotten his asking me, the first time we ever met, 'Do you think a man who hasn't got a university degree might be really intelligent?' (He hadn't got a degree, himself.) He asked the over-simple question, humbly. At the same time he was cunningly leading one into the trap of giving an over-simple answer — if I'd said 'Yes!' to his question about Norman, he'd have known that although I was an Oxford Professor my psychology was jejune.

I said I didn't know.

Herbert Hobbs was no fool. What he was getting at, put in the oblique, allusive way that more nearly matched life as I saw it, seemed to me somewhere near the truth about Norman. Norman Standsfield wanted power, and he knew what he wanted to do with it. So did Bill Taylor; so did Herbert Hobbs. But what seemed to give Norman, more than any of the others, the kick out of having power, was the actual sensation of exercising it. Mention of the whip-hand was not out of order.

'What an extraordinary man he is!' I said.

Bert nodded his large head. 'Many's the time I've had to

look after him . . .' He turned to me: 'You knew that, didn't you?'

I didn't know. I thought about Norman's insatiable demand for personal loyalty. It didn't surprise me that Hobbs had lighted on that.

'You know I was with him when he had his mental collapse?'

I didn't; and I can't say I was prepared to believe Norman had ever had one — not on the strength of Bert Hobbs's say-so. The story made a wonderful score for Bert over Norman, and I imagined Norman's rage if he knew Bert was telling it. To fox Bert, I deliberately didn't ask for more details.

'Yes . . .' he said, and his voice was breathy with emotion — with emotion and a sort of mystery.

We were silent for a little while.

His mood changed. He said ruminatively:

'You know . . . this morning I had a lot of sympathy with what Taylor said.'

I thought Bill would be delighted to hear more of this. I said: 'In what way?'

'His thought that his scientists ought to be allowed to carry their own can when they make a technical blunder. This I have sympathy with. This is the line I've always taken with my technical lads — though they're not scientific hot-shots like Nuclear Division's . . .'

I didn't see how that tied up with covering them from the outside while they put their blunders right. But thinking it was possible to tie up Herbert Hobbs's statements was a blunder in itself. Consistency was to be found in Herbert Hobbs on the level of intrinsic emotion, not of overt statement.

I glanced through the window. A dark sky: CUBITTS FITZPATRICK SHAND.

He went on. The emotion in his voice made its ruminative rumble sound comforting and inviting.

'Taylor said the Chairman's line of action does the Scien-

tists a disservice. This I agree with.' He paused and then
said in parenthesis: 'The Chairman doesn't *mind* doing the
Scientists a disservice.' He went on. 'It's stopping them
growing up. And my belief is very strong, Jack, that they've
got to grow up. The sooner they're allowed to grow up the
better. This is my belief, Jack. The Scientists are just as
capable of growing up as the Engineers!'

He spoke with so much fervour that I glanced at him. He
was looking at me intently with his bright hazel eyes — the
whites had reddened with emotion.

'Some of the youngsters have got a long way to go,' he
added.

I nodded my head.

'Especially in Nuclear Division,' he said.

I hadn't missed the earlier reference to 'scientific hot-
shots' in Bill Taylor's former Division.

'Oh . . .' I said.

I'd been thinking he was an old humbug, and I'd been
admitting to myself that I was not unsusceptible to his spell.
I stopped. For the health of the Power Board he was a
disaster. He exacerbated tensions and produced divisions
where they were not inevitable, all in the cause of playing
— under the guise of acting solely as the expression of
group-loyalty — an entirely private hand.

We were going down Piccadilly, and something reminded
me of Bill Taylor's denunciation of the lives we lead without fun. I thought about Herbert Hobbs. He had two grown-
up sons and a wife who was older than he was. A life without fun? Subject to my invariable rule that you couldn't
tell for sure unless you were actually there, I wondered. . . .
He interrupted my thoughts.

'I hope you're feeling like a good lunch, Jack.'

I indicated that I was.

'Because I'm going to see that you get one.'

I was amused. We were exactly the same age. But for the
moment he really sounded like an uncle, an uncle to me.

The snow was turning to sleet. A liveried man at the

D*

restaurant held an umbrella over us while Hobbs gave Binney his orders about picking us up again. I had always liked Jermyn Street, apart from the local hotel which Providence, in one of its occasional revulsions from excessive snobbism, had lately seen fit to eliminate. I should have liked to look in the shop where they sold artist's materials, and to consider the bootmakers' I could now enter, if I felt disposed, and order a pair of shoes — half a dozen pairs of shoes, why not?

'Come on,' said Bert. The prospect of the meal made him increasingly good-humoured. It even made him look more *embonpoint*ish. Walking with short steps, and paddling his arms out at the sides, he made his way indoors, leaving me to follow.

We went straight to our table. Bert ordered drinks. And then we began the palaver of choosing the meal.

It was the usual sort of place, semi-darkness, stiff white table-cloths, flickering chafing-dishes, waiters with a French accent although they looked as if they came from Cyprus. The room was more or less full, and there were only two women in sight. Men eating out on expenses. The place hummed with expense-account conversation, about the latest American musical, the latest Italian film, and so on — everyone was at the beginning of the meal. (Only expense account women start talking business straight away.)

It struck me that expense account men are more cultivated than anybody who isn't one, or isn't married to one, might think. I shouldn't be surprised if at least half, and probably three-quarters of the men in that restaurant on that day had social origins the same as Herbert Hobbs's and mine. Yet there they were, ordering to the manner born subtle and sophisticated dishes that until they got them on expenses they'd probably never even heard of. Good luck to them!

By recounting what we chose to eat I know I lay myself open to having you say you don't see anything out of the way in that. We chose *pâté mousse* followed by *sole*

véronique. All I can say is that the *pâté* was as bland as a
dream, with dark bits of truffle in it — which would improve
any dream, let's agree. The sole was light and fresh, the
sauce creamy and the grapes muscatels. We drank a white
burgundy — I'm hanged if I'll let myself in for more criticism by naming the vineyard and the year. I wondered
what Bert Hobbs had asked me out to say to me.

We ate with pleasure, beguiled for a few minutes by the
luminous pantomime of *crêpes suzettes* being cooked for the
men at the next table. (I wondered why nobody demands,
when the sauce is cooked under their noses, that the pancakes shall be cooked there too, instead of being brought
from the kitchen in a soggy pile.) Bert and I talked seemlily
about this and that. He'd certainly not brought me out to
tell me about his sympathy for Bill Taylor's point of view.
I presumed he would come to his objective when he offered
me the brandy, which I intended to refuse.

Apropos of nothing, he said:

'Have you been told about the date of the investiture,
yet?'

The dubbing — I thought of my scout. I said Yes.

'I wrote and told you how pleased I was to hear about
your K., and now I can tell you to your face.' Between
mouthfuls he lifted his glass to me.

I said: 'I was astonished by how many letters I got, some
from people I scarcely remember. With one or two omissions
from people I know very, very well.' Suddenly his expression
made me feel embarrassed. I went on: 'What I didn't know
was that the thing for chaps who've got a K. already to do
is to write "Snap!"'

And with that, of course, I made myself feel more embarrassed. Poor old Herbert! Norman, Bill Taylor, Amos
Wilson — they'd all got K.s. Plunging still further into
trouble, I tried to be funny. I said:

'With the Power Board on one hand and the University
on the other, I must be a classic example of *rising* between
two stools.'

Bert said in a low voice: 'I expect you're content, anyway.'

I looked at him and said cheerfully: 'On the Power Board's quota it must be your turn next, mustn't it?'

He was apparently occupied with extracting some bones from the fish on his plate. He didn't answer. I couldn't help seeing two large tears forming in his eyes.

I doubt if Emily Post could have told me what to say then. I knew he shed tears readily, but that was little help.

After a dreadful pause he said: 'Do you know what happened?'

I had to look at him. The tears had rolled down his heavy cheeks into, I supposed, his *sole véronique*. What a fate for *sole véronique*! What a fate for tears!

'What?' I said.

'It *was* my turn next. I was at the top of the Power Board's list when Amos Wilson got it.' He paused. 'I saw it, Jack, with my own eyes — *Norman Standsfield personally switched our names!*'

'What on earth for?' His tears made me believe.

'Just because he meant to. Amos and I are about the same age and seniority. The Chairman made a case for Amos but it wouldn't deceive a cat. Amos got it.' He paused and his breath came in a loud sort of sob. 'It *should* have been *mine!*'

Oh dear, oh dear. . . . I've heard some cries from the heart in my time.

I said nothing. After all, it might well not be true.

Bert Hobbs became steady again.

'Divide and Rule,' he said. 'This is Norman Standsfield's principle, Jack.'

For the moment I was thinking about myself — having said that when Norman was reputed not to have a friend in the world I should have liked to be his friend. I suddenly saw myself as grossly impetuous. However, I said:

'That could be true at Board level, I agree. But actually it isn't true lower down, is it?'

'I'm glad you've noticed this, Jack! Lower down, where it comes to the lads out in the Divisions, Norman Standsfield has done a wonderful job. Really wonderful. Though he may have all us members at each other's throats, he's pulled the lads out in the Divisions together nothing short of marvellously. I know my own lads think the world of him. They think he's really put the National Power Board on the map. And for this they'd go through thick and thin for him, this they would.'

I bowed my head at the thought of those lads, out there, going through thick and thin. Bert went on.

'If any man has succeeded in pulling the National Power Board together, this man is Norman Standsfield.' He paused. 'And *not* the Great Scientist who held the job prior to him, Lord Forbes!'

I was afraid he was right about that; but it was not, as it happened, because Lord Forbes had indeed been a distinguished scientist.

'You know, Jack,' — he became confidential — "the Power Board is really too big to be properly pulled together by any man. It's just an impossibility. A sheer impossibility.'

Of course he was now entirely right. The original concept of a National Power Board might have been justified on the grounds of its being grandiose; but it couldn't have been justified on the grounds of its being practicable. The general consensus of opinion nowadays was that the Prime Minister at the time favoured the grandiose.

'The Great Scientist, Lord Forbes,' said Bert, 'bit off more than he could chew. This is the top and bottom of it, Jack. He wanted the Power Board formed, because it would make a nice job for him. And then when he got it he was a wash-out in it.' He paused. He spoke in a friendly tone. 'I know chaps like you and Taylor think we oughtn't to have a non-technical man as Chairman. And I agree with you wholeheartedly. But you *have* got a Scientist to blame. . . . With the best will in the world I would have to say that my thought is the old Treasury was right when they put

in one of their own chaps, an Administrator, to replace
Forbes, the Scientist. People with administrative expertise
make a better job of pulling a big organisation together
than long-haired scientists.'

I kept my mouth shut.

'My friend, I don't count you as a long-haired scientist —
you know this. You've knocked about too much.' He leaned
forward and amiably put his hand on my forearm. 'You're
for all practical purposes,' he said, 'an Engineer.'

Then he called the waiter. 'Those *crêpes suzette* looked
good. Bring some for me and my guest!'

He sat back fatly, pleased with his order — and I was
not displeased with it, either. Then suddenly he looked
at me with an expression I hadn't seen before, as relaxed as
ever, yet wily and watchful.

'While we're talking about pulling things together in the
Board, Jack,' he said, 'there's one job ahead of the Chairman
that really wants doing urgently, in my opinion. I've had it
in mind for a long time now. . . . These recent happenings,
that we were talking about at today's meeting, have made
me think we oughtn't to put off doing something about it
any longer.'

He hadn't waited till we got to the brandy. As he spoke
he waved his hand with a reassuring, take-it-easy sort of
gesture.

'My thought is,' he said, 'about pulling the Scientists
together.'

I have to admit that I didn't catch his drift.

'My thinking goes like this,' he explained. 'As things stand,
each Division does its own research and development. Therefore each Division has its own group of scientists. So each
Division's group of scientists can make its own technical
mistakes independently.' He paused. 'All that the rest of us
can do is help pick up the bits afterwards. You see what I
mean, don't you, Jack? And I expect you see the way my
mind is working. Just in a practical way . . .'

I looked at him steadily.

'Now the way I put it is this — and I want *your* opinion on it. Do you think we should get on more efficiently if we united all the scientists, right across the board, in *one* organisation? We'd just have one Research and Development organisation for the whole Power Board. With its own Member — the entire responsibility for it would be his. And as a member, he'd be one of *us*.'

The trolley with the chafing-dishes on it was standing beside us and the light of the spirit lamp was flickering in our faces. I was thinking: This is it! I'd told Alice that when the repercussions of the row got going they'd be *something*, but she was to be prepared for the rumble of them to stay subliminal for quite a while. Then one day it would cross the threshold of audibility. . . . Well, if I knew anything about it, the rumble was crossing the threshold now.

The Scientists were to be hived off from the working Divisions — leaving the working Divisions to be run by the Engineers. (I couldn't believe the Administrators were meant to get much of a look-in.)

I looked at him.

'Well,' he said, 'Jack. That's my scenario for the future.'

And then he turned to start giving instructions to the *chef de restaurant* about the *crêpes suzette*.

I must say I admired the beauty and simplicity of his plan — or 'scenario', as the case might be. I hadn't the slightest doubt it would be taken seriously in the Power Board. In fact enough factions might line up behind him to put it into force. The Scientists, seen as arrogant, confident, new men, had not made themselves universally loved. Lots of people would like to see them put in the corner. Whether the plan had any actual merits or not was beside the point.

Herbert Hobbs turned back from the *crêpes suzette*, a smile of anticipation shining round his lips and dispersing into his wobbly chins. As if he were half-surprised to find my thoughts still engaged by his proposal, he said:

'Well, what do you think of my scenario? Get all those scientists off our necks, eh?'

Quickly he patted my forearm again. 'Just my little joke — I don't mean a word of it!' His small hazel eyes flickered brightly. 'You know what a lot I think of the Scientists. The Power Board couldn't run without them, and this is the truth!'

He paused, waiting for me to say something. He saw that I wasn't going to say something. His tone became especially quiet and wilily confidential as he leaned towards me and said:

'It's no use asking you for your reaction to a scenario for uniting our scientists right across the board without telling you the sort of person I have in mind for uniting them under . . .'

The white of his eyes reddened with emotion. Whatever he was going to say, I thought the odds were ten to one against its being what he had at the back of his mind. All the same I was fascinated to hear it, just to see how far he'd got the nerve to go.

'My thought about the sort of person,' he said, 'if only we could get him, Jack, is someone like *yourself* . . .'

You may think it served me right. It was not only his nerve, but his childlike faith in it, which made me feel as if I could burst with rage and laughter. There he sat, fat and nodding — there really was something childlike, even babylike, about him. If I'd said to him 'You lying old humbug!' he'd probably have cried.

He waited for a moment. He was good at waiting for moments — at waiting for months, for years if need be. One of the things he'd wait for years for was to get Bill Taylor down. What he was waiting for now, for a moment, was me to give away what I thought.

When I didn't give it, he turned to watch the pancakes being ignited, a smile of innocent satisfaction — with the *chef de restaurant*'s performance — illuminating his face. 'I told him to put a little more Grand Marnier in the sauce,' he said to me over his shoulder. 'I like it. And I'm sure you do, my friend . . .'

I was thinking about Bill Taylor. I remembered Alice's asking, when she'd comprehended the egregiousness of the Board's technical lapse, if Bill would be penalised. 'Penalised' wasn't the appropriate word, and I didn't know what really was the appropriate word. All I knew was that Bill's enemies would somehow — and certainly — take the row in the Board as an opportunity to try and 'do' him.

Well, looked at from that point of view, Uncle Bert's scenario for the future had its points. In fact it had more than points. (The pancakes flared with light.) It could be a winner.

Part Two

Part Two

CHAPTER ONE

After the Banquet Was Over

The events I've been describing so far happened in January 1962, and it's now the middle of 1963: I discover that it's not at all easy to write about the present — and there are plenty of reasons for thinking it's not wise, either.

One of the difficulties in writing about the here-and-now is getting over the thought of how dated the book will seem in the there-and-then, where 'then' is a decade hence. Nothing dates like the present.

As for its being wise, it clearly can't be. A wise man, before he expresses his views on events, or even sets about describing them, takes time to think them over. And by time I mean years, not months. A wise man, before picking up his pen, likes to give his head a chance.

Why, then, one might ask, am I picking up my pen?

In the first place there's an attraction in writing down what's in the front of one's mind. Immediacy seems to have a pull of its own. That, really, was what made me say to myself, when I felt tempted to pick up my pen without giving my head a chance: 'Risk it!'

In the second place, people nowadays seem particularly to want to read about the here-and-now, about *themselves, now*. Obsessed with it, they are.

'Egocentrics and narcissists,' I called them — to Brian Challoner, because I felt that he, as a sociologist, was somehow responsible for them. 'Why do they want to read about *themselves, now*?'

'I can give you the answer,' he said, 'that some of the philosophers are giving, if that's any use to you.'

'Give it and I'll see.'

We were sitting in the Senior Common Room after dinner, he and I and Alec Benda.

The gist of his answer was that everybody's focussing nowadays so concentratedly on 'the contemporary' is a backwash of Existentialism. Moral choice being entirely a matter of the present moment, the more you're preoccupied with moral choice the more concentrated you're bound to be on the present moment, the less interested in either the past or the future. And concentration on the present moment — this was Brian's own contribution to the theory — is infectious.

'It spreads,' he said, 'to people who don't know one end of a moral choice from the other.'

I listened. Whether it was any use or not, it was fun. Furthermore I was both relieved and pleased to hear that the Immanent Bomb hadn't been dragged in. I was going to say so, when Alec Benda sent serious argument flying.

'Oh, but how right you are, Brian! That's just how *teen-agers* are!'

My spirits fell.

Alec looked knowingly at Brian with brown eyes bulging under half-moon-shaped lids. Actually he had an excuse for dragging in his own favourite subject of conversation: Brian's current sociological enquiry was into the effects of television on adolescents.

'Teenagers live *entirely* in the present, you know. . . . It's perfectly fascinating. They seem to have forgotten *all* about their childhood. And they *refuse* to think about being adults.' He smoothed his hand over the side of his bald head. 'Perfectly fascinating creatures — the *boys* are, any-way. Not so much the girls . . .' The enthusiasm died out of his voice. 'They're just hangers-on to the boys.'

I let Brian cope with him.

I was thinking that even if the public's wanting to read

about itself in its own time really had got something to do with Existentialism, I still meant to take the risk of writing about the present. I told myself I was taking a Calculated Risk, which I'd gathered, from hearing the phrase in constant use at the Power Board, was a much less risky risk than an uncalculated one — in fact it was the sort of risk that was proper for a man to take who was generally agreed to be both Sound and Forward-Looking.

My calculations had to take into account the three main daunting facts; that current language dates, current ideas date, even current events date.

Over current language it was open to me to eliminate the slang of the day, especially from the text, in the hope of having left a timeless residuum. But that debarred me from the fun of reporting in particular the language of the National Power Board and its environs. However, it suddenly occurred to me that N.P.B. language is *in the present* something like what its speakers would unerringly identify in another context as a Period-Piece. Though it may be up-to-the-minute, its dating is so clearly written into it as to turn it into a sort of contemporary period-piece . . .

(A minor point: I decided to spell out certain very well-known words with dashes. This is to try and restore to them some of the impact they've lost through being of late incessantly printed in full. Get back some of the excitement, the suggestiveness, the force, of *what-mayn't-be-written*!)

Current ideas are a different matter. I've put my money on The Two Cultures and The Establishment, for instance. I should find it difficult to say concisely what I mean to say without them. If in a decade's time they're horribly dated — which I'm inclined to doubt, as there's no sign of their disappearing — so much the worse.

Incidental current events, however, are the most difficult of all to deal with, especially current events of the newsy kind. When Herbert Hobbs and I were having lunch in the expense-account restaurant we could overhear conversation at nearby tables about the Common Market. In

January 1962 lots of people were disputing: Will Britain get into it? Ought Britain to get into it? And so on. I'd bet that in 1972 those conversations reported in a novel will read as flat as the flat-earther's earth. By then our country will either be in the Common Market, in which case everyone will have forgotten we were kept out. Or we shall have been permanently kept out, in which case everyone will have forgotten we tried to get in. Or the Common Market will no longer be in existence in its present form, anyway. 'What's all this?' a 1972 reader will ask in pardonable boredom and incomprehension.

I took to writing about things before I had much chance to think them over; and to writing them with Time overtaking me every minute — blunting the edge of my comments and superseding the turn of my events. For example, anyone who wants to know who finally succeeded to the chairmanship of the National Power Board, if he hasn't seen the fellow on television, has only to ring up Power Centre and ask, instead of waiting for the end of my story.

And on the January day with which I saw fit to begin my story, all of us on our way to Alfred Matthewson's memorial service thought the succession to Norman Standsfield would not be settled for another four years, when he was due to retire. . . . I actually started writing the book shortly afterwards: while I know now, at the moment of writing these present words over a year later, that in the following June Time smote Norman with a coronary — as a consequence of which the question of succession had to be settled pronto.

Incidentally I may say that we're still arguing about whether Norman's decision to retire straight away was chiefly due to hypochondria and not to physical incapacity. The coronary is nowadays so woven into the canon of executive life that one takes it to be the sort of disaster a man comes back after. (Which is not to say also that it doesn't at the same time provide a commonly recognised way of rubbing in his not being indispensable. 'But look, Jimmy,' one says to him, 'I'm not being offensive or unkind or anything. But you — or Freddie or I, for that matter — might have a coronary one day and things'd *have* to go on . . .')

But I assume that at least some people may want to know *how* things fell out. So I will go on, by following up the meeting at which the Chairman settled the item on the agenda for which I had been specially called, without deference to anyone, least of all to me.

The sequel to be expected was a formal announcement at his next monthly Press conference that the Power Board had wound up the investigation for economic reasons. In fact the sequel occurred a week earlier. And was different.

I happened to be spending a night at the Club. I'd been to a meeting at the Royal Society during the afternoon and I had to go to another meeting in Whitehall on the following morning. I was sitting in the library late at night, working. I was still working on the proofs of the textbook I was reading when Stanley Forbes interrupted me in the 4.45 from Paddington a month ago. That, I am afraid, is the way we live now.

The library was very quiet. The only other person in the long dark room, its walls alternately interspersed with book-shelves and windows, its floor cluttered with sofas, little tables and standard-lamps, was a very elderly gentleman in gold-rimmed spectacles, dozing.

'Jack!' A loud whisper from the doorway. In the dim low light I saw the figure of Bill Taylor.

I was astonished to see him. He was wearing full evening dress. As he came into the lamplight I caught the gleam of his K.B.E. insignia dangling on its pink ribbon round his neck.

'I knew you were staying here.' His eyes were unusually clear and light. 'I'm glad you're still up. I've got some news for you.'

It first crossed my mind that he'd heard Herbert Hobbs's plan for reorganising the Power Board so as to get the

Scientists out of the way—Uncle Bert's scenario for the N.P.B.'s future . . .

But I imagined that Hobbs wouldn't have told Bill. That wasn't Uncle Bert's way of going about things. Uncle Bert dropped a word here and there to the less-interested parties, so that it got around to the more-interested parties through gossip. Then when the more-interested taxed him with it, he could throw them, straight away, by saying he'd been incorrectly reported.

Bill rang the bell for a servant, and then sat down on the sofa beside me. I was in two minds whether to tell him about Hobbs's scheme. I was repelled by the idea of doing Hobbs's dirty work, just as he'd planned, for him. While I hesitated Bill said excitedly:

'I've just come straight from the City, from this dinner . . .'

With an effort I recalled there had been a banquet at one of the Livery Companies. Bill said:

'Norman made his speech.'

I remembered that Norman was to be guest of honour.

'Do you know what he told them?'

At that moment the servant came: Bill ordered drinks for himself and me. I waited impatiently.

'His speech was all about life in the world of technology. He spoke as an expert, of course. From experience, of course . . .'

'Come on, out with it!'

Bill looked at me, his eyes seeming twice as large and twice as light as usual. (Alcohol, I thought.)

'To illustrate certain aspects, he gave them an example from current affairs. Technological advance, he said, inevitably involves some decisions which turn out to be wrong, as well as some which are right. And when a wrong one is made—listen to this!—you write the work off as soon as you find out. And like the National Power Board at this point of time, you say so!'

I looked at him harder, to make sure he wasn't making it up. He wasn't. Then we burst into laughter.

Despite the fusty reverential air of the room, we laughed
cackling laughter. In fact our laughter was a bit too cackling
for the event that provoked it, and we quietened down
quickly.

'Really,' I said. 'Really! What a man!'

'I told you. He's a b——!'

I put down my galleys on the low table in front of us.
This was the end of work for tonight. The servant came
and handed us our drinks.

'I expect Meg'll wonder where I am,' — Meg was Bill's
wife's name — 'but she's used to me coming in at all hours
after do's like this. You know, Jack, I'm a bit of a bastard
to her. Sometimes, anyway. Either she doesn't mind it or
she's got used to it. Which do you think it is? You have
a better understanding of women than I have.'

I thought he was drunk. His voice was more resonant
and his gestures more vigorous than ever — he suddenly
struck me as giving out energy like a generator, only in
all directions!

'Into that one you're not going to be drawn, I see,' he
said.

He leaned back against the worn leather of the sofa and
drank some whisky. His cheeks looked smooth and healthy:
the gilt on his enamelled cross of honour glittered.

'Well,' he said, 'you still haven't told me what *you* think
of Norman.'

'So far as I recall, you didn't ask me. You made a statement. Actually I doubt if I should express myself in quite
those terms about Norman.'

'My dear chap, you always did have a nice way of rebuking
me for using bad language. I know, I know! . . .' He turned
his square, solid-looking head so that he could watch me.
'But he *is* a b——, isn't he?'

I didn't reply. There was a pause.

The very elderly gentleman shuffled across the room to
the doorway. We watched him, not thinking about him.
Bill said:

'I'll tell you something, Jack. Something you don't know.'

I waited. His joking expression had disappeared.

'Tonight, while all this vote-of-thanks nonsense was going on, I realised something I hadn't faced up to before. This gave me a shock.' He paused. *'I've begun to hate Norman Standsfield's guts.'*

Silence. A clock somewhere ticked in a muffled way.

'This I don't like, Jack. I've got to work with him.'

I said nothing.

'It's mutual, too, I suppose.'

I contemplated one of the incidental realities of this sort of world — and of a good deal of the rest of the world, for that matter — that *I* didn't like either. I was used to it: I knew it was the way men were made: but I didn't like it. It was that men in this sort of world *liked* each other so little.

But that was not to say that they all hated each other's guts. I was very shocked by Bill's discovery that he hated Norman's. It was very unusual to hear one of them come out with that kind of remark: they might say another man was the Prima Donna Type or the Führer Type, or a b——!: but that was very different from *knowing* they hated his guts. Knowing their own deepest impulses was something for which they usually had, in my opinion, a negative gift — Bill certainly shared it. That's why I was all the more shocked. His hatred of Norman must be strong enough to crash through the barrier.

'Good Lord!' Bill interrupted my lucubrations. 'He's come back again.'

I looked up, and saw the elderly gentleman shuffling in.

'He must have come back to listen to the rest of our conversation.'

I drank some of my whisky. Bill's voice carried — he'd got into trouble before now for talking indiscreetly in public places.

'Do you suppose,' Bill asked me, 'he's One of Them? Too old, I should've thought, wouldn't you?'

In commoner London parlance at the time 'One of Them'

meant a homosexual; but in Bill's parlance it meant someone from the security services, a member of the spying-
classes.

Though I resented the interruption, I couldn't help
laughing. Bill had no more use for members of the spying-
classes than I had. Whenever anybody talked about Cold
War spying by scientists, he pronounced his clinching dic-
tum: 'The amount of scientific advantage that either side
really gets over the other by spying is negligible. The reason
they spy is to embarrass each other politically.'

We watched the old gentleman sit down again at the far
end of the room and hold up the *Financial Times* in front
of him.

'Must be One of Them,' Bill said.

His mood changed swiftly back to where it was before.

'I thought it would amuse you,' he said, drinking some
more of his whisky. 'To hear I'd just discovered I really
hate Norman Standsfield's guts.'

'Don't be a bloody fool!' I cried. 'I'm not amused. . . .
There are some games where I'm definitely not on the side-
lines, and this is one of them!'

I spoke heatedly. We were old friends. We liked each
other: we, at least, were allies.

Bill was leaning forward with his elbows resting on his
knees, looking down at his glass, his K.B.E. dangling over
it. Silent.

When he spoke he didn't look up — it sounded as if he
were speaking to himself.

'My wish,' he said in a low, strong voice, 'is that Norman
Standsfield would get out *now*! And that *I*'d get the chairmanship!'

I stared at him.

Suddenly he stared at me. 'This I want, more than anything. And the sooner the better.'

I knew, anyway.

'This I *mean*!' He put his glass down on the table with a
crash. 'The sooner the *better*!'

If I'd said 'I'm with you!' he wouldn't have heard.

He suddenly leaned forward again to pick up his glass — his K.B.E. clinked against it. He had a drink. Then he said:

'Do you realise that Norman Standsfield doesn't know what he's doing with the Power Board? He hasn't got a policy for the Board for the next five years, let alone the next twenty!' He rounded on me. 'How can he have? What basis has he got for building one on? He's not an engineer. He's not technical. He's *anti*-technical!' He paused. 'So how can he have any instinct for what's going to happen? How can he have any instinct for what the Power Board's got to be doing in the next five years? In the next twenty years? . . .' He beat his hand on the sofa between us — in his other hand the whisky sloshed about in its glass. 'Does he have any conception of how much Power the N.P.B.'s going to be asked to produce? And where it's going to come from? Other than as a bit of arithmetic somebody hands him on a slip of paper before he goes out to make a speech — and this he resents! This is true. I'm telling you!'

I shook my head. His voice grew louder.

'We're here to make Money. Of course we are. But above all, Jack, we're here to make Power. Because the country needs Power and is willing to pay us good money for it.' He paused. 'Do you realise how much Power this country's going to need? On their bits of paper they tell Norman the demand's doubling every nine years. Let me tell you, it's going to double in less, Jack, less. . . . And I want to see the country gets it!'

His eyes glowed at me with energy and rage — I might have been standing shoulder to shoulder with Norman in stopping him.

I thought: He *can* do it!

'You once told me, Jack, that I don't have a good understanding of myself — '

'No, Bill — '

'But this I do have a good understanding of! And I'm telling you — '

'Yes, Bill.'

He slowed down, and spoke with all his force.

'I'd give anything to see that the country gets the Power. I'd give anything. And I'd do anything. I know it's a feeling you tie up with Socialism. I'm Conservative, and it's just the same. I want to see this country *hum*!'

Suddenly everything, he, I, the elderly gentleman, the whole room, seemed to have gone utterly quiet.

He's got to get that chairmanship, I was thinking. There was no need for him to say more. I knew where I stood. He's simply got to get it!

Bill felt the need to say more.

'Do you know what it would be?' he demanded. 'Do you know?' He paused. 'A Major Breakthrough!'

We stared at each other.

'I suppose you think I'm drunk?' he said.

He *was* drunk. But he was speaking the truth. And what he wanted to see, I believed he could bring to pass.

CHAPTER TWO

Teenagers and Television

A few days later the Election Committee met in the college and elected M. J. Bowen to a Fellowship. A cable was sent off to him: we wanted to know how soon he could come, and until we got a reply we had to be prepared for his having accepted the offer from Berkeley to stay.

'I take it that if Bowen turns us down,' Stanley Forbes said to me, 'we shan't have to look any further than Mac-Robert.'

I cabled Bowen myself, telling him I could get him some more money for acting as a consultant to the Power Board. Together with his Fellowship stipend his total earnings would then be brought up as far as two-thirds of what he could earn in the U.S.A.

'Mike isn't mad about money,' Roz told me.

'So much the better for us,' said I.

Roz said lightly: 'So much the worse for him.'

I didn't pay much attention to her remark at the time.

Something new had happened. Roz had decided she was going to write a novel. Our plan had been for her to spend most of the time between now and September, when she was due to enrol at Stanford, in Italy. I had agreed to her indulging in a ladylike study of Renaissance painting and the Italian language because I liked going to Italy myself.

When she announced that she was going to write a novel I was oddly thrilled. I had just decided to try and write this present book, though I hadn't yet told her and Alice. I had no doubts at all about whether I preferred Roz to go to Italy for ladylike education or to stay home and write a novel.

Alice had some doubts. 'But what can she write a novel *about*? She's only eighteen.'

'About what it's like to be seventeen,' I said. 'Or sixteen. It might be fascinating.'

'She won't tell me what it's about. Has she told you?'

'I haven't asked her.'

Alice was thoughtful. 'I do hope she can write a novel.'

'Anybody *can*,' I said. 'What I hope is that she's got some talent.' I have to admit that in what I was saying during the next few minutes I was secretly speaking for myself. I said:

'If she wants to write a novel, why shouldn't she?'

'I still think it's too young all the same.'

'If anybody wants to write a novel, I wish them more power to their elbow, whatever their age.' I laughed. 'I mean literally their elbow. We all *think* of writing a novel. . . . It must be having the strength to put pen to paper continuously that makes the difference between that and actually writing it.' I paused. 'Alec Benda says it is, and he ought to know. Anyway, I think it's a terribly exciting prospect. I couldn't bear not to let Roz try it.'

Alice gave me a sidelong look. 'Do you think you could stop her, darling?'

So Roz began writing a novel, and we were waiting to see what it would be like.

I was in a position to infer just how long it takes to write a novel from my own experience of writing this book — I shall be lucky if I finish it by 1965. Roz announced that she wasn't going to show her novel to us till she'd written at least a third of it. To me the prospect was really exciting — my own child was doing something new, creating a work of art. (As an actor George was in my opinion only resuscitating something which somebody else had created.)

E

Alice continued to view the prospect with less excitement. 'You really do get fussed over her,' she said. 'I mean, don't you?'

I declined to reply. The relationship between a father and daughter is rather different from that between a mother and daughter.

'I wonder if she'll lose interest when Michael Bowen comes . . .'

I declined to show that I'd heard her.

The college got a cable from Bowen saying he would accept the Fellowship. I, on the other hand, got no cable saying if he wanted to earn some money from the Power Board. As young scientists like Michael Bowen were not in the habit of putting courtesy especially high on their list of moral obligations to society, I didn't take umbrage. I judged that he would arrive in Oxford expecting that as a matter of course I'd have an N.P.B. contract ready for him to sign.

A few evenings after the news that Bowen had accepted the Fellowship I dined in College, and the subject was scarcely referred to. The main topic of conversation now was a new argie-bargie with Skootz, Merridge and Potherill about the economics of storage-heating. However, Stanley Forbes took me aside before he left the Senior Common Room.

'Can you come back to the Lodgings with me, Jack? To give me your advice.'

I had no excuse for saying No. In the Lodgings we went towards the staircase, to go up to Stanley's room. Doris came across the sitting-room.

'I'll bring your *tisane*,' she said to Stanley — and then to me: 'Coffee keeps Him awake.'

'Sometimes one wants to be kept awake,' I said. 'Delicious though somnolence is.'

Doris glared at me. 'I hope you're not going to talk too long. He's got to get up early in the morning to go up to Town.'

'I think it's all right, Dearest,' said Stanley smoothly. 'Perhaps I can look after myself.'

As we went upstairs he said to me: 'To tell the truth, Jack, I know I couldn't look after myself as well as Doris looks after me.' It was the first time he'd ever made an intimate remark to me about Doris. It struck me that he was speaking the truth. Momentarily I thought about marriage, about myself and Alice, about all sorts of things . . .

'Come into my study,' said Stanley.

We settled down in armchairs and Stanley offered me a cigarette. His expression, lit by a single table-lamp on the desk beside him, was urbane as usual but serious.

'I want your advice, and possibly your help, if you can spare it,' he said.

'I'm sure I can,' I said — my help in doing nothing.

'I've had a rather surprising letter from John Farrow. A sort of round-robin from himself and several other Fellows. In fact all the Arts Fellows. Apropos the election of M. J. Bowen.'

'Oh,' said I. It didn't surprise me, for one.

'It was rather long,' said Stanley. 'John Farrow has never been known to write a short letter. By the by, don't you think his style, for someone who teaches English Literature, is perfectly wretched?' He paused, but not for an answer. 'The gist of his letter can be put very briefly. It expresses his belief that a strong minority opinion in favour of MacRobert — and the minority includes himself — a strong minority opinion found no representation on the Election Committee.'

I suppressed my inclination to say that's how it ought to be, and Stanley went on in his melodious even tone.

'Of course they're wrong, as you know, Jack. Their opinion was represented by the Dean and myself.' He stopped when I wasn't expecting him to.

I said: 'What do they want?'

'To speak for themselves *on* the Election Committee.'

I was silent.

'I want you,' said Stanley, 'to help me come to a compromise.'

As if Stanley needed any help to that! I said nothing. The only way of dealing with John Farrow was total, uncompromising *non*-compromise. Simply because Farrow had no conception of what compromise meant. People either gave him what he wanted, which showed they were momentarily impelled by their duty to society; or they didn't, which showed they were wicked. When he got what he wanted he demanded something further; and when he didn't, he demanded the same thing again. In my view he should be democratically accorded the privilege of demanding this particular thing over and over again for the next quarter of a century.

'They want me to receive them as a sort of deputation,' Stanley said. 'I'd like you to be at hand.' He waited. 'I think it would be for the good of the College.'

I thought it might well be for the good of the College. If they wanted a Two Cultures war, it would be as well for Clarendon if the scientific side carried the day.

'All right,' I said.

There was a bang on the door as Doris pushed it open with a tray on which were two of her Rockingham cups and saucers.

'Another ten minutes,' she said to me with a cheerful glare. 'His meeting in the morning is an important one.'

'Oh,' I said innocently. 'Where is it?'

'In Whitehall,' said Doris. 'And don't tell me you don't know with whom!'

She went out triumphant.

I left in two minutes. Stanley had already trapped me nicely.

I went out into the quad. It was a black, sludgy, hazy night, the sort of night which reminded one that the city of Oxford was built on a river. I noticed a light on in Brian Challoner's rooms — he was a bachelor and lived in college. As he was a signatory to Farrow's letter, I thought I'd go up and see him before I went home. On the staircase I could hear music coming from the room.

The outer door was open and I went in. The light in the room came from a reading-lamp, the music from a television set.

The occupant of the room, who jumped up when I came in, was a youth of seventeen or so. He was smallish, black-haired, with a sharp-featured pale face, handsome, almost pretty. He was dressed in light-coloured Levis and an Italian-looking jersey.

'I was just watching Brian's T.V.,' he said. 'He wanted to know something special about tonight's programme and our set's broken at home.' He spoke rapidly in a stylised version of the town accent — the son of a scout or something?

I said: 'Don't let me disturb you!'

Though I didn't seem to notice it at the time, I must also have observed, since I recalled it later, that his face, despite its being nearly pretty, was strained and slightly feverish-looking.

'Oh no, it's just over,' he said. 'The programme, I mean. I'm going now.' He darted across to the set and switched it off. 'And Brian said he'd be back . . .' He began to put on a short topcoat made of hairy, bobbly tweed.

There were sounds of footsteps and voices on the stair-case. It was Brian Challoner and Alec Benda, their academic gowns slung over their shoulders, just coming in from the Senior Common Room.

The youth passed me in the doorway and went down the stairs.

Brian said: 'That was one of my tame teenage viewers of television.'

'Tame, indeed!' I heard Alec Benda say. '*Really*, Brian!'

Brian said: 'How about drinks? What did you have with Lord Forbes, Jack?'

I said I shared his Lordship's *tisane*.

Brian went across to a cupboard. Alec said:

'You know you ought to ask *me*, Brian, about the effects

of T.V. on teenagers. I'm very much closer to them than most *croulants*, as the French boys call adults—it's what we are in their eyes.'

Brian was taking no notice.

Perhaps I ought to remark that Brian's choice of research topic was pretty surprising to me. I'd known him before he came to Clarendon, and I'd thought a lot of his work.

As a sociologist Brian belonged to a school that to myself I called humane sociologists. (I wouldn't have risked saying it in the company of professional sociologists.) Most sociology, the professionals might say, is motivated at least in part by social conscience. In the work of Brian and his colleagues, social conscience was manifest in a way that really stirred me: I felt I could readily go along with sociologists like that, where, I have to admit, I felt my footsteps dragging when I was required to assist in long Central European discussions of totemism and caste or Action Theory.

About a year before he came to Clarendon, Brian had come to the end of one stretch of research. 'If you were me, Jack, what would you do next? Something to occupy me for three years or so.'

I could still remember the incident very clearly. Brian and I were walking down the Strand to have lunch at Simpson's. I'd spent the previous hour with Bill Taylor in his office at Power Centre, inducing in him and myself the mixture of rage and despair that always overwhelmed us when we discussed the prospects of bringing the country up to scratch in technology and science. (I'd just returned from a visit to the Batelle Institute and was feeling my characteristic reaction to getting back from the United States to England—that I'd returned to a stagnant backwater, to a country of infinitesimal progress along well laid-down lines.)

We, Bill and I, were agreed that what we wanted to get done could only be done through education. He was sold on setting up a couple of M.I.T.s in England. I thought that wasn't starting anything like far enough back in the educational system. But that's not the argument I want to go into now. I merely want to account for the tone of my reply to Brian's question, in the Strand. I happened to have the answer ready, off-the-cuff and red-hot into the bargain.

'If I were you I'd do a study of the relationship between the class-structure of this country and its educational system.'

At the back of my mind was the idea that you couldn't give the country the educational shake-up it needed without giving the class-structure an equivalent shake-up. And that the essential class-structure was so ossified that giving it a real shake-up simply wasn't on. Ergo . . .

Brian said: 'Of course you're a Radical. You don't like the present class-structure.'

I didn't see what that had to do with it. However we were going through the doors of the restaurant.

I wasn't really expecting Brian to say 'That's a splendid idea, Jack. I'll start right away!' But I was dismayed when he let out during lunch the idea for research that was in his mind.

Teenagers *and* television! The worst of two corny worlds, as it were. 'Oh, spare us!' I cried.

Brian gave me a swift apprehensive glance, his little eyes very clear and sharp, his crew-cut hair standing up on end. He said:

'I think there's something to be got out of it.'

Had I been more concerned with listening to him and less concerned with airing my own views, I might have noticed his remark was ambiguous.

'It sounds like bringing sociology down to the level of feature-journalism,' I said.

'If *I* do it, Jack,' he said with a fleeting grin, 'it will be bringing feature-journalism up to the level of sociology!' He glanced at me again. 'And why are we knocking feature-journalism?'

He was harking back to a discussion we'd had some months earlier, about the way in which both sociology and the particular kind of journalism I meant had come to the fore in the period between the wars. From two different points of view, the one professional and compassionate, the other superficial and emotional, sociology and feature-journalism respectively covered the study of human beings in society which would formerly have been the province of novelists.

Our thesis was that in the period between the wars, novelists had abdicated from this province — in favour of concentrating on the human being alone, in isolation, chiefly occupied with experiencing the life of the senses. And when novelists abdicated, sociologists and journalists had taken the province over. More power to *their* elbow!

So I had to explain why I was knocking feature-journalists.

'I'll tell you why,' I said. 'Since the war, especially, teenagers have come to think of themselves as a race apart. And two bodies of people, for their own ends, have organised them into it. People in the advertising industry, in order to get their money out of them. And feature-journalists, in order to make sensational copy out of them.'

Brian tried to interrupt, but I went on.

'I don't need to tell *you* it's not a difficult operation to make people feel they're a race apart. A damn sight easier than making them feel a race together, which is what we've all got to try and be. As for teenagers — to organise them into feeling a race apart, when God knows it's difficult enough for the old and the young to get on together anyway, is bloody criminal!'

'How much part do you think television has played?'

'That,' I said, since it was clear that he meant to do it, 'is for your scientific investigation to discover.'

Anyway, all that was some months earlier. So far as the present moment in my story is concerned, you see why the youth was watching Brian's television set and why my attitude to the whole proceedings was cool.

Brian was getting down a bottle of whisky and a soda-water siphon from the cupboard. I glanced round the room.

I found Brian's taste in interior decoration puzzling. The college had provided him with two pleasant new rooms: he appeared to have furnished them at a cost of about £50. The sofas and chairs were second-hand and broken-springed. There were no rugs at all. He slept on what looked like an old hospital bed. Yet there was a large television set and an expensive hi-fi installation. I simply didn't understand, I thought, what made Brian tick.

Brian said: 'I suppose our President wanted to sound your opinion on the proposed delegation?'

I nodded.

Brian sat down, crossing one long leg over the other. His legs looked thinner and longer because he was wearing very narrow dark trousers. His trouser-leg went up, showing a short sock of the sort college-boys were at that time wearing all over the U.S.A., white with bands of red, white and blue round the top.

'I wish I could get out of the deputation now,' he said, pouring me a drink.

'Shame!' cried Alec.

'I'm glad Bowen was elected, Jack. He was the better man.'

I restrained some exasperation.

'You're just appalled at finding yourself lined up behind John Farrow,' said Alec.

Brian jumped, and looked as if he were going to run up the curtains.

'Let's have some music,' he said. He went across to the record-player and put on a record, of Billie Holiday — he was a jazz buff.

So that was the end of that. But it was not the end of the evening's events.

Alice and I were getting ready to go to bed when the telephone rang. I listened to her answering it —

'No, he's not here, I'm afraid. He hasn't been here for *days.* . . . I *know* my husband saw him earlier this evening. Yes. . . . Well, I'm afraid I really can't help you, then.'

E*

Alice put down the receiver.

'Who was that?'

'He said his name's John Minelli, or something that sounded like that. And he wanted Brian Challoner — whom he seemed to think was with *you*. . . . At this time of night.'

I exclaimed.

'Do you know who he is, darling?'

I had to think for a moment. Suddenly it struck me.

'I think that's the name of a youth who was sitting in Brian's rooms watching television earlier this evening.'

'But how extraordinary!'

There was a moment's pause. And then I said:

'I think he must be mad. Bonkers . . .'

I smiled to find myself using a word I'd picked up from Julia. But I hadn't liked the incident at all.

CHAPTER THREE

Raison d'etre of a Scenario

Next morning I had another disturbing telephone call, disturbing in a very different way. It was from Bill Taylor, in London.

'Herbert Hobbs,' he announced the subject of the call. 'Have you heard? Do you know what he's produced now?'

With great presence of mind I got the terminology right.

'A scenario,' I said, 'for the Power Board's reorganisation, R. & D.-wise.'

'Exactly.'

I said: 'He tried it out on me at lunch one day.'

'He's got the Chairman moving on it now.'

There was a pause.

'When are you going to be in London next?' he asked.

I said at the beginning of the following week, and arranged to meet him; and that was the end of the conversation.

I met him at Power Centre before lunch. He'd discovered that all the other members were going to be out, so we went to their dining-room to eat. It was a very large double-room on the corner of the building, one half being furnished with buttoned black leather sofas and low tables with dark marble tops, the other half with a long mahogany dining-table and a set of reproduction Hepplewhite chairs. The walls of the dining-room half were painted a Georgian pale green. The two corner walls of the sitting-room half were all window. The view was marvellous, including, as every skyscraper view of London seemed to include, St. Paul's.

A waitress served us drinks. I said idly that I was getting so inured to a gin-and-tonic before lunch that I could put it down without any appreciable effect.

'You're getting middle-aged, Jack. We're all getting middle-aged. We can't take as much drink as we used to.'

I nodded my head, and so lost my chance to forestall the inevitable follow-up.

'We can't take as much bed, either, Jack.'

'Er . . . no. Perhaps not.'

The sunlight shone on Bill as he stood, lightly balanced with his feet firmly apart, one hand in his trouser pocket. The sky was cloudless, filling the whole of the space above the roof-tops with a glistening, vernal blue — prematurely vernal, I may say: we were only in February.

I said: 'You seem to be in high spirits. How come?'

'Perhaps because the Chairman's out for the day.' He grinned at me. 'I suppose I ought to have said it was because you are in for the day. You always take me out of myself.'

'What's this the prelude to launching at me?'

'Nothing.'

'Actually,' I said, 'I thought I might find you in bad spirits.'

'Because of Bloody Hobbs's new scheme?' He drank some gin-and-tonic and then put down his glass on one of the small tables. 'I'm used to Herbert Hobbs's scenarios by now.' (The Hampshire 'ow' grated round the room.)

'Are you?' I said. 'And is Uncle Bert's latest effort a good idea?' I sat down on the window-sill.

Bill stepped up to the window, and thrust both hands into his trouser pockets. He was wearing a Glen Urquhart tweed suit which gave him a sporting air, and he looked as if he'd had a fresh haircut. Small, forceful, large-eyed.

'Is this the question, anyway?' he said.

'It's *a* question,' I said. I stood up hastily. I'd forgotten the radiators were embedded under the window-sills.

We finished our drinks and strolled across to the long dining-table, where two places were set.

'*I* sit in the Chairman's place,' Bill said sardonically.

I said: 'I asked you if Uncle Bert's latest effort is a good idea?'

'And I replied: "Is this the question, anyway?" In other words, do you expect anybody's scenario, for anything, to be considered on its merits in *this* place?'

In *this* place — glancing down the empty table I imagined all the other members there. '*Quot homines* . . .' I thought, which being translated N.P.B.-wise, meant: However many members, that many hands being played independently for personal reasons.

The waitress came in bringing us each a tub of potted shrimps. She asked Bill if we wanted to drink wine. I shook my head. Bill ordered himself a bottle of Vichy water. (It was an N.P.B. member's fashion. Bill said that in his case it was to flush out his kidneys, but I suspected that Vichy water seemed to the members just that bit classier than tap-water. I looked forward to the day when I came upon aspiring young engineers down below in the Board displaying a taste for Vichy water in readiness . . .)

'Now,' I said, when the waitress had shut the door. 'Give me the low-down!'

Bill looked at me steadily with no facial expression. He said:

'What's *your* story for why Hobbs wants to form this other Division?'

I said: 'To hive off the Scientists into some sort of glorified purdah, with the courtesy title of Research and Development Division.'

'O.K.' Bill ate some shrimps. 'Carry on!'

'I call that Intention No. 1. Then there's Intention No. 2, which in my opinion really takes precedence over Intention No. 1. Intention No. 2 is to deliver a grand, public smack-in-the-eye to *you*, grand, public and lasting — an R. & D. Division set up now would be a permanent memorial to a lapse of judgement in your Nuclear Division days.'

'This is true.' He ate some more shrimps.

'Well?' I said. I thought I'd done fairly well.

'You've covered Hobbs's taking a crack at the Scientists. And his taking a crack at me. Is this the whole story as you see it?'

'It is.' I looked at him. 'Now, you shoot!'

Bill shot, as it were. The story within the story.

As Member for Coal & Oil, Herbert Hobbs had two men working immediately under him, referred to as his No. 2's. Carried away by personal imperialism and desire to be a father-figure, Hobbs had promised his own position, when he retired, to *each* of them.

Two into one won't go. Even Herbert Hobbs's cunning and wiliness couldn't get him round that. Two men, one Division — and both promised it. There was only one solution. Each man had to have a Division; so a new Division must be carved out. Simplicity itself! Positively child-like simplicity . . .

My mouthful of shrimps nearly choked me.

'Do you mean to say he's going to turn the National Power Board upside-down for that?'

'Who says he's going to? This is only,' Bill said, 'the scenario-stage.'

He methodically finished his shrimps.

We were both silent for a little while. Then Bill sat back in his chair and we talked again. Having got the low-down off his chest, he was prepared to agree that I'd been on the right lines as far as I went.

A new Division for Research & Development would certainly 'get those Scientists off our necks'. We could see that, all right. We could also see that Hobbs, as member, would lose least in parting with his own Division's R. & D. men — because his own Division had least of them. (Nuclear Division, of course, had most.) And we could also see that for the Scientists to have a member of their own might, despite their being kept in a sort of purdah, be troublesome for Uncle Bert on the Board—but that was nicely taken care of by the Scientists' member being one of his, Uncle Bert's, own men!

I contemplated the scenario *in toto*. 'It's got everything,' I said.

'Right,' said Bill.

The waitress came in, but we scarcely noticed her serving us with lamb chops and grilled tomatoes, though I just found enough attention to turn down, remembering Alice's injunctions, the chipped potatoes.

I said:

'What are the chances of its going beyond the scenario-stage?'

'The Chairman.'

'What line is he taking at the moment?'

'None. He's *moving*. But he's got no *line*.'

I was put off, by the look in his eyes, from going on. I began to eat. Bill did the same.

The normal assumption in the National Power Board was that as the Chairman felt antipathy towards both the Scientists *and* the Engineers, he took the line which made the most bad blood between them. That meant he would automatically be disposed *not* to throw Bert Hobbs's scenario out.

As leader of the Administrators, Norman would be unquestionably supported by the Member for Finance and Administration.

Equally unquestioningly Bill, as leader of the Scientists, would be supported in whatever line he took by the present Member for Nuclear Division, who was called Trevor Darwin. (Incidentally I may say Darwin was a very good scientist.)

We paused a moment to discuss Darwin. If the N.P.B. had to have a Member for Research & Development, Trevor Darwin was the obvious man. And his place could be filled by promoting the scientist who was currently Chief Superintendent of Courtenay Bagpuize.

We took it that Herbert Hobbs would be no slower than we were to see that that arrangement meant the installation of two of Bill's men. Two more Scientists! Not likely.

'What line is Amos Wilson going to take?' I said, thinking of the Engineers. Would he go in with Hobbs, their leader; or would he fight to keep his own R. & D.? We didn't know.

We munched our chops. Bill abstractedly helped himself to more Vichy water. To change the conversation, I said:

'How did you know what had been going on at Uncle Bert's headquarters?'

Bill gave me a look of sarcastic triumph. 'From one of the girls in Hobbs's office. She used to be in Nuclear Division.'

'Really!' I said.

His eyes shone with harsh amusement. He said:

'It's been going on for a long time — I mean Hobbs's favouring first one and then the other of his No. 2's . . . But it's hotted up during the last year. One month it's been one of them who's been called into Uncle Bert's room for private confabs. Next month it's been the other. The poor bastard who was left out had to go round and quiz the girls in the other poor bastard's office to find out what had been going on.' He paused. 'Before all this started they were reasonably happy and on reasonably good terms with each other. Now their girls say both of them are getting near to a nervous breakdown.'

It wasn't difficult to imagine, Uncle Bert sitting in his room, looking tall and fat and wily and father-like. He had a long handsome table at one end of which, for reasons unknown — but frequently guessed-at — stood a huge terrestial globe.

'I can't help pitying the poor bastards,' I said.

'Then your pity will be wasted,' said Bill, 'if this scheme goes through and a whole new Division is carved out for the bastard who doesn't inherit Coal & Oil Division! A whole bloody new Division. . . . Even if Hobbs doesn't mean it to amount to anything.' He thought it over. 'You can't say Herbert Hobbs is not a creative thinker!'

The waitress came in to see if we had finished.

'Sweet or cheese?'

Despite Alice's further injunction, I said ice cream. Bill, whose weight always stayed exactly right for his fine mesomorphic build, said cheese.

'Well, after all that,' he said, 'do you still think the thing ought to be discussed in terms of its merits?'

'I do,' I said. 'Even though after all that it'll seem a bit of an anticlimax.'

'All right, then. Let's have a brief run-down of the pros and cons!'

For the next quarter of an hour we had a brief run-down of the pros and cons. After judgematically considering all the aspects, weighing all the angles, going back where necessary to Square One, we concluded that research and development run the present way, and research and development run Bert Hobbs's projected way, would probably work out just about the *same*.

The fact of the matter is that given a large body of men to do a certain job, there are several ways in which they can reasonably be organised to do it; and between those ways there's very little to choose. But that doesn't stop people who are organised in one of the ways from seeing the remarkable attractions — in the nature of efficiency, logic, and God knows what-all — of being organised in one of the other ways. I found those attractions somewhat less than remarkable, myself.

'I know it makes a *change*,' I was inclined to say, 'but does it *help*?'

'You don't know how unpopular you've made yourself around the Power Board and elsewhere,' Bill told me when I said it to him, 'by saying this.'

'Oh!' I was wounded by the thought of anything I might say making me unpopular anywhere. Especially when it was both sensible and true. How could it make me unpopular?

Bill and I agreed that if we were setting up the National Power Board from scratch — admittedly one of the most ill-advised things to do — we should probably organise its research and development in Hobbs's projected way. Only probably: it was a near thing. But the fact that the N.P.B. was already in existence, with its research and development already going satisfactorily, put the choice on an entirely different footing.

'I've had enough of this,' said Bill. He'd finished his cheese and he meant the discussion. 'Let's have some coffee — black. And talk about something else. It's time we talked about *you*. Instead of about me.'

We got up and strolled back again to the sitting-room. On the way I glanced at a new picture, a gouache by John Piper. It was only when I got close to it that I saw it was not an original.

The sunlight was still shining through the glass: the vernal blue of the sky was fading, now, from the horizon upwards.

The waitress poured our coffee and Bill took a cigar. When he'd lit it he said:

'With *this* place I was pretty fed-up, *prior* to Bert Hobbs getting out his new bloody scheme.'

'Which place?' I said innocently, not quite seeing how we were talking about me.

'This place.' He waved his cigar-hand through the air.

'Oh.'

I thought he certainly ought not to leave the Power Board. I said:

'I grant that Norman is a bit much to put up with.' The time would come when Norman must retire.

'With the whole place I'm fed-up, not just with Standsfield.' He sat down and I sat opposite him. 'Unless you're in it, you don't know what it's like.'

'No . . .'

'Don't say No like that! Of course you don't. You're an academic. You've got your freedom —'

'Come off it, Bill!'

'What it's like here you don't know. Bloody frustrating! This is true. . . . Here am I, Sir William Taylor, Deputy Chairman of the National Power Board, and I can't do any of the things I want to do!'

I am afraid my sympathy for him wilted. I remembered him in his different mood, the evening when he was drunk at the Club, and said: 'I want to make this country *hum*!' and I knew he could do it.

'Every morning,' he said, 'when I come to the office my staff gather round me, as if I were an ox.'

'Good God!' (He was much too small for an ox.)

'And the *yoke* is put on me!'

I said Good God! again.

'The motions required of me,' he said, 'I then go through.'

He saw that I was going to say something and got in first.

'The truth is this, Jack.' He looked at me with a clear, penetrating gaze. 'I'm a Prisoner of the System!'

I have to say that as an old friend of his I felt bound to listen but not to do anything more. The truth was, so far as I was concerned, that he really was a man who wanted to make the country hum and really could do it. Prisoner of the System, my foot!

'Some day,' he said, 'I shall burst out!' He looked at me menacingly as a new image occurred to him. 'They can't sit on a volcano for ever!'

If I was supposed to believe that he really would leave the Power Board, I didn't believe. I thought his desire to see the country get the Power it needed was so strong, and so possible for *him* to realise, that he would stay.

A minor question puzzled me, though. I'd heard a rumour that Matthewson's had asked him to join the oligarchy that was going to rule the firm in succession to the Old Man. I was surprised he hadn't mentioned it.

I said: 'Even so, Bill, even though you're yoked, frustrated, imprisoned, et cetera, most people would say you haven't done so badly for yourself.'

'My dear chap, this is identically what they say about you, too.'

'Really?' I must say I couldn't see the slightest grounds for such comment.

'When you come to think about it, *you* haven't done so badly, you know. This is a nice scientific field you've picked yourself to work in. Materials. When you picked it it was the coming thing, and now it's right bang In. And you're in it—and at the height of your powers!'

I laughed in a wry sort of way.

'Materials is due for a crop of Nobels, isn't it?'

'That's for the Swedes to say.'

'Let's have a run-down of the total situation!' he said. 'This is interesting. You picked a nice field to work in, and you're practically one of the founder-members of it. And you picked yourself a wife who's a damned nice woman, with a title and some money as well. This is pretty good, you know.'

There was no missing the inference. The Universal Climb. Wot me?

'I've often wondered how you've done it, you know,' he said, clearly not having the faintest idea where to stop. 'Meg and I talk about it . . .'

Only a few minutes ago I'd remarked that his present mood was not indicative of his true self. I felt that it was time to change the subject of conversation.

Before I could do so, Bill said: 'My dear chap, I haven't offended you, have I?'

'Not at all.'

He took a puff at his cigar. He thought for a moment, and then he looked at me. 'You're going to stick around, in this place, aren't you?'

I laughed. 'If *you* do.'

Bill stood up and walked across to the window. I watched him and then followed.

We looked through the glass.

'This thing of Hobbs's is only at the scenario-stage,' I

heard him saying, 'but if it really gets going. . . . Do you see any of the immediate consequences that won't be destructive?'

An aeroplane was flying across the clear blue, leaving a vapour trail behind. I didn't answer. I wasn't required to.

CHAPTER FOUR

K–Day

In March the great day arrived, and brought with it a question. Had I come to the time in my life when I ought to have a morning suit of my own, instead of always hiring one from Moss Bros.?

Alice was in favour of my having one of my own, largely on class grounds, I thought. '*Our* sort of people have their own.'

I was in favour largely because I saw a way of avoiding the fuss each time of trying on innumerable pairs of trousers and jackets.

Roz, on the other hand, said:

'The question is whether you'll wear it often enough for it to pay for itself.'

I was delighted to hear her. The concept of one's breaking even, financially, through using an inordinate number of times some article, be it a morning suit or an I.B.M. 7090, that one hasn't the faintest need to buy in the first place, possesses for me a singular beauty.

I said: 'I should try to wear it as often as possible.'

'Where?' said Roz.

I began: 'At Garden Parties . . .'

'You're only invited to one of those a year.'

I said: 'And I could wear it at weddings and funerals.'

'You're scarcely ever invited to a wedding.'

'But it would be easy to go to more funerals. And memorial services. There are lots of memorial services.'

Roz began to laugh. 'Every morning Alice and I could look up what's on in *The Times* for you.'

'Exactly,' I said enthusiastically. 'I should be not only the best-known mourner in London. I should be the best-*dressed* one!'

That was the end of the discussion. It was obvious that I should be going to Moss Bros. as usual.

There was only one more embarrassing moment to come. One morning at breakfast, Julia said:

'Why can't I come with you?'

The rest of us looked at each other, no one having a reply ready. Julia said:

'You know I can behave very well.'

Alas! poor Julia . . .

We hired a car to take us to the ceremony. Ever since the afternoon when we went to a Garden Party in a taxi and were directed by a policeman to a back entrance of the Garden, Alice had insisted on our going by hired car, preferably with a sticker stuck on the windscreen.

The morning was greyish and rawly cold. 'Rather inauspicious, don't you think?' I said.

'Terribly,' said Alice. 'But you'll feel better afterwards. I mean, won't you? . . .'

It seemed to me that I was being asked to get there at a somewhat early hour. My idea would have been noon, just right for a pre-accolade drink; and then off to lunch. (We had booked a table at the Connaught, to celebrate.)

'Don't forget,' said Roz, giving me a last look-over when we got out of the car. 'Just before you go in, hitch your coat forward!'

I'd got tired of trying on jackets and had escaped with one that tended to ride back on my shoulders.

I gave Roz and Alice a last look-over, and found myself without a word of exhortation for either of them. I had gained nothing financially by going to Moss Bros. They had both made the occasion an excuse for getting new out-fits for themselves, and as neither of them had won any money on a horse or a dog, respectively, I'd had to pay.

Alice was wearing the pearls she'd inherited from her mother. 'I really must look like everybody else, mustn't I?' she'd said. But at the last moment she had jibbed, and had left off her diamond brooch. She was wearing a hat made of fur. Roz was wearing no jewellery and her Zulu top-knot.

We were waved into one of the entrance corridors by a functionary of presumably lowly order. As we went along I re-experienced the shock of recognition with which I had seen these corridors for the first time. The crimson carpet, the dark cream walls, the subdued lighting. . . . It was an unforgettable shock of recognition. 'Why, *now* I know what those huge old cinemas round Leicester Square were modelled on!'

I said to Roz: 'This'll make you a scene in your novel.'

'I'm not writing about *this* sort of people,' she said huffily. But when we separated she gave me a sparkling grin.

'You're on your own now!'

I replied in the proletarian vernacular of the times. 'Watch it!' It served her right, I thought.

I went past several rooms — I presume all palaces must have lots of spare rooms for official purposes — and ended up in a large sort of corridor-room which was roped off into pens. I was directed to the appropriate pen, which already contained some score of middle-aged and elderly gentlemen assembled for the same purpose as myself. I was suddenly struck by how being married to Alice debarred me from being wholly one of them — I couldn't say I was really accepting a Knighthood in order to please my wife who wanted to be called Lady. No matter, I loved them all the same, in their black jackets, grey striped trousers, light grey silk ties — some with a pearl-headed pin — with their grey hair, their thinning pates, and their smiling pink faces.

We were all waiting. All agog. It was a happy sight. I pondered on the marvel, the miracle, that had brought us all here, that in another six months would bring another score or more middle-aged and elderly gentlemen with grey hair, thinning pates and smiling pink faces here; and in another six months another score or more, and in another six months another, and in another six months. . . . So long as the country didn't become a republic, and I saw no signs of the likelihood of that, the marvel would repeat itself at six-monthly intervals *ad infinitum*. It was a marvel of steadily sustained administration. Only the dear old Civil Service, I felt with a burst of enthusiastic vicarious loyalty, could have pulled it off.

I recalled a remark made to me during the war, when I was in the Ministry of Aircraft Production, by a woman colleague. It was a variant of 'Woman's work is never done'.

'It's like the Honours List,' she cried. 'You've no sooner got one out than you've got to start on the next!'

I wondered how many other people were feeling, at this very moment, the same thing, doing the same thing, as she. Echelon beyond echelon of them I saw. With their motto shining above them: EVERYBODY IS LOOKED AT.

It must, it couldn't help but, entail jolly hard work for all concerned. All over the country names were being fed into an integrated complex of systems, a vast wondrous industry, for sifting and weeding. For sifting and weeding according to the highest principles of fair-mindedness and justice. I asked myself if it was surprising that the Civil Service was entrusted with it — and found it was not. (If you happen to think otherwise, let's hear you suggest something better!)

Such a charge obviously couldn't be entrusted to the lower orders, and in fact the highest were called upon to occupy their time with it. I've already remarked that the holder of the office of Joint Permanent Secretary to the Treasury and Head of the Civil Service reigned at the top. Then of course the Ceremonial Officer of the Treasury. Then some chosen senior Permanent Secretaries, chosen, as you're bound to see at once if you've got the hang of it, according to Department so as to cover Aspects of the Nation's Life. All in committee. In committee of course! (If the Civil Service was going to do it, or any other organisation in our country, how else but in committee? It's necessary to face facts — and also, come to that, the combination of common sense with order-liness.)

I was put off momentarily. I suddenly realised that in a parochial way I was thinking only of the Prime Minister's List of Honours, parochial because it was the one I was on myself. There were other Lists that the Civil Service didn't do: the Diplomatic Service did its own, the Armed Services, the Palace with the Order of Merit and the Royal Victorian Order. On the other hand the Prime Minister's List was by far the biggest parish, and above all the one for which Almost Everyone was Looked at — a parish and a half! . . . I was put on again. (The arrangers of the ceremony had allowed lots of time, I assure you.)

Contemplating, then, the vast wondrous industry, I was taken with a fancy for getting out a flow-sheet for the manu-facture of the Prime Minister's List. Clearly the first sifting-plant installation was at No. 10 Downing Street: the next at the Ceremonial Officer's place at the Treasury: then, coming to the heavier stuff, now, a group of committees in parallel, composed of Permanent Secretaries and their equivalents, each committee covering — guess what! — an Aspect of the Nation's Life. I didn't know what all these committees were; one for industry and its dependants; one for something like local government and affairs; one for science — knowing the Norman Standsfields of this world I imagined this one was honoured with somewhat lower prestige than the others; and of course the famed Maecenas Committee, which processed the names of the Great and Good Ones outside the scope of the other committees, names from the universities, the arts, the entertainments and so on. And then, heaviest stuff of all, the truly master committee, from which the final product flowed direct to the Prime Minister himself for him to present to the Monarch. (Actually the P.M. could at that point then short-circuit the whole shooting-match by adding names entirely of his own.)

The raw material of the industry, i.e. the names of Everybody, flowed into the first stage, No. 10, if they were not State servants, whom therefore nobody had looked at already —names of persons recommended for Honours by their friends or their colleagues or their relations or their own selves. The names of State servants flowed directly into the second stage, as they'd already been pre-treated, as it were, in the Civil Service—sifted according to the jobs they did, some of which carried Honours automatically; and measured out according to preordained quotas.

Enough. There were lots of devices for circulating papers, getting official opinions on people, making cross-checks on reputations, even producing fresh names: and I've missed out altogether the political list, got together by the Chief Whip from local party organisations. . . . EVERYBODY IS LOOKED AT. You can see for yourself. Ill-disposed people, scanning the Prime Minister's List, might remark on the Treasury looking after its own. Just the sort of thing they *would* say! If they said it to me I counselled them to look at the Armed Services' List. Certain individuals, Herbert Hobbs for instance, thought that in the N.P.B. you had to be a grade higher to get the same Honour you'd get in the Civil Service. He overlooked the fact that when a Civil Servant moved to the N.P.B. he was usually put up a notch. (Both Norman Standsfield and Charles Quain, the Member for Finance and Administration, were earning more now than they would have done if they had stayed in the Civil Service.)

Altogether, I thought, still feeling vicariously loyal to whoever had provided today's list, the dear old Treasury probably did the job as well as anyone could be expected to.

But any system of selection that is operated by human beings is fallible. There was no doubt about that. On the borderline of choice there *must* be mistakes. In this room, now, it occurred to me, there must be a middle-aged gentleman with thinning pate and confidently smiling pink face who ought not to be there.

While in some other room, alone, sat some other middle-aged gentleman with thinning pate and miserably grey face who might have been there equally well. 'It *ought* to have been *mine*! . . .' Poor fellow. Poor, poor fellow.

But that was the way of a world which was run by fallible men. Informed though it might be to perfection by fair-mindedness and justice, the Honours Industry could never produce a List that was faultless.

Good God! I suddenly wondered if the one who ought not to have been there was *me*. I went on smiling confidently like the rest. If I was the mistake, it was too late to get me back now.

But then I thought a bit more sophisticatedly about fallibility. Although it was true to say that in general the Honours List was not faultless, Chance ensured that a faultless one would come up sometime. I looked round at my smiling pink-faced colleagues with hope and relief. I felt sure it was today's.

Among the growing crowd I saw a couple of men I knew vaguely. They saw me. Vague though our acquaintance might be, we exchanged salutations of unusual vivacity and cordiality, not to mention satisfaction. There is nothing more satisfactory on such occasions than seeing somebody one knows. One looks at the other people, glumly standing alone or trying to start up meaningless conversation with strangers, and thinks: 'Those poor sods don't know anybody.'

At last our roped-off pen must have been up to complement, for a new functionary, of presumably higher order, came on the scene to brief us. He was a cheery, hearty fellow who might well have been a Naval Commander. He gave us our instructions decisively. With our faces all turned the same way I noticed that some of them were not as pink as I'd thought to begin with. Some of them were nearly green. I supposed the functionary's cheeriness was calculated to take some of the awesomeness out of the occasion.

Our instructions, so far as I can recall them at the moment, were to walk to the centre of the room, bow, take three steps forward and kneel down. Afterwards rise, take three steps back, bow, and walk out at the opposite side of the room.

Our instructor surveyed us as if he might be going to say: 'Everybody got that? You can't miss it! Jolly good show!' He looked at his watch. We all looked at our watches. We'd been there for ages. It was just the moment when a waiter with glasses of champagne would have fitted into my ill-conceived pre-accolade picture.

We were then led off into another long corridor-room which clearly opened into the great room where the ceremony was to take place. We were marshalled into a queue. The man at the head of it was a little way down the room from a doorway in the wall along which we were lined. In due course the door was opened and through it came the sound of music, buoyant music, played by the Guards, I supposed. Zero hour was at hand.

Slowly our queue moved up.

The man in front of me was hopping in readiness.

I remembered to hitch my coat forward. Prematurely. I waited. Then I hitched it again. The music seemed to get louder.

My turn. I stepped forward. It was like the moment when one's in a television studio and sees ON THE AIR. The music was playing —

> *The flowers that bloom in the spring, Tra la,*
> *Breathe promise of merry sunshine. . . .*

My name was spoken. I was on my way to the centre of the room, in six-eight time —

> *As we merrily dance and we sing, Tra la,*
> *We welcome the hope that they bring, Tra la,*

I bowed; saw the hassock; made for it and knelt down. I felt the tap on my shoulder.

Of a summer of roses and wine. . . .

Time to get up again. The hassock had handles on each side — to help poor old chaps, I thought, who didn't have it made till they were tottery.

And that's what we mean when we say that a thing

I stood up. The Monarch, I suddenly perceived as if I'd never known it before, was a woman. I took my three steps backwards, bowed.

Is welcome as flowers that bloom in the spring.

I was on my way to the other side of the room. Sir Jack.

Tra la la la la la . . .

The music, now that I was relieved of strain, simply wafted me to the door on the other side of the room. It gave into another corridor-room like the one in which I'd queued up. A functionary waved me through it. And the music seemed finally to soar —

And that's what I mean when I say or I sing,
Oh, bother the flowers that bloom in the spring!

An excellent ceremony. Heigh-ho, off to lunch!

I suppose I might have expected to wait where I was until the remainder of my confrères had been dubbed, when Alice and Roz would join me. But there weren't any of the men who'd been ahead of me in the queue waiting. Another functionary waved me on, and still swinging in six-eight time I obeyed, to find myself going back to join Alice and Roz in the room I'd just quitted.

Inside again, I had a chance to observe that the ceremony had taken place at the top end of a long narrow room. There were rows of seats for relations and friends of the Honours recipients down each side, and also across the bottom end, under a minstrels' gallery — in which the minstrels, were now embarking unless I was mistaken on 'I'm in Love with a Wonderful Guy'.

I saw Alice and Roz among the spectators sitting under the gallery.

I was of course pleased to join them. They looked at me with their cheeks pink and their eyes sparkling. 'I'm in love with a wonderful guy!' Alice whispered. I squeezed her fingers.

The band had started playing 'There's Nothing Like a Dame'. My middle-aged and elderly confrères, instead of waltzing across, were now marching by in brisk four-four time.

Not as excited as all that by the spectacle, I looked round the room. There was more crimson carpet, more buff-coloured walls with gilt, more chandeliers. It all had a faintly shabby look.

'Don't you think it has a faintly shabby look,' I said to Alice.

'Sh! . . . It ought to. Everybody knows *that*. It's a *royal* palace.'

I realised that we were watching the last few of my pen-full. However, I noticed that the men who'd been behind me were still being shown into the spectators' seats.

'Extraordinary,' I whispered to Alice.

After a final reprise of 'I'm in Love with a Wonderful Guy' the Guards finished with 'South Pacific'. They paused, and then started up 'Annie Get Your Gun'. What's more, after the last of my confrères had bowed and made for the door, there was a slight hiatus and then the first man of what must be an entirely different pen-full made his appearance, then a second. . . .

'Good God, this is sinister,' I whispered, looking again at our nearby doorway, where yet another man was being shown in—and nobody, nobody at all, was being shown out.

We were stuck. Literally to cut a very long story short, we seemed to be sitting there for hours and hours. Goodness knows whom we didn't see invested with goodness knows what. More middle-aged and elderly gentlemen went rolling past. . . .

There was momentary flutter among us when the middle-aged and elderly gentlemen gave place to three Queen Alexandra's Nurses, looking delightfully clean and gay in their uniforms. After that, back to the grind.

It ended, of course. We got out, and went for an excellent lunch at the Connaught, after which we caught the 4.45 from Paddington. All in all, though, it had been an excellent day. I was Sir Jack, now, for the whole world to see.

When we got home I found a letter awaiting me. It appeared that as Sir Jack I'd been seen by something called the Imperial Society of Knights Bachelors. The letter explained its aims, life-work and fees.

The Society was founded, it appeared, to maintain and consolidate the Dignity of a Knight Bachelor — in this case, me. And after eighteen years striving, it had achieved the first great step towards that end, namely getting royal permission for every Knight Bachelor, i.e. me, to wear a badge, three inches long by two inches wide — 'upon an oval medallion of vermilion, enclosed by a scroll, a cross-hilted sword belted and sheathed, pommel upwards, between two spurs, rowels upwards, the whole set about with a sword belt, all gilt.'

'Gee whiz, that's *something*!' I said to Alice, who was reading the letter with me. 'I can't wait to have one.'

'I don't see that a practical joke's *practical* if it costs ten guineas. I mean, darling, *is* it?'

'But if I wore it all the time it would pay for itself.'

'Read on!'

Among the things it did, we read, the Society registered every duly authenticated knighthood, advised knights on heraldry and etiquette — 'As me and another Knight was walking down Victoria Street . . .' — and periodically published a knightage. It also offered country members a room in its offices in London in which to hold interviews and transact business. All for twenty guineas.

I hadn't got twenty guineas. 'Well, can I have the Authentication Certificate?' I said to Alice. 'Only one pound. Not even a guinea.'

'They *say* it's valuable as a family *record*.' She couldn't keep a malicious spark out of her eye.

'It's the idea of being authenticated that *gets* me,' I said. 'And wouldn't *you* like me to be authenticated? Be honest! . . .'

I am afraid the badge, authentication certificate, knight's private room in London, went the same way as my family tree and coat of arms.

I didn't ask Alice if she was going to drop the Alice and call herself just plain Lady Carteret.

But when we got to bed that night she said:

'I really am in love with a wonderful guy!'

F

CHAPTER FIVE

The Golden Boy

After the excitement of K-Day, there was a lull in my affairs. At last I finished correcting the proofs of my textbook and sent them in. There remained only the title to be decided. My publisher, *artiste manqué*, not being in a position to change a word of the text, but wanting to exercise his will to participate in creation, proposed to alter the title.

I had called the book *The Mechanical Properties of 2-Phase Systems*. What, I wanted to know, was wrong with that? I thought it was both apt and inspiring.

My publisher thought it didn't indicate that the book was theoretical.

I said anybody who knew enough about the subject to be buying the book would know it was theoretical. If he wanted to dot i's and cross t's, I suggested *A Theoretical Investigation of the Mechanical Properties of 2-Phase Systems with Particular Reference to Metals Containing Non-Metal Precipitates*. How about that?

He said it was too long.

When I had nothing further to suggest, he gave me to understand that the matter would rest for a time *sub judice*. Who, I wanted to know, was the judge?

I now had all my time available for my research, which was going well. One day I got home from the lab to find there was news for me.

'Darling,' said Alice, 'a few minutes ago Mr. Bowen rang up.'

'Where is he?'

'Here. In Oxford.'

I said: 'Good Lord!'

Alice said: 'It *is* just a teentsy-weentsy bit off, isn't it, darling, not to let you know he was coming.' She paused. 'I mean, I'm not criticising him.'

'You bloody well are.'

The corners of her mouth flickered. 'Well . . .'

I said: 'There's nothing to worry about.' I didn't want her to take against him before she actually saw him. (He was quite handsome.)

'They all go on like this nowadays,' I explained, by 'they' meaning bright young scientists — and possibly not so bright young scientists as well. 'It's because they're so much in demand. Anybody who's wildly in demand behaves badly. It's a pity but it's true.'

She was silent, and I felt I must lay down the law, right from the start. I went on.

'Being wildly in demand is something human nature just doesn't seem able to stand up to. One might as well get used to it. If it were young Arts graduates who were wildly in demand, they'd behave just as badly as the young scientists do now.'

'Oh,' said Alice.

'Michael Bowen's only like the rest,' I said. 'And we've got to put up with it — in fact we've got to like it.'

'The *rest*? I thought you said there was nobody to *compare* with him.'

'There are thousands to compare with him for manners. Nobody to compare — or very few — for talent. Come on, darling, don't be disingenuous. It would be pleasant if their manners were nicer, but we're looking for talent.'

'And Mr. Bowen has it . . .'

I nodded my head and changed the subject. I asked her where he was staying. Though I didn't say it to Alice, it occurred to me that Bowen might well be assuming I'd have rooms ready for him in College.

Alice said he was staying with another young Australian. 'He says he's going to '*bunk down*'. I rather *imagined* on the floor.'

While she was speaking Roz came in.

I said: 'Why not?' I paused. 'I envy him. Just to turn up. Not mind where you sleep. What freedom!' As I said it I'm afraid I heard faint echoes of Bill Taylor's phoney speech about being a Prisoner of The System.

Rosalind smirked and said to Alice: 'Theoreticians are gypsies, you know, Mummy.'

Alice said to me: 'Darling, don't get romantic about the freedom young people have to sleep on each other's floors. You know you wouldn't like it, if you had it. It's not your *thing* . . .'

'I'm not so sure,' I said.

Roz said: 'When you came back from Australia you grumbled like mad about not being able to get proper service in expensive hotels.'

'That's not the same.' Somehow Mike Bowen's bunking-down without warning or care in the other man's rooms took me back to when I was his age.

Alice read my thoughts. 'And darling,' she said more gently, 'don't get romantic about being young, either.'

I said: 'Why not?'

Roz replied: 'There's no future in it.'

I felt they were both depriving me of something. I said nothing more.

Alice resumed her drawly tone. 'The *rest* of the message is that he'll come in to *see* you, in the lab at nine thirty to-morrow morning.' She moved away from us, saying over her shoulder: 'I don't know *what* he said to *Roz* . . .'

I turned to Roz. 'Oh, he spoke to you, did he?'

'Yes.'

'What did he say?'

Roz watched her mother go out of the room. 'He asked me to meet him tonight.'

'That's pretty quick off the mark.'

'You can say *that* again!'

'What did you say?'

'I said I couldn't.' She stared at me: 'It's perfectly true. I've got behind with typing my manuscript and I really must get it up to date again tonight.'

I was momentarily nonplussed. It had never occurred to me that she could put novel-writing before courting, though I should have been the first person to say she ought to. On the other hand I needed nobody to tell me that this was just the sort of move to bring a young man on.

Roz said: 'I told him if I got it done tonight, I'd meet him tomorrow night.'

'I see . . .'

She moved as if she too were going out of the room. I said:

'By the way, I suppose you don't know if he's brought that motor-bike with him?'

'I shouldn't think so.' She paused 'It was right for Berkeley but it wouldn't do for here.'

My spirits rose. She said:

'I suppose he might get a Honda or something . . .'

My spirits fell again.

'Anyway it's *his* business,' she said. 'It isn't mine.'

I was thoughtful. I'd had my way, over bringing Michael Bowen to Oxford. While he was five thousand miles away it had been easy to confine myself to thinking of him sheerly as a scientist. I realised that I'd now got him on my hands as a person.

Punctually at nine thirty the following morning he presented himself at my office in the lab.

When I was Mike Bowen's age — he was now twenty-seven — I expected Australians to be rather undersized and prone to lose their hair and teeth rather early in life. As a representative of the next generation he showed me how things had changed. He was tall and slender but quite strong; he had short curly brown hair; and his teeth were good enough for a toothpaste advertisement.

It was the first time I'd seen him after a relatively short encounter in Berkeley six months ago. What I remembered was a trace of gangliness and jumpiness. And about his face, which was longish, chinny, slightly concave, I remembered having thought how it was easy to imagine it when he was my age, with the slightly ravaged, burning cadaverous look that some women seemed to find peculiarly attractive. For the time being, though, his eyes, which were large and in colour a grey that was nearly green, merely glowed; and his complexion looked dazzlingly healthy.

He came into the room blushing with nervousness, and with anxiety to make a good impression making sweat come out on his upper lip. (I wondered if he knew I knew he'd already tried to date Roz.) We shook hands.

'It was very good of you to get me some extra money from the National Power Board,' was his first speech. 'I'm grateful for this.' He relaxed a little. 'I sure am!'

'That's O.K.,' I said.

He glanced round my office and looked at the view through the window. The room was long and narrow, with glass all the way down one of the long sides and blackboards on the opposite wall. The view was of the Parks; and on a sunlit morning in spring it was misty and luminous and green. The trees, only just sprouting leaves, were still; and one sensed the river in the distance. There were a few dark figures, Lowry-like, making their way along the paths.

'This is my first visit to England,' he said.

'It has its charms . . .'

'I *know* I'm going to like it.'

It struck me that after five years in the U.S.A. — three at Brown, doing a Ph.D., followed by two at Berkeley — he seemed more like a young American than a young Australian. The rotund opening speech, the ingenuous expression of enthusiasm. But he kept some of his Australian accent — 'guid' and 'collerdge'.

'Well, how was Berkeley?' I said, taking a chair by my table.

He sat down beside me, and wiped the sweat off his upper lip.

'The physicists at Berkeley are not very mathematical,' he said. 'They prefer to use their instincts.' His nervousness had completely disappeared.

'Oh,' said I, feeling we'd got down to business pretty quickly. At Melbourne he'd started off as a mathematician himself. Whereas I, if one felt inclined to put it that way, definitely 'preferred to use my instincts'.

'Don't *you* prefer to use your instincts?' I said.

'This is a very *difficult* question.' He glanced at me sideways.

'You'd better answer it,' I said, laughing at him.

He replied after a pause. 'What the mathematical people want to do,' he said, 'is to find more and more exact and general solutions, for simpler and simpler problems . . .'

'Yes? And you?'

He suddenly laughed back at me. 'I want to find rougher and more specific solutions, to more and more difficult problems.'

If he'd been trying to bowl me over he couldn't have done better. It was what I wanted to do myself. In my field of research there was no option, anyway — not as I saw it. The problems in metallurgy, in mechanical properties situations, can't be precisely formulated. And it's only problems which actually can be precisely formulated that lend themselves to exact and general solutions. My life was made up of rough and specific solutions to imprecisely formulated problems — specific solutions often enough to *practical* problems!

'There were plenty of field-theory people around,' he went on. 'Field theory deals with linear situations. But linear approximations get you nowhere in the problems I want to solve —'

'I agree,' I said. 'Let's talk about the problems you want to solve!'

First we talked about the problems he'd already solved, and then about those he'd got lined up. He was an authority on 'cracking'. At Brown he'd done an excellent piece of work that enabled him to get out some new fundamental energy principles which controlled cracking. And at Berkeley he'd defined an effective surface energy for the production of a crack in an inhomogeneous medium — that, I must explain, being a much more difficult problem than doing it for a homogeneous medium. His theory depended on certain relationships between stress-strain curves and velocities of deformation, and in order to cope with them he'd had to put them on to computing machines. So he had useful machine experience.

Enthusiasm took charge of him. He got up from his chair and went to the blackboard. (Actually it was an up-to-date plastic white-board, on which one wrote with a coloured wax crayon.)

'The aim of the exercise is this,' he said, beginning to deliver me a lecture. 'To find criteria for sorting media into three categories.' He wrote on the board:

1. Dead brittle
2. Effectively brittle (controlled by surface energy principle)
3. Essentially tough

He read them aloud to me as he wrote them, rather as if I were a foreign student. Then suddenly he turned to me.

'You see it's ultimately the real world I'm interested in.'

I laughed.

'If we can get abstract mathematical criteria for them . . .' he said, turning back to survey his three categories. He paused.

I said an encouraging Yes. He went on reflectively:

'It means developing fancy methods for solving partial equations which are not linear.'

I said: 'I hope you will develop them.'

He turned to look at me again and gave a laugh. When I'd said I hoped he would, I knew that in point of fact he already had.

He looked as if he were going to sit down again. But suddenly he went back to the board. He spoke quickly:

'I had an idea coming over in the plane! I'll try it out on *you* . . .' He began to write some equations down on the board.

'*Now*,' he said, and his greenish eyes were burning slightly, 'I think we can get at it this way—'

The excitement he was feeling came over to me. What he was doing was not as it were marshalling a complete set of facts and logically deducing a general underlying pattern. With a manifestly incomplete set of facts he was having a hunch that there might *be* an underlying pattern. And that was the essence of a discovery—the jump his imagination had taken over a lot of gaps. If he actually had made a discovery he would be able to fill the gaps in.

'What do you think?' he asked.

I started to point out where the gaps were.

His mood shifted. He wasn't deflated: he was too tough for that. And anyway I was doing what at that moment I was required to do.

But the moment was after its fashion a critical one. I was fifty-five, and he was twenty-seven. He'd had a very bright idea, and I should have been glad to have had it myself.

He was standing back from the board, looking at his mathematics.

'You must admit,' he said, 'it's so pretty it must be true for the real world.'

It was a remark I didn't normally allow to go unchallenged. I should have found examples of mathematical theories generally accepted as true for the real world that were awkward, if not to my mind frankly ugly.

Instead I said nothing. I suppose I must have smiled at him, but suddenly my thoughts were moving elsewhere. They were focussing in a vague yet compelling way on the future. I felt disturbed. For a few minutes I was listening to him with only half my attention.

He stopped with surprise, caught in a gesture that summed

F*

desire for my approval with complete confidence in himself.

I recognised the source of my sadness and alarm. It was nothing to do with envy of his talent, nothing to do with fear of being superseded in my work — I felt careless of both. I thought:

'He's come to take Roz away from me.'

I pulled myself together.

'Yes, yes,' I said. 'It *is* so pretty it must be true for the real world.'

He gave me a sharp look, no doubt seeing signs of a wandering mind in an aged person, and then promptly picked up his lecture again at the point where I'd lost touch with it.

CHAPTER SIX

Az Uborkafán

The language is Hungarian. You'll think I'm being a show-
off; but I consider it's worth it, in order to bring one of
the most beautiful expressions in any European tongue to
everybody's notice. And useful as well as beautiful — in-
finitely more useful than *Verfremdungseffekt*, and practically on a par with *raison d'être*.

Az uborkafán is translated as 'on the cucumber-tree'. And
it means 'on the make', 'on the climb'. An image, as I'm
sure you'll agree, of lasting poetry for a human occupation
equally lasting and equally poetic. 'On the cucumber-tree'
— you will now see why I've chosen *'Az Uborkafán'* for the
title of this chapter.

'Joan's having a party,' said Alice. She was opening the
day's correspondence one morning at the end of Term.

'What for?' I asked.

'To show off her Rothko, of course, darling.' She handed
me the card. 'It doesn't say so, but she must *want* everybody
to see it, mustn't she?'

We were all sitting round the breakfast-table.

'Am I invited?' asked Roz with rather more interest than
I should have expected.

I said: 'Yes.'

Julia said: 'Who's going to stay and look after me?' Her
large grey eyes were wide open. As it was early in the day
her lock of silky fair hair had not yet flopped over her
brows.

'You *know* who'll come in to look after you, darling. Now *who* do you think? . . .'

I went on looking at the card.

'It's very grand,' I said for Roz. 'Could we afford cards as grand as that?'

Alice was pouring some coffee and didn't see fit to indulge me with an answer. I stroked Julia's delicious little head. Then I said to Alice:

'I really approve of a party for the Rothko. It will be a test, won't it?'

'Test?' said Alice, with inattention that amounted to innocence: 'Of what?'

I was triumphant. 'Of whether the colour' — Alice quickly joined in unison — '*brings us to our knees!*' We paused, delighted with each other.

Julia said: 'Will you say your prayers?' (It was my belief that she already had intimations of sarcasm.)

Roz was laughing. She said: 'I like Joan, all the same. I wonder what other young people she's going to invite. I think I'll call her and ask.'

'How you do get *on* with Joan, don't you, darling! . . .'

'I'll ask her,' said Roz, 'if she's invited Mike Bowen.'

Julia looked from one to the other of us and said in a girlish ha-ha tone:

'I think she loves him.'

Rosalind blushed. Alice said: 'Julie, if you've finished your breakfast, you may get down. Very quickly.'

Julia promptly got down from her chair and then stood beside it folding her table-napkin in slow motion.

Alice took back the card from Roz, 'I like parties so much,' she said. She glanced at me. 'I love coming home *tipsy*.'

I said: 'That's one of the pleasures of the middle-aged.'

Alice said she would order a hired car, so that we could both come tipsy if we wanted to. We did not discuss who would bring Rosalind home. (In the last four weeks I'd

only once heard the shuddersome word, Honda — and then,
mercifully, in a tone of dismissal.)

The party, when we came to the day, began at eight thirty
and Alice and I arrived punctually.

First of all let me say that Joan's house was magnificent.
It was large and spacious — it was in the country — and
beautifully decorated, whether the taste was Alice's or her
own. With very little money, poor people can achieve a
charming effect: with a lot of money rich people can
achieve an lawful effect. Also with a lot of money rich
people can achieve an effect beyond compare.

There were pictures and lights and servants and champagne and guests from London.

The Rothko temporarily enjoyed a place of honour in the
entrance hall. The colour was . . . if you'll go and look at
some Rothko's you'll see what I want to say.

And Joan looked marvellous. ('I think that's the dress
she got from Courrèges,' Alice whispered.)

I contented myself with saying 'Oh my!'

Alice and I separated. At parties she always talks to everyone she doesn't know. I tend to sit down with someone I do
know. We both enjoy ourselves.

The first person I ran into whom I knew was Alec Benda.

'I simply love Joan's parties,' he said. 'She's such a marvellous person, isn't she? So splendidly *dans le coup!*' (I
gathered that society must have reached that point in the
history of its advance when it was not quite the thing to say
'with-it' any more.)

'I suppose so. Let's find somewhere to sit down.' I moved
towards a comfortable sofa.

Alec said: 'Do you see who she's got over there? That
handsome dusky little man? That's Hussein Awad!'

'Who in God's name's he?'

'Don't you know? He knows more about the newest
pictures than anyone else, *but* anyone! . . . He's an Egyp-
tian. Everybody calls him Hussy.' Alec giggled. 'But the
funny bit is that actually he *isn't* . . .'

'Is he *dans le coup*, too?' (I adopted Alec's idiosyncratic way out of society's current dilemma.)

'My dear Jack, he practically makes *le coup*. He's just going to open a gallery in South Moulton Street or South Audley Street, South somewhere, anyway. He's got *all* the newest painters — you know, the *under*-thirties, the real trend-setters and pace-makers. You'll find Hussy's right out in front, straight away.'

We each took a second glass of champagne from a waiter. I saw my chance to ask him a question.

When in the world I inhabited a young man of extraordinary talent, Michael Bowen, for example, appeared on the scene, his published work was read by all the experts in his field and was available to everybody else who cared to try and understand it. The shock of recognition of his talent passed round a widely-distributed stable set of men. And they it was who made his reputation. My question. What about a comparable young painter? I wanted to know who it was who decided whether *he* was the newest, or the greatest, or the most *dans le coup*? Scarcely anybody could see his paintings in the flesh. (I may say I knew there was a growing pressure on him, especially in the U.S.A., to circulate colour transparencies.)

'Oh, I can tell you that!' said Alec. 'The shock of recognition that really makes *his* name *here* goes round a circle of people that's positively tiny. Hussy Awad's actually one of them . . .' He gave me a sideways look. 'Of course it doesn't include any Establishment people. I mean, it couldn't, could it? Though one or two Establishment *gallery* people are terribly quick at catching on — *after* the event, that it. . . . But they don't *make* what's In. Not really!' He paused.

'So? . . .'

'What's In is made by Hussy Awad, for one. Then there's the people at —— and ——.' (He named an art school in London that I supposed I must have heard of and another in a provincial city.) 'And there's ——.' (He named a youngish, that is to say fortyish, art critic.) 'Though he's in Los Angeles at the moment.'

'Isn't that too far away?' I said, meaning from a London cucumber-tree.

'Not at all!' said Alec with enthusiasm. 'Their communications are so wonderful. The shock of recognition gets around in no time at all, wherever they are.' He paused. 'And then they have their contacts for transmitting the news outwards, to the people in provincial art schools who are really waiting to hear. . . . And the people in London who are waiting to buy.'

I considered that I had been educated. To tell the truth I enjoy being educated. Always have.

'So you see,' Alec wound up, 'That's how any young artist who's recognised can be right out in front at once.'

I was prompted to ask a second question. Is visual art now some kind of *race*? Like a French bicycle race, in which the *maillot jaune* for being the most In is passed from one young painter to the next? But Alec suddenly jumped up, saying:

'Do excuse me — I see the young man who's staying with me looking rather bewildered. He's a young American folk-singer, terribly talented, you know. We met in Tangier. I must go and introduce him to some more people. I'll come back. There's something I want to ask you.'

With his bald head flashing under the light of a chandelier, Alec moved into the crowd and left me.

Out of propriety towards Alec, I must say explicitly that when he said the young man was staying with him he meant he was sleeping with him as well. Alec Benda was a descendant (in the metaphorical sense) of the great Victorian gondolier-chasing men of letters who referred to homosexuality as The Problem. The great Victorian gondolier-chasers kept The Problem to themselves. Alec, their mid-twentieth-century descendant, made it public. It was not The Problem for him alone: it was The Problem for Society. It was Society's duty in the first place to acquaint itself with the facts. (Alec would insist, for instance, in giving evidence before any public body set up to enquire into the subject.) And in the second place to be helpful.

It seems to me you may wonder at the wisdom of an Oxford college appointing such a man as a Fellow to teach young undergraduates. Alec Benda was not my own choice. I had pressed for us to have a Fellow to teach Creative Writing, knowing I was at the tactical disadvantage of not having a nominee, because I didn't know the literary world well enough. And Stanley Forbes had responded to the loudest voices.

Brian Challoner had once explained to me that in the literary world there were three identifiable pressure-groups: the Roman Catholic, of course; the Jewish, especially in the U.S.A.; and the homosexual, everywhere. The voices for Alec Benda were unusually loud, since he was Jewish in origin, homosexual in practice, and currently under instruction for the Roman Catholic Church. Alec Benda left, as one might say, no stone unturned. *Az uborkafán!* . . .

On the other hand, fair's fair — Alec Benda's books were distinguished both in scholarship and in art. He'd been awarded some prize or other for a story set in the Venetian Republic during one of its palmily corruptest decades in the eighteenth century. Furthermore, speaking for myself, I found Alec a lively, amusing companion.

'Hello there!' I looked up to see Brian Challoner standing beside me, dressed in a nearly black suit and looking about seven feet tall and a few inches wide. From a passing waiter he swiped a glass of champagne which he neatly exchanged for my empty glass. Then he sat down.

'I saw you talking to Alec.'

'Yes. He threatens to come back.'

We sat for a few moments, surveying the crowd. I noticed Alice talking to Joan's husband, a tired-looking man. He always looked tired. He was an Oriental languages don. The most interesting thing about him was that he was reputed to have a very fine collection of Oriental erotic literature.

Alice and I used to speculate about whether he collected it because he was tired or was tired because he collected it.

I glanced at Brian. His small bright eyes were sparkling. (My own rather larger protruding grey eyes were probably getting brighter by now.) 'It's good champagne,' he said.

'It's a good party.'

'Did Alec tell you about *my* problem?'

'No. He didn't mention you.' I must say the word 'problem' jarred with my earlier thoughts. I said: 'What is it?'

'You remember the boy who was watching television in my rooms that night you and Alec came round? John Minelli.'

I said I did. And I remembered his telephoning us after Alice and I had gone to bed. 'Your tame teenager . . .' I said.

Brian glanced furtively at me, and rapidly looked away. I waited. I noticed a few silver gleams in his dark furry haircut.

'I'm afraid he's not tame,' he said. 'In fact he's quite violent.' He paused. 'I'm having a job to stop him watching television in my rooms all the time.'

'Oh dear,' I said. It was not unusual for undergraduates to get smitten in this way. In my Cambridge days in the thirties the disease used to be known as Don's Dread. 'You'll just have to get him out,' I said. I was thinking that the boy's being a townsman rather than an undergraduate made it easier. 'Throw him out, if necessary.'

'I'm afraid that's what I tried,' Brian said. He looked away. 'Last night . . .'

'And?'

'First of all he went down on his knees and begged me to let him watch just one more programme.'

'Well, T.V. programmes fortunately end before midnight —'

'He wept.' Brian paused. 'And then he became violent.'

'Did you actually try to throw him out?'

'I'm afraid I did. He began to struggle. And then he

broke a window — deliberately smashed his hand through it. The College porter came up. . . . The gash was bleeding so much I thought I'd have to take him to get some stitches put in it. Fortunately I didn't have to.'

'Good God!'

'It was a wildly masochistic act. You know . . .'

I remembered being struck by the strained, feverish look in the boy's face as well as his brightness of eye — both of which I'd put down to homosexuality. I wondered exactly what Brian's relationship with him was.

'I particularly want to avoid being the centre of a public scandal.' Brian looked me in the eye momentarily. 'You probably don't know there's likely to be a Royal Commission on the effects of television on adolescents. I'm an obvious person to be asked to sit on it.'

I couldn't help bursting into laughter. I have to record in Brian's great favour that he laughed too. As my test of a full sense of humour is to see that one is funny *oneself* — you only need half a sense of humour to see that other people are funny — my sympathy for him glowed up.

'Oh, you'll be all right,' I said, for the simple reason that I couldn't think of any action he might take that would improve matters.

Brian drank some more champagne. He said nothing.

I noticed that Joan's husband, who was still leaning tiredly in the same place, was now talking to Stanley Forbes. Stanley caught my eye and waved his glass at me.

Brian stood up, swiped two glasses of champagne from a passing waiter, gave one to me and kept the other for himself. He really was adept at it. As he did it Stanley Forbes left Joan's husband and came towards me.

'His Lordship wants to talk to you,' said Brian. 'I'll get out of the way.'

It occurred to me that Forbes might want to talk to me about the window-breaking. 'Hello!' I shouted to him cheerfully, and drank some of the fresh champagne.

His Lordship looked distinctly drunk. 'Lovely party,' he

said as he sat down, aiming his behind with great delibera-
tion at the chair-seat.

I cannot pretend I wasn't beginning to feel slightly drunk
myself.

'Lovely party,' I repeated.

We both watched Roz and another girl, a very pretty girl,
go by.

'Lovely girl,' I said.

'You must be very proud of her, Jack.'

'I meant the other one, not Roz. I wonder who she is.
Wonder if she comes to Roz's parties.'

Lord Forbes sighted them both along his upturned nose
for a moment. 'I should say,' he said, weighing his words
carefully, 'they're equally lovely.'

The sight of Roz had made me wonder where Mike Bowen
was.

'I came to tell you something,' Stanley said. 'About a
friend of yours.'

For a moment I thought it must be about Challoner. I
tried to look singularly unperturbed.

'Bill Taylor,' said Stanley.

I must say I was surprised.

'A very good man.' Stanley turned a steady blue-eyed gaze
on me.

'Excellent man.'

'A very good man. . . . Jack, the news is good.'

He went on with his blue-eyed gaze — he was drunker
than I'd thought.

'I've no doubt,' Stanley said, 'that we shall one day elect
Taylor to the Society.' He paused. 'No doubt, now.'

He meant to a Fellowship of the Royal Society, to the
crème de la crème of the scientific world. Being in it myself
I sometimes said it ought not to exist — I leave it to other
people to assess my degree of sincerity.

On the other hand, let me stress at once that my present
conversation with Stanley about the Royal Society had nothing whatsoever to do with a cucumber-tree.

'You don't mean to say —— is going to change his mind!'
I said. —— was the chairman of the committee which dealt
with the category of candidates into which Bill came. Bill
had been up for election for several years: —— was opposed
to it and had rallied enough support to keep Bill out each
year so far.

'I happened to see —— this morning,' Stanley said. 'And
he gave me that impression. In fact he expressed himself
more strongly, though I doubt if I'm at liberty to repeat
his words.' He nodded his head. 'Between ourselves, he now
has grave doubts about the election from *his* category this
year — he thinks they made a mistake. Would have done
better to elect Taylor.' He went nodding his head, happily.
'I think we shall see a successful outcome to our endeavours.'

Though I was struck by the bizarreness of his telling me
all this at a party, now, when any time during the next six
months would do well enough — and would also be more
reliable — I nodded *my* head happily at the prospect of
Bill's success.

'I know how much you believe Taylor ought to get the
chairmanship of the National Power Board,' Stanley said,
his eyes glowing with their characteristic intimate look.

I gave him a glowing look in return.

But I was not agreeing off the cuff that Bill's getting into
the Royal would necessarily enhance his prospects at the
N.P.B. For one thing, if it did anything but stir Norman
Standsfield's envy and spite, I was going to be surprised.
One might have thought that, with Norman not being a
scientist and therefore election to the Society being something which he couldn't possibly have for himself, he would
at least be neutral to Bill's election. Alas, Norman Standsfield was not made that way — nor, for that matter, were a
lot of other men. Envy is not only deplorably common to us
all: it is also maddeningly irrational. Drinking some more
champagne I lugubriously felt that envy could scarcely be
regarded as rational at all, judging by the frequency with
which everyone, myself included, experienced its pangs over

things which they could not, by any stretch of the imagination, have for themselves.

'What's the matter, Jack?' Stanley's mellow voice sounded beside my ear.

I made myself grin. 'Nothing, Stanley, I'm just drunk.' And then I thought about the effect of Bill's prospective success on Herbert Hobbs. 'Oh God!' I said aloud.

We were interrupted.

'Now then, Dearest. It's time to go!' Stanley's wife had come up behind our sofa, and I looked up to see her glaring opaque stare fixed on me as if I were engaged in the criminal act of corrupting Stanley's will to leave.

Stanley and I stood up. 'Thank you, Doris,' he said.

Doris turned her attention to me. 'It looks as if it's time for you to leave, too.'

'Alice has ordered a car . . .'

'If you'd had any sense, you'd have shared ours. That would have cost you nothing!'

'No more it would,' I said.

Doris looked at me in a puzzled way.

'Yes,' she said shortly.

I watched her and Stanley move away through the crowd. Her arm was firmly linked through his. Protecting him, as usual; seeing that he conserved his energies.

Protecting him for what purpose, come to that? Conserving his energies for what actions?

Whatever happened, Stanley was not going to do anything.

The room buzzed with chatter. The lights were softly shaded. People pushed their way to and fro, women trailing auras of perfume, men auras of happy intentness — *az uborkafán!* . . . I felt happy, myself.

> *Oh! cucumber-tree,*
> *Cucumber-tree,*
> *How I love thee!* . . .

I had no intention of going home so early. There was lots more of the evening still ahead.

I suddenly noticed Michael Bowen. So Roz had got him invited after all. But she was not with him. He was standing alone, entirely absorbed with examining Joan's piece of sculpture by Giacometti. . . . What was going on?

Before I could get up from the sofa to go and find out, I found Alice beside me. Her eyes were very bright.

'Darling,' she said, examining my face, 'you're getting tipsy!'

'I'm not.'

'I can always tell by the way your eyes begin to bulge. I mean, they do bulge, don't they?'

'Are you tipsy, yet?'

'Nearly . . .'

We looked at each other in the way husbands and wives who are slightly drunk often do look at each other.

Alice said: 'Joan's husband asked me if I'd like to borrow his copy of the *Kama Sutra*. He's heard it's going to be published; you know, *publicly*, for *everyone* to read. . . . He thought we might like to read it in advance. You *know* . . .'

'Somebody once showed me a copy in Cambridge. It enjoins you to perform with your right ankle twisted round your left ear. I can see that that makes a *change*, but does it really *help*?'

Alice, not given to giggling, nevertheless made a sound that approximated to it. 'It sounds *interesting* . . .'

'That's as may be. But in my opinion, it has to be taken more as an erotic fantasy on the part of the writer than a practical proposition for the reader.'

Alice drank some champagne. 'I think I'll take the book, all the same . . .' There was a pause. 'It won't be long before the car's due.'

I said: 'Alec Benda wants to talk to me about something first.'

'I saw him in the next room. I'm going there. I'll tell him to come to you.' She turned back. 'By the way, Michael Bowen is taking Roz home now.'

As she moved away, a waiter came by. I helped myself to something and sat down.

In a moment I saw Benda coming to look for me. His large bald head flashed; drink had made the half-moons of his eyelids sink lower; his fleshy jaw seemed to be held up by a constant smile. It struck me that when one was not hearing his absurdly twittering speech, it was a good deal less difficult to remember that when he was an undergraduate he had been quite a successful athlete — he had only just missed getting a Blue for cricket. Nowadays he carried too much weight, but he still played the game. I asked myself, as I often did about sharers of The Problem, why? . . .

'I'm terribly drunk,' he said. 'Isn't it *gorgeous*? . . . And my folk-singer is having marvellous success. I'm so glad. He's such a *sincere* person. I mean, this is one of the things about folk-singers, isn't it? They're really *sincere*.'

'What did you want to ask me about, Alec.'

The smile which seemed to hold up his jaw disappeared. His eyelids lifted and he looked at me with a dramatic stare.

'It's about my being under instruction.'

'Are you having your doubts?'

'*I'm* not. But Father Cyprian is.'

'What's the trouble?'

'It's hard to put into words. I think Father Cyprian feels I'm not sufficiently *concentrated* on it. It's not that I'm *divided* . . .'

'Lots of people must have felt like that about it,' I said comfortingly.

'I know, I know. But all the same I can see what Father Cyprian means, and I agree with him.'

'What would Father Cyprian say about, for example, your young American folk-singer?'

Alec looked at me sideways, his brown eyes large and unveiled. 'He's terribly *understanding*.'

I didn't think much of that, from Alec's point of view.

As I understood it, the Roman Catholic Church said NO to all copulation, except in the extreme case of child-begetting. I could only believe that Father Cyprian's 'understanding' amounted to getting Alec into the Church first and then putting the screws on afterwards.

'H'm,' I said.

We said nothing for a little while.

'I suppose,' Alec said, 'if he feels I won't *do* . . .' He shrugged his shoulders slowly and sadly, and didn't complete the sentence. 'One's religion is a serious matter, isn't it?'

Having no religion I was in no position to answer.

'I feel it will be a terrible loss,' he said.

Again, in the religious sense, I was in no position to answer. In the secular sense, on the other hand, I was. It meant that he wouldn't gain the whole-hearted support of the Roman Catholic pressure-group. Also it often looked to me as if, above a certain level of social class, conversion to the Roman Catholic Church carried a bonus of social, as well as spiritual, elevation: for example, if one were fortunate enough to be within striking distance of knowing the aristocracy in general, entry into the Roman Catholic Church got one to know the Roman Catholic aristocracy.

'And one will miss the little things too,' Alec said reflectively. 'It would have been nice to send one's books to Evelyn and Graham and Alfred *automatically* . . .'

'I know,' I said. 'And you might have been invited to play cricket by the Duke of Norfolk.'

Suddenly he gave me a look that made me fear I'd made an enemy for life — which, I admit, I'd asked for. But after all, I was drunk. And so was he. His expression changed.

'Jack, you're as bitchy as one of *us*!' And he laughed with satisfaction.

I laughed too, somewhat thinly.

'Oh well,' he sighed, 'I see your advice is the right advice.'

I hadn't the faintest idea what advice I'd given him. In

fact I was pretty sure I hadn't given him any. Had I? I asked myself. I said:

'I think it's time we all went home.'

I saw Alice appear in the doorway and start signalling to to me. We stood up, and swayed a little.

'I must go and find Brian,' he said. 'Poor Brian! But I did warn him, you know. He really shouldn't have slept with this boy.'

'*Has* he?' I asked.

Alec looked at me with amazement. 'But what *else*! . . .'

I could have given him several alternatives, actually. Alec said:

'Anyway, I'm sorry it's happened to him now, just when they're going to ask him to sit on a Royal Commission, which was what he'd counted on, I'm sure — in a *way*. . . . I mean he doesn't really *care* for teenagers. You know that, don't you? He only chose them for his research because he knew they were an In subject. They were bound to have a Royal Commission of some kind or other on them. Dear Brian doesn't miss any tricks. And quite right, too!'

Alice was coming towards us. I saw that she was carrying a book.

'I really must go,' I said. 'We've got a car waiting for us.'

Alice said: '*Dar*ling, do you think you can get to the door?'

'Of course I can.' Australians, I thought, were not the only ones who could carry their liquor.

I got to the door and into the car.

By the time we got home I was able to go upstairs quite easily, to take off my clothes and get into bed.

'Well, how about that?' I said to Alice, who was still moving about the bedroom.

'You've done terribly well, darling.' She glanced down at me. 'You still are.'

Finally she sat down on the edge of the bed. Tipsy. Holding the copy of the *Kama Sutra*.

'Just *look* at the first page I've opened it at!'

I half sat up, and looked over her elbow.

'It's called The Top,' she said. 'When the woman turns round and round on the stem of the *lingam*, it says.'

'What did I tell you!'

She went on: 'This can only be learned with practice.'

'By you, my darling,' I said with some triumph. 'All I have to do is to lie back. It's you who gets the hard bit.'

Alice looked away. 'Oh . . . I thought *you* had it.'

I scarcely know how to describe what happened next. I can only say that a few moments later we were trying The Top. Alice sat facing me.

'Now I have to spin round and round. Isn't that what it *said*, darling?'

'You should have remembered before you put the book down!' I began to laugh. 'Anyway, *can* you?'

'It's easier said than done, I do agree.'

She managed to get round through 90 degrees, after plunging her knee into my diaphragm.

'It said it required practice,' I said.

Alice had started to laugh. 'You can say *that* again!'

At the expense of nearly falling off on to the floor, she managed to get as far as 180 degrees. 'It seems funny to be looking the other *way*,' she said.

'Never mind which way you're looking, my darling. Get *on*!'

'That would only be easy if one didn't have any legs.'

'Darling,' I cried, 'if you don't get on a bit faster, I shall lose it!'

'Then'— she managed to get as far as 270 degrees —'the only thing I can think of is that you wind a piece of string round and round my waist and pull!'

We were simply shaking with laughter. 'Please, please, get *on*! . . .'

'It said if I'm tired I can lean my forehead against yours.'

'*Anything*! . . .'

360 degrees — relief in sight! She leaned forward; we stopped laughing; the fantasy gave way to a practical proposition. At last!

'Well,' I said, when we had recovered ourselves. 'What did I tell you?'

Alice lay quietly beside me and said nothing.

After a while I said: 'Do you think the room is spinning round a bit?'

'Yes. From left to right. Only it never gets any further. You know . . .'

'Tipsy.'

'The pleasures of the middle-aged.'

Alice switched off the light and turned towards me. At that moment the telephone began to ring.

Alice reached for the receiver in the darkness. I couldn't hear what it said. Alice said: 'No, he's not here.' There was a pause and she put it down.

'Asking for Brian Challoner?' I said.

'Yes. But somebody different this time. With a foreign accent. Welsh or West Indian. And then he rang off.'

'Damn his eyes!' I spoke angrily, but I felt oddly jarred.

After a moment's pause Alice said: 'I think it was rather nasty of him, don't you?'

I put an arm round her. 'That's just how I felt.'

We kissed, to restore each other's tranquillity.

There was a creaking sound as the bedroom door opened, and in the light of the lamp on the landing we saw the shadow of Julia. She came to the bed.

'I had a horrid dream. The telephone was ringing and I couldn't stop it.'

I stretched out my arm towards her. 'It *did* ring. . . . Poor little sweetie.'

She came and put her head on the pillow beside mine. I petted her for a few moments. Suddenly, in nostalgia, I was taken back to the days when George and Roz were Julie's age. Oh, to be there again! . . .

Alice said: 'I'll take her back to bed.'

I lay alone in the darkness.

Alice came quietly back to me. 'What a long and extra-ordinary evening! . . .'

'You,' I said, 'can say that again, too . . .'

CHAPTER SEVEN

Emotion at Courtenay Bagpuize

During the Easter vacation I stayed firmly in Oxford, working. Michael Bowen had settled down very well and we were doing a joint calculation that looked as if it might be exciting. One day I took him over to Courtenay Bagpuize to meet the members of the computer group. At the end of the morning I left him to have lunch with them; and instead of driving straight back to Oxford and getting on with an afternoon's work, I stayed. There was a new canteen where the food was good and the view attractive.

The part of the canteen for senior people and distinguished visitors was on the first floor. I went up the wide spiral staircase, minus risers so that you saw through it; past tall potted palms; past the lavatory which had wall-to-wall carpet — installed, it was said, to accommodate future visits by Royalty — to the lofty dining-room, in which the outer wall consisted of a long curved window.

It was a beautiful April day and sunshine glittered on the polished floor, on the afrormosia-topped tables, on the silver-plated salt-cellars and pepper-pots, and butter-dishes shaped like scallop shells. Vases of early roses stood on the tables and a warm smell of fried onions floated in the air — there was a minor flaw, as yet uncorrected, in the ventilating system. Everything looked pretty wonderful, and it all ran, I can tell you, at a profit.

I seemed to be early: a few tables were occupied by people I didn't know. The Chief Superintendent knew I was on

the site, so I went across to the curved window while I
waited for him. It looked out on to a sort of piazza from
which radiated avenues between long streamlined buildings
in light-coloured brick — the high, glass-topped engineering
hall; the building that housed reactors for materials-testing
and exponential experiments; and so on. In the distance,
though one couldn't see it, was the river.

At last the Chief Superintendent came in. With him, in
addition to some of his superintendents, were Bill Taylor
and Herbert Hobbs.

'Quite a party,' said the Chief Superintendent. 'And' —
his voice took on an eager tone — 'we're expecting the Chairman this afternoon.' Turning to Bill and Herbert Hobbs,
he added: 'But not on the same business as our friends
here.'

It was all news to me. I waited to learn what the business
was that brought 'our friends here' to the site.

I learnt it. Bill Taylor and Herbert Hobbs, together with
the Member for Finance and Administration, who was
lunching with someone else, formed a working-party deputed
by the Chairman to study ways and means of integrating
the Power Board's research and development.

They were on a fact-finding visit to Courtenay.

When nobody else was listening during the lunch, Bill
said to me:

'Meet me in the D.C.S.'s room' — he meant the Deputy
Chief Superintendent's — 'at about two-thirty. We shall have
it to ourselves.'

I looked at him. His stare was clear, light-eyed, unemo-
tional as usual. And yet I suddenly felt menaced.

During the lunch everybody talked as if nothing out of
the ordinary were in the wind. Just a trio of chaps were
doing a day's job on the site. It was a good lunch, as I
expected, but I was too disturbed to enjoy it.

Punctually at 2.30 I was in the D.C.S.'s room. It was on
the first floor, not a specially distinguished room. The trees
and bushes and sunshine gave it, as they gave all the rooms

and laboratories on the site, a countrified air. At 2.35 Bill came in.

'You've gathered what's going on?' he said.

'I imagine I have. Norman's playing it as if he means to follow Hobb's scenario. Right?'

'Right.'

'How far have you got?'

'As far as all the members writing acrimonious letters. On this subject we were asked by the Chairman to write privately in our own handwriting. Supposedly so that even our secretaries shouldn't know what we're saying. Actually so that we shouldn't know what was in the other members' letters to him and in his letters to them.'

'Is he going to follow the Hobbs scenario as far as installing Uncle Bert's No. 2 as Member for Research & Development?'

'God knows! This is the way he's playing it — for the hell of it, of course.' Bill looked at me. 'There'll be a hell of a row in Courtenay if it ever happens.'

He glanced through the window. The bushes below it were rustling softly.

'At the moment the scientists and engineers here are threatening that if it ever happens, Courtenay will secede from the N.P.B.'

I said: 'Bloody ridiculous — they couldn't!'

Bill shrugged his shoulders. 'They could make a hell of a nuisance of themselves. And something like this could start,' he said, 'a Chain-Reaction.'

I thought we were wasting time. Bill looked at me.

'Anyway, to tell you this isn't what I brought you here for.'

'I know.' I stared back at him.

There was a pause. Bill drew in a breath. The bushes went on rustling.

'There's been an offer from Matthewson's,' he said, 'to me.'

I said nothing.

'This doesn't seem to surprise you.'

'No. I heard about it. What surprised me was that you didn't tell me.'

'Why did you think this was?'

I saw no point in not getting the worst news out straight away. I said:

'Because I thought you must be seriously considering taking it.'

'Right.'

I said: 'Oh blast!' I looked through the window.

We were both silent.

I said: 'I suppose they've offered you a lot of cash?'

He nodded.

'More than you'd get if you got the chairmanship here?'

He didn't answer.

I said: 'Is it cash you want most?'

'In the present circumstances, yes.'

'If the circumstances were to change for the more reasonable?'

'To this you know the answer!' He looked at me steadily. 'What I want to do you know — I don't have to tell you again, do I?' He spoke as if he were furious with me as well as with Norman and the rest.

There was another silence.

I had reached the point where I was no longer sure I knew what he'd do. I'd heard his outburst about being a Prisoner of the System before and I hadn't believed in it on either occasion — it was just the volcano letting off a bit of steam.

But now. . . . His situation really was becoming intolerable.

I said: 'For God's sake, hang on!'

'Is this *all* you can counsel?'

'It isn't trifling!' I cried.

Bill looked down, thinking.

'You've seen, and I've seen,' I said, 'surprising reversals of fortune come to people, as a result sheerly of hanging on. . . . I could name at least three men — and so could you, if you tried — who've pulled off highly successful careers, who at one time or another were written off by everybody else.'

At least he listened. And I meant it. He lifted his head slowly to look at me.

'If it comes to that,' I said, 'think of Winston Churchill in his dark years! In fact, isn't he the prime example of hanging on?' The name of Churchill, I thought, must surely have some effect on Bill.

'My dear chap!' He laughed harshly.

'Well?' I said.

His lips tightened. Then he said: 'One's got to weigh up the *chances.*'

At that moment one of the telephones on the D.C.S.'s desk rang.

'Damnation!' I cried.

'You'll have to answer it. They know we're here.'

I was the nearer to it so I picked it up.

It was the Chief Superintendent's secretary tracking me. The Chairman had just arrived and was going to dine that evening in Oxford with Lord Forbes — would I wait here and travel to Oxford with him?

I was put out on two counts, one at being interrupted in talking to Bill, the other at being kept all afternoon on the site. Alice and I were going out to dinner with Joan. I explained to the secretary that I had a dinner engagement in the country, and so should be happy to drive back to Oxford with the Chairman provided we left the site by five-thirty.

The secretary said she was sure that would be all right.

I put the receiver down. 'Blast Norman!'

Bill had stood up — our conversation was broken. He said:

'This will give you the opportunity to see if *you* can find out what Standsfield's got in his mind.'

I shrugged my shoulders. As we walked out of the room

G

I wanted to say again: 'For God's sake, hang on!' but I could see he was no longer in the mood for it.

We parted, and for the rest of the afternoon I kept myself occupied by talking to people on the site about science. It was a bit of a struggle. I felt oppressed by events. For the first time I really could see Bill leaving the Power Board.

My rendezvous with Norman was in the Chief Superintendent's office at five-fifteen. He was already there. He was sitting on the edge of the table, reading a memorandum.

'Thank you so much for waiting for me,' he said, standing up. 'I realise you've had to change your plans.' His voice was high-pitched and honey-sweet — laying it on, as usual. 'What are you doing about your own car? Can we give you any help?'

I said Michael Bowen was driving it back for me.

The Chief Superintendent was getting a decanter of sherry and some glasses out of a cupboard in the lower half of a glass-fronted bookcase. I noticed that he was getting out two glasses. 'I'm terribly sorry I shall have to leave you almost immediately. I've got to catch the charter-plane to the North. . . . Sir Norman says he's happy about my deserting you both.' He was an exceedingly polite-mannered man, so polite-mannered that I wondered whom the rôle of spokesman for the Courtenay seceding-party had fallen upon.

Norman put down the memorandum. 'Your point of view has been grasped, I think,' he said to the Chief Superintendent, giving him a sidelong smile that looked to me ambiguous if not sinister.

A few minutes later Norman and I were left alone.

The room was a little larger than the D.C.S.'s but otherwise very like it. On the first floor, of course. The first floor was where the bosses' rooms were always to be found in the Power Board's research establishments — as it were the *piano nobile*. The casement windows were open, and the bushes and trees beneath them were rustling a little more loudly. The sunlight was slanting through them at a lower angle. It was going to be a radiant evening, by the look of it.

I drank some sherry and glanced at Norman. I thought he was both tired and hunted. His face looked longer and hollower, and his glance was darting about restlessly. Although his cheeks were as rosy as ever his complexion as a whole seemed to have a greyish tinge. Exercising the whip-hand, for all its joys, must take it out of you, I thought.

Norman drank a very small amount of sherry, and with his head tilted forward looked at me from under his eyebrows. He said:

'I thought it would be agreeable to talk to someone who's . . . outside all this.' He made a gesture with his hand.

I was not specially pleased at being told I was outside the N.P.B. — he'd said it intentionally. I replied:

'I always find it interesting to talk to someone who's inside.'

'You have the advantage of not *being* inside.' He gave me a swooping, from the waist, bow. His eyes suddenly gleamed, apparently in a friendly way.

The advantage of not being inside. . . . For the second time that afternoon I recalled Bill Taylor's outburst about life in the Power Board. I thought: Oh God, the Chairman's going to do it now!

'Yes, indeed,' he said, and drank a little more sherry.

I mustn't give the impression, in forecasting an outburst, that I was visited by superhuman prescience. It was repeated experience which led me to regard it as one of the natural hazards of conversing with somebody in what was called a top job, that in a brace of shakes he'd be saying he was dissatisfied with it and thought of leaving it. 'Here am I, Sir Norman Standsfield, Chairman of the National Power Board; and I'm prevented from doing the things I really want to do . . .'

I was ready for it. I sometimes felt it was only a matter of being in the vicinity of the Throne to find oneself listening to: 'Here am I, Monarch of England, and I'm prevented . . . etc.'

I was accustomed to listening with a sympathetic air,

simply hoping it would soon stop. In the first place I had
never seen any of them give up their jobs for that reason.
And in the second place The System of which they were
Prisoners was very properly evolved to stop them chucking
their weight about *ad lib.*

On the other hand I must add, in justice to them, that
I'd never heard any of them say what they're always supposed to say; that being at the top turns out to be hollow
and empty, and they wish they were back again in those
exhilarating, striving days down at the bottom.

Norman was waiting for me to say something. Surprised
that the cue was mine, I said:

'I'm partly inside, you know.'

'Yes, indeed!' He was smiling in his most friendly way.
'And of course a friend of Bill Taylor.'

What was this gambit? I said: 'I am.'

Norman paused. Then he said directly: 'He's one of my
problems. Perhaps you can help me.'

I was pretty astonished. His tone was intimate. I could
have thought he meant it.

'I want to know what you think.' He started to bow again,
elegantly and smilingly. 'I should like to talk to you about
Taylor, so that you'll see how he comes to be a problem.'

'Please do.'

Norman said: 'Then I'll come to the point straight away.'
He lifted his chin a little, still smiling. 'It's generally admitted that Taylor is brash.' He paused. 'And that he makes
remarks that are unconsidered.' He made another pause —
and then came the venom. 'And he's known to make
mistakes.'

I simply couldn't decide what he was up to. One alternative was that he was trying to make bad blood between
Bill and me. The other was that he genuinely wanted
a confidant. (He wasn't likely to find one *inside* the
N.P.B.)

Although all the members would have said it was the first
alternative, I couldn't help feeling there was at least an

element of the second. You'll recall my saying that even if
he hadn't a friend in the world. . . . Though I must say
that abusing Bill Taylor was a bizarre way of opening up
a friendship with me.

I said with as little anger as I could manage:

'I don't think brashness is as serious as all that — it ought
to be what you say that matters, not the way you say it.'

'If only it were!' he interpolated. I went on.

'What Bill Taylor says only appears to be unconsidered.
There's usually a good deal more thought behind it than
there is behind the considered remarks of a lot of people
I could name.'

Norman's eyes glinted.

'As for mistakes,' I went on: 'Who *doesn't* make them?
The only people who never make any mistakes are those
who never have any ideas at all!' And for good measure I
added: 'And there *are* occasions when not having any ideas
actually does more damage than making a mistake!'

His eyes glinted again — more so! But I was going to
have my say about Bill now, now or never.

'To sum up about Bill Taylor,' I said. 'One: I think his
brashness doesn't matter — especially among men whose
general *sensitiveness* isn't the first thing that strikes one
about them. Two: I think his remarks are more considered
than they see fit to pretend — because they don't really want
to hear them. Three: for a man with his fertility in ideas,
the proportion of ideas that are mistaken is remarkably
low!' I paused a moment. 'The case *against* Bill Taylor is
what he's like, what his personality is. The case *for* Bill
Taylor is what he can *give* — to the Power Board, to the
country! . . . The fact that people can let that case
against *weigh* more than that case for, is a demonstration
of how contemptibly *petty*' — I spat the word out — 'they
can be!'

Norman looked down at his glass, and then had a sip of
sherry.

'Well,' he said, 'with these well-chosen words, my dear

Jack, I think the air may be said to be cleared.' He nodded his head. 'Thank you for clearing the air.' He smiled, absolutely furious with me.

But I wasn't ready for what he said next. He said:

'To hear you convince the *Minister* of this. . . . This is what I should like to hear.'

(On the spur of the moment I thought I might find it easier to convince the Minister than to convince his civil servants — the Permanent Secretary and the rest.) I said:

'Yes?'

Norman said: 'If you're thinking *I* haven't tried, let me assure you I have. As a formal step one takes, perhaps you're thinking? No. Further than a formal step, a good deal further. . . . As far as there appeared to be any chance of his giving a favourable response.'

I said: 'That's good . . .'

'Don't you think this would be to my advantage, to have Taylor beside me, in my support, when I'm trying to deal with the Ministry?'

I looked at him. So he was at loggerheads with the Minister and his civil servants? Nobody in the N.P.B. seemed to know exactly how much Norman parleyed with the Minister and on what terms. He kept it to himself with remarkable skill — which was not surprising, since in his touchy, imperious way it must have irked him to have to keep parleying with the Ministry at all.

Norman went on: 'Taylor may have complained to you that he's kept away by me from what I believe he calls 'the places where the real decisions are made'. Isn't that so?'

It was so.

'I should like you to know that it's entirely because of his own defects. For our own safety, I feel that he *has* to be kept away!'

It was my turn to be furious. Norman went on.

'Taylor is a man of great gifts — I am sure this is seen by us all. In other circumstances I've no doubt they'd take him a great deal further. But in the present circumstances,

I'm afraid they will not. Because of his defects we must
accept the fact, and he must accept it too, that he's reached'
— Norman looked at me — 'his Ceiling!'

With even greater fury I heard the fatal expression, the
expression by which a man's chances of getting a job were
dished. There were three such expressions, which, in ascend-
ing order of dishingness, ran:

1. It wouldn't be in his own best interests.
2. I'm worried about his judgement.
3. He's reached his Ceiling.

My fury was the greater through believing that to say it
about Bill was nonsense.

'I've had my say,' I said.

Norman looked at me steadily. He must be ruining Bill's
prospects in the places where the decision about who was to
be next Chairman was made.

I glanced away, and caught sight of a clock. We were
already ten minutes past the time I'd said I wanted to leave.
Norman noticed my glance. I stood up. Norman remained
where he was, sitting on the edge of the table. Slowly he
drank another tiny sip of his sherry. The inference was
clear — he knew I was late and intended to make me later.

'It was good of you to stay,' he said. He paused. The sunlight glinted on the clipped grey hair round his temples.
There was a smile on his lips. I went across to the window
and leaned against the sill — it was obvious that he didn't
mean to hurry.

'You see that problems exist, even for me,' he said.

I said: 'I suppose what we get our money for is trying
to produce the solutions.'

'I have my solutions to some of them.'

I looked at him sharply. He was looking sharply at me.
He put down his glass on the table.

'Such as,' I said, 'for the problem of how best to get the
Power Board's research and development done?'

'This is one of them. For this the solution is to hand, I

believe — though with some of your friends it won't find favour.'

'You mean to hive off all R. & D. into one Division?'

'To do it right across the board.' He nodded his head. 'Is there any alternative, in the present circumstances?' He lifted his chin, and smiled.

'That's for you as Chairman to decide,' I said, and glanced at my watch.

Norman sat where he was.

'The Minister is continually getting at me,' he said, 'about the size of the National Power Board. About its unwieldiness.' He paused.

'Yes? . . .'

'With this I am not in agreement. *I* could "wield" it.'

There was a moment's silence. He said:

'This may not be surprising to you. Yes, *I* could wield it — I could wield it but for one thing. And do you know what this is?'

I looked at him. He said with extraordinary emotion:

'I could wield it if I could rely on the loyalty of my staff. Especially on the loyalty of my nearest colleagues!'

Silence. When the way he treated them, I thought, made it practically impossible for them to *be* loyal. Divide and rule. The whip-hand.

'My nearest colleagues seem to possess an inability to be loyal to their Chairman,' he said bitterly. 'This, not its unwieldiness, is the National Power Board's tragedy.'

I said nothing. What was there that I could say?

Suddenly he said to me:

'Perhaps you think this is *my* tragedy?'

I was astonished by the remark, and I simply didn't know what he meant by it. I just went on looking at him, I hoped, expressionlessly.

Norman's mood changed. In a business-like tone he said:

'In point of fact, giving consideration to the Minister's criticism, a very simple solution for this, too, is to hand. For reducing the size of the National Power Board. If the

Minister so desires it. Again, with your friends it won't find favour.'

I was damned if I would ask him. He stood up, looking giraffe-like and elegant, in order to launch it:

'The Power Board's research and development could be envisaged as being done, on our behalf, by a body of scientists and engineers *outside* the Power Board.' He paused. 'Outside altogether.'

He watched me. He went on.

'Possibly by some nationally-sponsored body, you know the sort of thing.'

I still said nothing.

'A list of the Board's technical problems could be fed into it; and the solutions paid for.'

His eyes seemed to be glittering with triumph.

I stood facing him, too outraged to utter — certainly too outraged to ask myself, as I did afterwards, if he meant any word of it.

'It's a scenario,' he said, and I assumed he was quoting Bert Hobbs's word with malice. 'A scenario which I think we owe it to ourselves to discuss exhaustively in the near future.'

I looked at my wrist-watch. 'I'm afraid I've really got to go.'

'My dear fellow, I must apologise! I've kept you so late . . .'

For the moment I didn't see how we could stay on speaking terms during the drive to Oxford.

When we got to the car Norman was all charm and solicitude. The driver was instructed to keep up a good pace. The sun was going down, and in the fading light the hedgerows looked denser. From the ledge behind his headrest Norman took a small tin and opened it. He offered it to me. It contained Marie biscuits.

I shook my head. Norman chose a biscuit and slowly ate it.

After a pause he started conversation — on a gossipy level,

about Stanley Forbes and Clarendon College. I'd always known that he must have Stanley pretty well weighed up.

'You know,' he said to me confidentially, 'between ourselves, my dear Jack, Lord Forbes was not a success as Chairman of the Power Board.'

'Oh,' I said.

'He's a very fine scientist — or so I'm told. But he's useless as an administrator.'

He was leaning his head against the headrest, speaking to the roof of the car. Something made me look at him suspiciously.

'You know,' he said, 'Lord Forbes is an object lesson to people who talk about Scientists running Whitehall. The fact is' — he turned his head towards me — 'they can't do it. They'll never do it. It's a nonsense.' He paused a moment. 'It will never come to pass.'

I turned and looked away through the window. I thought: This is really the end. The very end. The last and final end.

The hedges and trees flashed by, and a thin stripe of clouds near the horizon was glowing with fire. During the remainder of the journey we both leaned our heads against the headrest and said nothing. I couldn't wait to get home and unburden myself to Alice.

Norman had made me late, of course. Alice was all ready, carrying the copy of the *Kama Sutra* to return it to Joan's husband. I dumped my briefcase in the house and we started.

'*That man!*' I kept saying.

'Yes, darling,' said Alice, who was driving.

'You can't imagine what he's got in mind now.'

'Do you remember the night you came home after that meeting, and told Roz and me that when the repercussions got going —'

'Don't say it!' I interrupted. 'It's on the cards they're going to be *more* than f—— something! That Man is everything he shouldn't be. Talk about being *against* the Industrial Revolution! . . . He not only hates scientists and engineers. Bill Taylor was right all along — he *scorns* them, too. What he'd really like to do is hive them off from the N.P.B. altogether. Talk about them being 'On Tap but not On Top'! He'd like to relegate them to the rôle of servants. *Feed* them a list of the problems, and *pay* for the solutions! . . .'

Alice said: 'Darling, you must try and calm down before we get there.'

I said: 'How the hell I'm going to talk to Joan and Perry' — Joan's fatigued and scholarly husband was called Peregrine — 'I simply don't know. I shall be thinking about That Man all evening!'

I thought about Norman all that evening; and during much of the next two months, when a lot of things happened in the N.P.B. But during the next two months I didn't see him again. In fact I hadn't set eyes on him again before the news came that he'd had a coronary.

Part Three

Part Three

CHAPTER ONE

Alice Takes a Hand

During the next two months a great deal happened in the N.P.B. I was kept apprised of it by Bill Taylor. A great deal happened. Please let me remind you that none of it was necessary. It happened in the course of a purely organisational shake-up, which was to conclude with a new disposition of the Power Board's research and development marginally better, or marginally worse, than the previous one, and which, while it was actually on, brought that research and development to a standstill.

Incidentally I must remark that I had *not* apprised Bill of what the Chairman had said to me at Courtenay and on the way to Oxford.

The small working-party, consisting of the Deputy Chairman, the Member for Coal and Oil, and the Member for Finance and Administration, had put in its report on ways and means of achieving the reorganisation. The report was unanimous. Obviously there *were* ways and means of integrating the Board's research and development, and there was not much basis for difference of opinion over *what* they were — from an administrative point of view they were relatively simple.

But although they put in a report that was unanimous, one of its signatories, the Deputy Chairman, Bill Taylor, then ceased to be on speaking terms with the other two, the Member for Coal and Oil, Herbert Hobbs, and the Member for Finance and Administration, Charles Quain. (It is fair to say that Bill had never had any use for communication of any kind with Quain — 'the Chairman's catspaw' Bill always called him.)

'We've had it,' Bill said to me, shortly afterwards. 'All the Administrators have to be certain of is that a change is feasible administratively. It's stupid to make it, scientifically. But it's feasible administratively!'

'Well,' I said in what I judged to be a moderating tone, 'you don't want to get paranoiac about it.'

'*Why* not?'

For a moment I thought I'd given him the opening to quote one of my own aphorisms against me — that people who suffer from persecution mania usually are being persecuted: they somehow seem to be asking for it, and they get it.

'It doesn't help,' I said, with a singular ebb of confidence as I thought of all the world's great figures who had got where they'd got with the aid of paranoia — A. Hitler, J. V. Stalin, *et al.*

Bill seemed to be satisfied with my answer. He merely said:

'This I'm telling you. Standsfield will do it, and he'll get away with it.'

That was that.

With the inevitable in view, Bill began to come round to it. The reorganisation had some gains to offer, as we'd always admitted. Hobbs's own research scientists and engineers, a depressed class in Coal & Oil Division, would get a lift from being united with the 'hot-shots' in Nuclear Division. And so would Amos Wilson's men, though they were a much better lot than Hobbs's. (To do Amos Wilson justice, Generation Division, despite his supposedly not being personally very interested in R. & D., had somehow managed to get two exciting projects on the go — one for automating the control of power-distributing systems, the other for direct conversion of heat into electricity, eliminating all the inefficient stages of steam-raising and so on.)

And *all* the research scientists and engineers might get a lift if the new Member for them were a really first-rate applied scientist. *If.* You will take the point, if you remember the reason why Uncle Bert had to get out his scenario for a new Division in the first place.

'The idea of a single Division for R. & D. I can swallow,' said Bill Taylor. 'But the idea of Beckett as its member I'm damned if I'll swallow!' (Beckett was the name of Uncle Bert's second No. 2, the second man to be promised Uncle Bert's own Division.)

'Well, that's something,' I said, relieved to find him accommodating himself to the major issue.

He went on. 'Do you understand that?' He lowered his chunky-looking head as if he were going to butt someone. 'Beckett's getting it I don't swallow. This'd be a bloody insult to R. & D. And a bloody insult to *me!*' He paused.

'I see that.'

'This I've thought over as long as I mean to. And this is my conclusion, Jack. If Trevor Darwin gets it, I'll'—he gave me a sharp look—'"hang on". . . . But if Beckett gets it, this place has had it, so far as I'm concerned.'

I said nothing. His decision had attached itself to a minor issue, but it was still there. The only consolation was that we stood a better chance of carrying the minor issue—or so I thought at the time.

Bill said: 'Matthewson's are "hanging on" too. They want an answer from me.'

I said nothing to this, either. There was no point in going over the same old argument.

To my surprise Bill said: 'You see, I've admitted your side of the case for my staying here.'

I nodded.

'And you,' he went on promptly, 'have got to admit my side for quitting.'

I said: 'Let's leave it there for the time being.'

When I'd parted from him I felt very perturbed. Talking about it to Alice, I argued that if Hobbs had carried the major issue I couldn't see what was to stop him carrying the minor one.

'And if he does,' she said, 'Bill Taylor goes? I mean, it *is* definite, isn't it?'

'I guess it's definite.'

Alice said: 'Isn't there anything *you* can do?'

I shook my head.

'I think you *ought* to do something,' she said.

I shook my head again.

'You've always said Sir Amos Wilson ought to support Bill Taylor,' she persisted — you remember what I said about her nagging persistence. 'Why don't you *ask* him? I mean, why *don't* you? . . .'

'Because I don't play politics.'

'Why not?'

'Because I don't fancy my chance as a politician. It's not *me* . . .' I paused. 'As a matter of fact, I haven't got any gift for it and have never made a start. I love to watch other people *at* it. But that's as far as I go. I don't even pretend to know the game, let alone be able to play it.'

'Well, *I* think you ought to try. Just for *once*, anyway. . . . After all, it would be worth it.'

I felt I was definitely being nagged. I said: 'I'll think about it. But I'm not going to promise.'

That evening I thought about it at length. I'd been absolutely honest when I'd told Alice I didn't fancy my chance as a politician. Other people might have the gift for it, but not I. I may say that among scientists the word 'politician' was generally used as a term of abuse, meaning a scientist who had abandoned his 'scientific integrity' in the course of advancing himself in worldly affairs. Such scientists existed, all right. But for the rest of us to call them 'politicians', and define 'politics' in terms of them, was in my opinion short-sighted as well as mistaken. For one thing, it discouraged scientists who actually had the moral fibre to remain scientifically honest — and *they* existed, too — from going into affairs at all. And for another

thing, it suited only too well the Norman Standsfields —
'Scientists in Whitehall is a nonsense' — to point out that
any scientists who actually had gone into Whitehall were
disowned, under the term 'politicians', by all their fellow-
scientists.

Though Alice didn't really know what she was talking
about, I admitted to myself that there was something in
what she said. If Amos Wilson could be persuaded to stop
not giving a damn, he obviously could be of some use to us.
If Generation Division weighed in on Bill Taylor's side,
the Chairman might feel compelled to have second
thoughts.

The following morning Alice returned to the charge.

'You've thought about it,' she said, 'haven't you, darling?'

'I said I wasn't going to promise.'

The fact of the matter was that I felt nagged, now, by
my conscience as well as by her. Either I went and had a go
at Amos Wilson, or I just sat by while events went against
Bill Taylor.

Alice sat looking at me, simply waiting.

I said: 'Oh, all right, then. I'll have a go.'

'I knew you would,' she said.

'You did *not*!'

Her hazel eyes flickered brightly. 'I mean I *guessed*. It's
all right to *guess*, isn't it? . . .'

The occasion for me to have my go fell out quite naturally.
I was having lunch with Stanley Forbes at the Club, and
we saw Amos at another table. Stanley was going to a meeting immediately afterwards, so I went over and asked Amos
to have coffee with me. Stanley observed me with interest.

'What do you think of Amos Wilson?' I said.

Stanley sighted Amos along his nose. Then he gave me a
peculiar smile.

'Amos looks,' he said smoothly, 'rather different from
what he is.'

'Meaning?'

'I always found I could deal with him straightly.'

I laughed. Why *did* Amos Wilson look the way he looked? With his small eyes, over-bright and sly, just that shade too high up on his long face and too near to his long nose; with his mouth curving just that shade too far down at the corners into a wolfish leer; he looked as if, the moment he came up to one, he would touch one for a fiver or volunteer a hot tip for the 3.21 (greyhounds).

I wondered what Amos thought in return of Lord Forbes.

Ten minutes later I was sitting alone in the drawing-room when Amos came in and joined me. His eyes were bright and his complexion was red — I thought he'd probably drunk half a bottle of wine with his lunch.

'Sir,' he said, in a matey tone, 'what can I do for you?'

I half-shut my eyes to survey him. 'Nothing, I should think.' I glanced at the coffee-tray on the table. 'Do you want a brandy?'

'H'm. Rich today, Jack? All right. Throw your money about if you want to!' He grinned at me. 'I'm not going to stop you, am I?'

I called the waiter and ordered two brandies.

Amos lit a cigar, blew out a small cloud of smoke, and said:

'What's in the wind?'

He then leaned back in his chair and turned his matey gaze at the ceiling.

I said: 'You always strike me as not giving a damn for anything, Amos.'

'This could be true.' He went on looking at the ceiling.

'I think it's time for you to come off it.' I paused. 'As a matter of fact, time to give a damn for what's going on in the N.P.B.'

He turned his head towards me. 'I said it *could* be true.'

'Thanks for the concession.'

He paused a moment and then said: 'I'll ask you the same question again. What can I do for you?'

'Nothing for me. Something' — I was going to say 'for the

Power Board' and then changed my mind — 'for Bill Taylor among others.'

'Does the great Bill Taylor need my support?'

We were interrupted by the waiter, bringing our brandies.

I said: 'You know as well as I know what goes on. How the Chairman runs the Board. "Divide and Rule" and all that. . . . It's the Administrators who rule. And it's the Scientists and the Engineers who are divided.' I paused. 'Are you willing to put up with that?'

Amos drank some brandy and then took a puff at his cigar. I went on.

'If *you* took charge of the Engineers, instead of letting it go to Bert Hobbs —'

'Who says?'

'And then if the Engineers and the Scientists had the wit to sink their differences and see that they're —'

'Look, you're a nice chap, but this sort of stuff I don't go for.'

I held on to my temper — his tone had been amiable. But I thought that if he knew his onions as well as he thought he did, he ought to go for this sort of stuff. I might have expressed myself too theoretically for him, but there was nothing seriously wrong with the theory.

'All right,' I said. 'Do you want to know what it boils down to in terms of action?'

He gave me a swift glance. 'O.K. Let's hear what it boils down to in terms of action.'

I said: 'If Bill Taylor became Chairman, would you be willing to serve under him?'

'This is a question, not a line of action. Suppose I said Yes?'

'All right. Would you rather the Board had Taylor as Chairman than another non-technical person like Standsfield?'

'Who have Whitehall got as their candidate?'

'I don't know. Bill and I have talked about it. There's

nobody obvious, the way Standsfield was, as far as we can see. But that doesn't mean they couldn't find one. And *wouldn't* find one promptly, if Taylor got out.'

Amos drew a long breath through his nose.

'And the way the Chairman's playing it now,' I said, 'looks like resulting in Taylor's getting out.'

Amos gave me a fleeting, private look. He must have calculated regularly the odds, if Bill Taylor were eliminated from the Board, against his getting the chairmanship himself. They couldn't have been longer than the odds that Bill would have given him — Bill thought he'd scarcely be considered.

'As I understand it,' I said, 'Bill Taylor really will get out if Beckett's made the new member.'

'So you want me to join this caucus that's rooting for Darwin?'

'Right.'

'What's the case for it?' Amos was matey and cheerful again. 'I'm willing to listen to sense.'

I said impatiently: 'You know all that.' I couldn't see that I was making any headway.

Amos paused, thoughtfully, while he had another pull at his cigar. Suddenly he said:

'Listen, I'll tell you something, eh? . . . I've no use for Beckett. He's a competent, useful engineer — and he's damned good at getting things done. That's his forte.' (Pronounced 'fort'.) 'But he's no good for R. & D. Never has been. C. & O.'s R. & D. has done sweet Fanny Adams since its Foundation Day. I'll tell you something else.' He leaned towards me with a Member for Generation's leer. 'I'd rather have sweet Fanny Adams than Beckett.'

'Then why haven't you said so?'

'The great Bill Taylor never asked me.' He sat back.

I said: 'Oh well, I'm asking you *for* him.'

Amos grinned at me. He knew as well as I exactly how true my remark was. He said:

'This I'll accept.'

I said: 'Then I think you ought to do something about it. If you went in with Taylor and Darwin —'

'Yeh,' he said impatiently. He knew it all: he'd known it all before I started.

'It's urgent,' I said. 'And serious.'

'Yeh,' he said again, without looking at me. Then suddenly he did look at me. 'Yes, it is.' He picked up his glass and finished his brandy.

I was provoked. 'Damn it, doing this sort of thing isn't *my* line. Nor *my* job!' I stood up.

Amos stood up in a more leisurely fashion. 'I don't know about that.'

'I've got to do it,' I said, 'because I think a lot hangs on it.'

Amos glanced at me unblinkingly. 'The good of the cause, eh? . . .'

I grinned wryly.

Amos walked across the room close beside me. 'Taylor for Chairman,' he said with good-natured sarcasm. And then he added: 'You know, Jack, *I* wouldn't mind being Deputy Chairman.'

I acknowledged, as we used to say in Cambridge, his remark.

At the doorway we paused. 'Can I give you a lift anywhere?' he asked.

I was going to the Ministry of——, which was in a different direction, so we went downstairs together and then parted.

Throughout the next hour or so at the Ministry of —— I felt irritable, and anxious. The minutes seemed to pass extraordinarily slowly. And what was there to do, anyway, when the meeting was over?

When the meeting ended, I was relieved of any necessity to answer that question. I was handed a telephoned message by a secretary. It said:

'Sir William Taylor and Sir Amos Wilson are going to see the Chairman tomorrow afternoon.'

CHAPTER TWO

Waiting for a Call

From about four o'clock on the following afternoon I was waiting for a telephone call from Bill.

I had still not heard from him when I left the lab at about five-thirty, and there was no message awaiting me when I got home. It was a night when I'd arranged to dine in College: I left it till the last moment to set out. I thought: He'll ring from his house, later. And I told Alice to take the call if I wasn't yet back.

There were a lot of Fellows dining, and I was too late to get a seat beside anyone I knew especially well. Some distance away from me I saw Alec Benda; he was engaged in a conversation, embellished by theatrical gestures, with our local Luddite, the Eng. Lit. Fellow, John Farrow. I had a feeling he failed to meet my eye.

Brian Challoner did meet my eye, in his usual furtive way. I thought he was looking particularly harassed. Was he worried about getting on the Royal Commission or about being pursued by his un-tame teenager? (Alice and I had not had any crazy telephone calls in the night for the last two weeks. But Stanley and Doris Forbes *had*!)

Michael Bowen was there, sitting with our pure mathematician, with whom he seemed, surprisingly, to have struck up a friendship. I say surprisingly because our pure mathematician, a very clever and engaging young man, was at the opposite end of the professional spectrum to Mike Bowen: his line was classical analysis and geometry — not much sign, there, of an inclination to formulate problems as abstractions from the physical world!

I saw Reg Popper, farouche as usual, entertaining his theoretical physicist friend from Courtenay Bagpuize. I simply couldn't remember the man's name: I could only recall his blushing when I asked him his father's profession and he said: 'A merchant . . .'

When dinner was over we all went into the Senior Common Room, but I didn't mean to stay there. At any time I somehow didn't like the way it was decorated. After the Hall's cool brightness of a Swedish day, the S.C.R.'s cosy dusk seemed to be aimed at evoking the mewed-up intimacy of a Finnish night. For me its atmosphere was tinged with the claustrophobic and the perverse. The walls and ceiling were panelled with dark-coloured wood, but it was the chairs which most affected me. They were teak-framed with seats and backs made out of broad black leather thongs, fastened ostentatiously with brass buckles — made for relieving the tension of interminable Arctic night by a bout of Nordic flagellation.

Tonight I especially didn't mean to stay because I wanted to go home and wait for Bill Taylor's telephone call undisturbed.

Popper saw fit to catch me.

'Hi, Prof, can you sp-p-pare us half an hour of your valuable time?' His companion, sleek and handsome and smiling, stood beside him. Suddenly I remembered the man's name — Harry Sinkins.

'What's it all about?' I said.

'He' — Reg indicated his friend — 'needs your advice, I guess. So do several other chaps at Courtenay.' There was the usual menace in his voice, as if he were passing moral judgement (unfavourably) on whomever he was talking to or of.

'Courtenay?' At once I suspected they wanted to talk about the idea of Courtenay's 'seceding' from the N.P.B., and I also saw my own means of escaping them. 'Surely,' I said, 'it would be more proper for Dr. Sinkins and his colleagues to ask the advice of the Chief Superintendent?'

Through the concentric rings of his thick spectacle lenses I got a glance combining starkness and beadiness. 'I,' he said, 't-t-told him to consult *you*.'

'Then,' said I, 'you'll have to come home with me. I'm waiting for a telephone call there.'

'Thank you, sir,' said Sinkins.

When we got back to my house I took Popper and Sinkins straight to my room, which was the tail of the L-shaped drawing-room that Alice had altered. It was a very small room and I attempted to keep all my books there. I switched on a reading-lamp by my desk and made sure that the telephone extension was switched through. I noticed that Alice had put a little vase of philadelphus sprigs on the desk — their scent was wafted in the air. I sat down in my desk chair; Reg Popper took the armchair, and Sinkins sat on the edge of the divan. They lit cigarettes. I offered them whisky and they both refused.

'Now,' I said, 'what is it?'

Sinkins looked politely at Popper: in the low-powered light his eyes looked darker and more deeply set in their orbits. Popper's spectacles flashed. He said:

'You t-t-tell him. It's your s-s-story.'

There was a brief pause, and Sinkins said:

'Well, sir, we're worried about the future of Courtenay.'

I suppressed amusement at his innocent pompousness. Loftier persons than he, I thought, were worried about the future of Courtenay. But for one thing he was only speaking in the vein in which the young scientists at Courtenay always spoke; and for another thing, it was well that they should think, not yet lofty though they might be, seriously about their establishment's future. After all, they *were* its future.

'We've heard, of course,' he went on, 'about the integration of R. & D.'

I nodded my head.

'There was a lot of feeling,' he said, 'when we first heard about it.'

I said: 'Provided it didn't express itself as a plan for Courtenay to secede from the N.P.B., I'm ready to sympathise.'

Sinkins smiled. 'There was talk of seceding from the N.P.B., but it petered out. The Chief Superintendent told us, very politely indeed, not to be silly.'

I hadn't known the Chief Superintendent had had to quell them.

'He's a bit of an administrator, the C.S.,' said Reg. *'Used* to be a scientist, though.'

I ignored him by looking encouragingly at Harry Sinkins. He responded.

'The problem's different now. I think we're all fairly sure of Courtenay's future after the reorganisation, provided we're confident in the . . .' — he hesitated — 'Leadership.'

'In other w-w-words,' said Reg, hindered by a stammer but not by tact, 'we've heard we're going to get as Member for Research and Development that chap from C. & O. Div., name of Beckett. *Research manager.'*

(In case you may not know, 'research manager' was Reg Popper's idea of the ultimate term of abuse: 'managing' research was the antithesis of 'doing' research.)

'You've heard that, have you?' I said.

'Come off it, Jack!' said Reg. 'Of course we've heard it. They say old Hobbs wants to get *his* chap, Beckett, on to the Board. But *we* don't know what goes on up there.'

'You seem to have intimations,' I said.

For a moment we confronted each other. And then neither could help bursting into laughter.

'If I've got i-i-intimations, it's your fault. I was just an academic, till you got me a part-time Fellowship at Courtenay.'

Suddenly I remembered that I was waiting for a telephone call from Bill Taylor. I was impatient to get rid of these two young men.

'We've got off the track,' I said. I turned to Sinkins. 'What were you going to say?'

'There's an offer come in from the States.' Embarrassment made him incoherent. 'I mean, if we're not confident in the Leadership. . . . It's an offer not just to me. It's for a group of us — our team as a whole, if you see what I mean.'

'Offer where from?'

He told me. I did see what he meant. His whole story was entirely and deplorably plausible.

'I think there'll be quite a few more as'll go to the States too,' said Popper. 'From other sections.'

'Oh?' said Sinkins, his head on one side.

I felt I'd heard enough bad news for the time being. I said, not quite knowing whom I was hitting out at:

'You don't seem to have rehearsed your story.'

'This is unkind!' said Popper. 'Bloody cruel, in fact.'

Harry Sinkins stood up. 'I know you're waiting for us to go.'

'Aren't you going to ask him?' Reg said to him.

Sinkins looked at me, his clever sleek face overshadowed with concern. 'I think the question is already put.'

'To go or not to go?' said Reg. 'This is the question!'

I was getting more than tired of him. I said: 'So far as I know, who becomes Member for Research and Development is by no means settled. If I were you I should wait and —'

'Do you mean to say,' Reg interrupted, 'there's still a chance it'll be Trevor Darwin?'

For a moment I was too taken aback to reply. How on earth did these two know? Had Bill Taylor been down to Courtenay and slipped the news into the grapevine? Impossible.

'Look,' I said. 'When the appointment's made, if you still feel the same, come and put the question to me then.'

Reg gave one of his harsh laughs. 'Do you think, Harry,' he said, mimicking Harry's earlier speech, 'the answer is already put?'

I said to him: 'Don't be too clever by half!'

'Is that possible? I mean, just let's consider it intellectually, Jack.'

'We will not consider it intellectually or any other way,' I said, standing up. 'Come on, Reg, it's time to go.'

'All right. I know I've got to go, but don't hurry me!'

'I'm sorry,' said Sinkins, 'we've taken so much of your time.'

I glanced at my watch. Still no call from Bill Taylor.

They left and I waited.

There was no call from Bill Taylor that night.

If there is any generalisation about the interpretation of news to be drawn from my own experience, it is that no news is bad news. I went to bed very depressed.

Alice tried to cheer me up. 'Perhaps he didn't get a chance to telephone you. Did he say he was going to?'

Bill hadn't said so. But if the news had been good I was certain he would have telephoned. Bill rarely failed to express himself in terms of action. It was only in the face of a really impossible situation that his will to action sometimes seemed to crack.

I wondered if his will to action had cracked now.

'Perhaps he's written you a letter,' Alice said, with nagging optimism.

'A letter?' said I. 'Is Bill ever known to *write* a letter from one day's end to another? He only *signs* letters.'

'I thought you said he wrote to the Chairman.'

'That,' I said, 'is not the happiest thought of the evening.'

'Oh . . .' said Alice, consolingly.

I switched off the light.

The following morning I took to telephonic action, myself. As soon as I got to the lab I rang Bill.

'What's happened?'

'Nothing.'

He sounded both sombre and tense.

'Do you have to be so curt?'

'On the telephone, yes.' There was a pause. 'You'd better come up to London, if you want to talk.'

Not pointing out how men in affairs always seemed to assume that academics had nothing to spend their time on, I agreed to meet him in the Club that evening.

'I'll tell them to lay on a car to drive you back to Oxford,' he said, 'so you needn't worry about trains.' The effect of the offer was only to make me more apprehensive — disposing of the least of one's worries seemed to make the greatest of them seem greater. I prepared for the worst of news.

When we met Bill delivered the news in the tone in which he'd spoken on the telephone: somehow its sombreness and tension made what he was saying sound less dramatic.

'I'm going to join Matthewson's.'

Even so, it struck me as dramatic enough. I restrained myself from saying anything straight away. As we walked up the stairs I asked:

'Have you actually told them, now?'

He turned his head angrily to look up at me: 'Do you think I'm just *playing* this game?'

I draw back. There was a mood of frustration and failure in which men like Bill seemed to be impelled, entirely off the rails of reason, to turn round and quarrel with someone who was an ally or a friend. The look in his eyes made me realise that unless I was lucky it was going to be with me.

At the same time I noticed that he hadn't said Yes to me, perhaps hadn't been able to bring himself to say Yes to me — or, it occurred to me, perhaps he still hadn't been able to bring himself to say Yes to Matthewson's. Not that it mattered if he had made the decision and had reconciled himself to it. Reconciled himself to it. . . . That seemed to me important.

We were going upstairs to have our before-dinner drink in the library: the usual room, after being closed to us for redecoration for four months, was still inexplicably not open. However, we gained in privacy by being in the big room. We went to the furthest corner and sat down on a sofa.

As he sat down and then leaned forward to move an ash-tray, I suddenly saw a gesture superimposed from the past, the night he came in from the banquet where Norman had made his surprising speech, when Bill leaned forward and his K.B.E. insignia clinked against his glass — on that night, vigorous and combative, optimistic, self-revealing, intimately friendly: tonight . . . everything seemed to be all over.

A waiter brought us drinks. The desk-lamps and standard-lamps were glowing around us, but the curtains were not yet drawn. Through the tall windows in between the book-shelves came the tender light of an early summer dusk.

Bill sat still, silent. I said:

'What happened yesterday afternoon when you and Amos saw the Chairman?'

'Standsfield's got us cold.' Bill looked at me. 'The Minister and the civil servants are all set for the reorganisation. And the Minister thinks Beckett is the man.'

'Is that what Norman said? I —'

'Of course it's what Norman said.' Bill interrupted. 'Be-cause this is what's going to happen. This damned reorgan-isation will be proceeded with because it's gone too far for us to go into reverse. If the Chairman and the Minister dropped dead tomorrow, it wouldn't make any difference. . . . If we tried to go into reverse *now*, we'd look as if we were making more of a balls-up than if we went ahead!'

'I see that,' I said. 'I meant, is that what Norman actually said about Beckett?'

Bill went on looking at me without deigning to say Yes. I said:

'Norman may be lying. It wouldn't be the first time.'

'This is the Amos Wilson line!'

'None the worse for that, Bill. Amos Wilson's the reverse of a fool — and he happens to be, temporarily, an ally.'

'So what?'

'So Norman may be lying. The Minister may not think

Beckett's the man — or more likely, the Minister may never have been told there's an alternative. Who, on the Board, except the Chairman, has seen the Minister about it?'

'No one. You know this is Norman's technique. He never lets any of us get near the Minister. This is the way he's always played it. You've got to give him credit for a brilliant performance.'

'It seems incredible.'

'This is true.' Bill paused. 'A demand to see the Minister could be made by Amos and me. But is it worth it? Standsfield has the support of two of the other members, which would be enough to impress any Minister.' He paused. 'And whatever Standsfield's relations are with the Minister, he's O.K. with the civil servants, through being' — his voice resounded — 'a Whitehall man!'

I shook my head. I didn't see it quite like that. but there was no point in arguing with Bill in his present mood.

Bill said in a slightly different tone: 'One thing happened yesterday afternoon that would amuse you, as an outsider.' Though he eyed me with sarcasm and contempt, I guessed at that moment that we'd passed the turning-point away from quarrelling. 'When Amos and I came to the end of our row with him, Norman picked up his phone and said to his secretary: "Will you ask Mr. Hobbs to come in and see me?" Doesn't this appeal to you?'

'In that high sweet voice, I suppose.'

'Right.'

There was a pause.

'He's intolerable,' said Bill. 'I'm going to quit.'

He sat still. I'd expected him to jump to his feet, as he usually did when he thought of something to be fought, rattling his keys in his trouser pockets.

I watched him steadily. A moment ago I said that in the face of a situation in which action seemed impossible, his will to action cracked. In using the word 'cracked' I don't mean to infer that there was anything pathetic or weak about it. He was not as it were a broken man, far from it.

For the moment, the man in him just seemed to be not there.

'You're going to Matthewson's,' I said.

He nodded.

We drank a little in silence, and then he began to tell me about what Matthewson's had offered him. Certainly it was attractive. The oligarchy which was going to run the firm in succession to Alfred Matthewson was going to carry on with his imaginative and realistic policy — in fact they were going to carry it further and at a greater pace.

I was amused by my own discomfiture: in a conventional way I had assumed that an oligarchy would base its policy on the lowest factor of imagination and realism common to its members. An oligarchy, a machine, a bureaucracy . . . the end, I'd thought, of the splendid Old Man's creative touch. Wrong again.

'They're hoping to go ahead,' said Bill, 'with some of the ideas that got bogged down during the Old Man's last few years. He got a bit obstructive and quirkish towards the end. Actually gaga . . .'

I recalled his eulogy of 'the last great paternalistic tycoon' only a few months ago. Times change . . .

'I think they can be helped,' Bill said, 'by me.'

While he spoke he returned to a more normal mood. The man in him, offered scope for expressing himself in action, began to be there again.

'And the money's all right.'

I said I was glad of that.

'It means we shall have to go and live in the Midlands. Meg doesn't want to leave London. *I'm* not worried — I shall have to spend several nights a month in London, anyway. I suppose she doesn't like the idea of my being off, on my own. Though she's always saying she doesn't want me at home. . . . I shall never have a complete understanding of Women.'

Alice and I had always felt his marriage was not harmonious, though we hadn't enough information to under-

H

stand why. Alice thought Bill would be impossible for any woman to live with. On the other hand, his wife, whom we met occasionally, didn't seem to have any alternative partner in view.

I contented myself with just drinking without replying. I could not help reflecting on how quickly his mood had changed. We were occupying our concern with the domestic consequences of a change in his career which shocked me, which was a loss to the country as well as a private defeat for him.

Suddenly he said: 'This is not good.' He paused. 'It's not good, Jack, is it?'

My spirits plunged again. At the beginning of the conversation I had been hopeful because he might not have reconciled himself to the break and so might finally not make it. I was now faced with his not having reconciled himself to it, but being forced to make it all the same.

His light eyes looked large and transparent. He too must have recalled our night here together — 'I could have made things hum,' he suddenly said. His lips tightened and his little moustache went shorter. 'I could have made things hum, damn their eyes!' He paused. 'It was a Challenge.'

I spent the rest of the evening with him, and it was in the early hours of the following morning when the car got me back to Oxford. Alice was lying in bed, reading.

'You're *so* late, darling. But I thought you'd be in a *state* . . .' She stretched out her hand. 'Well? . . .'

I sat on the edge of the bed and undid my tie. I took her hand.

'Well,' I said. 'I suspect it's all over bar the shouting — the shouting that in this case may be done by me and a few other chaps.'

The grip of her fingers tightened.

'But,' I said, 'the way things fall out is really pretty odd. It's all over, but I'm not sure it ought to be.'

I told her some of the story, meanwhile disengaging my hand so that I could take off my shoes.

'Has Bill Taylor actually resigned?' Alice said. 'I mean, he's decided to. But *has* he? Actually? . . .'

I looked up and grinned at her. 'You know, you *are* a civil servant.' I paused. 'What's more, you're right.'

She looked surprised.

I said: 'Though I've spent the whole evening with him, I still couldn't tell you whether he has or he hasn't, *actually*. . . . In the circumstances a civil servant would 'call for the papers'. And I admit that's what I should have to do now — to see if there's a letter of resignation there.' I paused. 'Even to me Bill Taylor doesn't tell everything. Perhaps he'd be making a tactical mistake if he did.' I paused again, and sacrificed loyalty to honesty by adding: 'And even to me he doesn't necessarily tell the exact and complete factual truth.'

'How extraordinary! . . .'

'You should be the last person to feel there's anything extraordinary about it. You're the one who knows he's only really resigned if there's a letter of resignation in which he says so among the papers.' I paused. 'What he says in conversation is *autre chose*. . . . The Civil Service depends on writing.'

'If he had *sent* a letter, could he take it *back*?'

'Oh, please!' I said. 'At this time of night . . .'

Alice looked away with a dissatisfied grimace.

I stood up, smiling at her: but I must say that, although I wasn't going to tell her, I didn't know whether Bill had told me the exact and complete factual truth on the particular point.

I didn't see that it mattered, though. When I went to bed that night, I definitely though it was all over bar some shouting from the side-lines.

It was just inside a week later that I got a telephone call from Bill Taylor at the lab.

Norman had had a coronary the preceding afternoon.

Bill had just come back from seeing the Minister.

'Standsfield may be out of action for quite a while, according to the quacks. In the interim,' Bill said, 'I've agreed to be Acting Chairman. He' — he meant the Minister — 'was very pressing.'

'Pressing!' I cried.

'He's not a bad chap,' Bill said rather shortly. 'This is the first time I've had a session with him on his own — his Permanent Secretary wasn't around.'

'But what—' I began.

'Do you mind if I ring you back later, Jack? Perhaps tomorrow. I've got to go back and spend the afternoon with him. He's whistling up his civil servants. There'll be a succession of meetings.'

'Yes,' I said. He sounded like a different man.

'This sort of thing sets off, Jack,' he said, 'a Chain Reaction.'

Resolutely putting out of my mind the idea of a chain reaction ending with an almighty bang, I said:

'I'm sure it does.'

Bill rang off. And I, I may say, was left feeling somewhat breathless.

CHAPTER THREE

Curious but not Queer

I reflected again on the concept of 'hanging on'. When I counselled Bill Taylor to do it, I hadn't had anything in mind apart from a general conviction that time produced its unpredictable turns of fate. Being random they might comprise one or two turns that were in one's favour.

It struck me as strange that in middle-age I had come to recognise a degree of unpredictability, not only in turns of fate, but in the actions of human beings, that I would have scouted when I was a young man. I had counted myself as having matured, in one sense at least, when I came to realise that the essential nature of a particular human being was individual, of course, but also changeless. From one of one's students, for example, one couldn't hope for *anything*, but only for certain limited things which were really determined by an essential nature he'd been born with. He might do a bit better with such talents as he'd been born with, but he wasn't going to grow any fresh ones. When one was a student oneself one felt one could become anything. The effect of Time was to whittle down what one thought one could become — to whittle it down to what was consistent with what one actually was.

And having recognised that a man's essential nature is changeless — and its different elements definable, if one has mastered a technique of defining them — I had argued that his actions must be consistent with it. What else had he got to act *from*? And so I had scouted the common idea of a

human being acting 'out of character'. The out-of-character
action merely indicated that one hadn't comprehended his
character.

In middle-age I had come to think differently. I had
decided one had to allow an element from which to expect
the unpredictable, out-of-character action. It was, to my way
of thinking, an element of the sheer *random*.

I scarcely need comment that most people found my picture of their essential nature comprising an element of the
random no less offensive than my earlier picture of its being
determined from the start.

But I have got away from my immediate point about
'hanging on'. Nobody had acted out of character on this
occasion. My immediate point was that there *is* an element
of unpredictability in human affairs, and on occasion it will
happen to show in one's favour. It is unrealistic, not to say
foolish, to rely Micawber-like on something turning up. It
is also unrealistic to presume that nothing can turn up.
Hanging on may well be fruitless, but sometimes it won't be.

Now that Norman was temporarily removed from the
scene, Bill would certainly hang on.

'He' — the Minister — 'was very pressing.'

I couldn't help smiling in recollection at Bill's sudden
lapse into official stuffiness and innocence. How did he think
the Minister was going to face the prospect of being responsible for a National Power Board that was suddenly
without either Chairman or Deputy Chairman. So far as
Bill and I had been able to discern, the Treasury had no
top civil servant hanging around whom they would take
the opportunity to plant on the N.P.B. as they had planted
Norman Standsfield.

'So Bill *hadn't* resigned,' said Alice.

'I haven't seen the papers,' I replied.

'*I*'m sorry for the Chairman,' said Alice.

'That shows a sympatheticness of nature which is shared,
if you ask me, by none of his board members.'

I wondered how many of his board members wished, at

the bottom of their hearts, and possibly quite near the top
as well, that his stroke had carried their Chairman off
altogether. I said:

'He'll recover. He's not old. He'll probably be back again
in a few months.'

'And then they'll all be *back* where *they* were.'

'A lot can happen in a few months. Bill,' I said, 'has got
into "the place where the real decisions are made."' I recalled Norman's telling me Bill's phrase for it. 'If he doesn't
get flung out again, we shall see some action.'

'Will he get flung out again?'

Alice simply would ask that question.

I said: 'No.' And I added: 'He already expresses the view
that the Minister is not a bad chap.'

'That's *good*, isn't it?' she said.

I was ready to bet that as Acting Chairman Bill would
make a go of it. The fact that days began to pass without
my hearing from him again made me guess he was doing
so already. Action, in a man such as Bill Taylor, often
looked to be on the level of metabolism — acting, he expressed his whole being naturally and at its best. And Bill
at his best could easily make a go, a superb go, of it.

My guess was confirmed incidentally by Stanley Forbes,
who asked me into his Lodgings one evening for dinner, in
order to talk about College affairs. He had just returned
from London, from one of his Whitehall committees.

'I hear,' he said, 'they're talking about a successor for
Sir Norman Standsfield, in case he isn't fit to take up the
Chairmanship of the National Power Board again.'

I guessed he must have been asked for his advice — he
was likely to be consulted. I thought I'd tease him, by
saying:

'Surely Norman'll be fit. Everybody comes back after a
coronary.'

'Of course they do.' Stanley spoke blandly and convincedly. I looked at him sharply — we were sitting in the
drawing-room after dinner, waiting for Doris to bring in

his *tisane*. The way he said 'Of course they do', blandly and convincedly, lowering his uptilted nose and giving me a fine sincere stare with his bright blue eyes, somehow conveyed another emotion as well. . . . It was *satisfaction*. He looked radiantly pink and healthy. He actually was radiantly pink and healthy. Seven years older than Norman Standsfield — and he, Stanley, had *not* had a coronary!

'But one has to be prepared, you know, Jack.'

'I'm sure,' I said, nodding my head. The stately way in which men of affairs, Stanley and his like, prepared themselves for the succession of their colleagues always seemed to me an example of how to be sensible, how not to spend unnecessary emotion in — shall we say? — regret.

I wondered how many people were preparing themselves to find a successor to the Dr. Gurney's Chair of Natural Philosophy in the University of Oxford. Preparing? Boy scouts had nothing on *them*. . . .

'I hear our friend being well spoken of again.'

'Bill Taylor?' I noted the 'again'.

Stanley nodded.

I thought he was being especially stately with me tonight. I said: 'I'm not surprised. There's nothing like having *got* there for making people see that you *can* get there.'

Stanley smiled as a man smiles when you have said something to him which he hasn't understood and which he wouldn't have liked if he had.

'Yes, yes,' he said, nodding his head again. His wavy hair threw off bright silver gleams. Although the evening was still light — we had dined early — the lamps were on.

We were silent for a few moments. The green brocade curtains were undrawn and I looked into the garden, thinking that despite Doris's grumbles, the window wall was delightful. A cloudy sky was still flickering with summery twilight; the small patch of grass, catching the luminousness that English lawns seem to catch just before dusk, was strewn with the fallen pink flowers of a blossoming tree nearby. Although one could see the top of a neon sign adver-

tising a garage beyond the far wall, everywhere seemed unusually tranquil.

'Are you feeling warm enough?' Stanley said solicitously
— one of the windows was open.

'Quite warm enough,' I said. 'The floor's doing its stuff.'
I thought of Doris's feet, and letters to Skootz, Merridge and
Potherill.

Stanley brought me smoothly back to business.

'There's another matter in the College coming up over the
horizon.' He paused. 'In fact it's with us already.' He
watched me blandly and innocently, with his nose pointing
upwards. 'Our friends on the Arts side . . .'

'Don't say they're getting up on their hind legs again?'

Stanley said: 'I'm afraid so.'

'They got their representation on the Fellowship Election
Committee.' (Stanley had given in to them, of course.) 'What
do they want now?'

'They want to play a full part in the life of the College,
and that's very understandable. And very desirable —'

'Full part in the life of the College! Now, what, might
I ask, does that mean?' I could guess.

'Apparently they feel — most strongly, John Farrow tells
me — that they are not playing a full part in the life of the
College as long as they are denied pupils of their own.'

'You mean they want the College to take in undergraduates reading nothing but Eng. Lit., Philosophy, and so on.'

Stanley nodded.

I burst into rage. 'Which means taking in that many
fewer scientists and engineers!'

Stanley nodded again. 'My reaction is to feel that we've
taken,' he said, 'a Cuckoo into the Nest.'

'I'll *say* we have!'

You will recall my first describing Clarendon as something
new in the University, Oxford's attempt to go along with
the Technical Revolution by raising the proportion of
scientists and engineers. Handing out places to Eng. Lit.
students would immediately lower it again — which, I had

H*

no doubt, was exactly what Farrow, our D. H. Lawrence-worshipping Luddite, wanted.

'What have you said to them?' I demanded.

Stanley observed my rage emolliently. 'I asked them to prepare a case on paper.' He gave me an intimate smile. 'I hope they'll take a long time.'

'If Farrow does it, it will be intolerably badly written but it won't take a long time!'

'I think,' said Stanley, 'the idea is that Benda will write it for them.'

'Well, f—!' I said. 'That's real Creative F—ing Writing for you. No wonder he couldn't meet my eye the other evening!'

Stanley lifted his hand. 'I think I hear Doris . . .'

Then he gave me another intimate smile that turned into a laugh.

I said: 'I suppose when you get the case on paper you'll call a college meeting?'

'After you and I have discussed it, Jack. And planned some tactics.' He was looking expectantly towards the door. 'We must get together, Jack. . . . I don't need to remind you that the proposal is contrary to the terms of our foundation.'

Proposal! I thought that in view of the way it combined the fantastic with the deplorable it too ought to be called a scenario.

Stanley turned back to give me a special smile of slyness and complicity, which I presumed was supposed to be re-assuring. I wasn't for one moment reassured.

Doris came into the room with her silver tray. On it were three, not two, Rockingham cups and saucers. I realised that Stanley had not taken me up to his own room. Doris served Stanley first.

I took one of the cups of *tisane*, which I detested.

Then Doris took the third cup and sat down with us. There was a moment's silence.

Suddenly Doris turned to me. 'Has He told you?'

I was taken aback. 'Told me what, Lady Forbes?'

'Not yet, Dear,' Stanley interrupted. 'I was waiting for you to join us.'

'Telephone calls,' said Doris to me. 'Has He told you about the telephone calls?'

'Oh,' I said. 'The penny's dropped . . .'

'An unfortunate metaphor,' said Doris. 'They come from public boxes.'

If the *tisane* was supposed to have a soothing effect, it needed to have it on Doris.

'From that mad little pansy-boy,' she said, 'of Dr. Challoner's!' She glared at me. 'Is he an *actor?*'

I said: 'I don't know. I've only set eyes on him once.'

'His name's John Minelli. It sounds like an actor.'

'It sounds like the son of an Italian coffee-bar owner, which is what I was given to understand he is.'

'You know,' she said, 'he telephones using different accents? Last night it was American. Like an *actor.*' She sipped her *tisane*. 'Even if he is the son of an Italian coffee-bar owner.'

In the pause Stanley said: 'Has he troubled you recently?'

I said he'd left Alice and me alone for a little while.

'He began by ringing the College,' said Doris. 'Of course the porter learnt not to put the calls through. And then he began ringing our private number. It's ex-directory — how d'you account for that?'

I was at a loss to account for it.

'Two o'clock in the morning. Three o'clock in the morning. Of course we've told the police.'

That was new to me. I think I said, when I first mentioned it, that both Alice and I found the youth's telephonomania unexpectedly disturbing — creepy as well as just annoying. The mention of the police, now, made me a good deal more worried on Brian's behalf.

'He must have a bicycle,' said Doris. 'As soon as he's made the call he jumps on it and rides off before the police can catch him. The police tell us to hold him in conversation.

What,' she demanded of me, 'am I supposed to hold a mad pansy-boy in conversation about, for *half an hour?*'

I was tempted to say I was sure, in view of the several American best-sellers which consisted of nothing else, that she could hold him in conversation indefinitely by starting him on a detailed account of his sexual experiences.

'At two o'clock in the morning?' she reiterated.

At any time of the morning, noon or night, I thought.

I said to Stanley: 'What does Brian Challoner suggest?'

'He has nothing to suggest, Jack.' He paused. 'It's rather serious, too, for him. I might say dangerous. I expect you heard that he's being thought of as a member of the Royal Commission on the effects of television on adolescents.'

'Benda said something about it.'

'They sounded me about him.'

'I hope,' said Doris, 'you didn't conceal anything!'

'Am I the sort of person to be disingenuous, my dear?' Stanley said — thus making, I thought, the most insincere remark of the evening.

'*Yes,*' said Doris.

She turned to me. 'Are you cold? Shall I shut that window?' I felt as if she thought I must be cold through weakness of moral fibre.

I shook my head.

She turned back to Stanley. 'Yes,' she repeated. 'You're too kind-hearted, Dear.'

'I think Challoner's a good man,' Stanley said to me.

Doris snorted.

I was going to say 'He certainly knows his subject', and thought better of it. If getting on to the Commission was Brian's aim — and I assumed that for once Alec Benda had been truthful as well as snide — I wanted Brian to achieve it. I said:

'Can't we do anything to put this business, this persecution by a boy, to an end?'

Stanley shrugged his shoulders. 'The porters are instructed to prevent the young man from entering the College, of course. But if the telephone calls are stopped as a result of police action,'—he made a gesture, turning up the palm of his hand—'we shall have a job to avoid a court case.'

I nodded my head without commenting. For once there was a great deal to be said in favour of Stanley's capacity for not doing anything. I guessed it was Doris who had gone to the police.

'Poor old Brian!' I said.

'Poor old Brian, indeed!' said Doris.

'I'm afraid,' said Stanley, 'I can't speak for him as unreservedly as I should like. One has to think about these things, Jack.'

I looked reflectively at the cup of *tisane* I was holding. I was stumped.

We must all have been looking reflectively at our cups of *tisane* or at each other. Because a sound at the window made us turn suddenly to see somebody already standing by the open doorway.

'Good God!' I cried; and 'Who's that?' shouted Doris; simultaneously. Stanley stood up.

I had observed a short furry overcoat and tight dark trousers.

Minelli said: 'May I come in?' Actually he was now over the threshold. '*Please* may I come in?'

He stood there, palpitating. His face was inordinately pale. He looked startlingly handsome.

'Leave at once!' said Doris. 'Whoever you are!'

'No, let him stay,' said Stanley.

The youth appeared not to hear or see Stanley. He kept a brilliant, raging glance on Doris.

'Please, Lady Forbes! It was you I came to see. I had no other way. Please excuse me! I want to speak to you. I must speak to you.'

His brilliant raging glance was met by Doris's opaque glare. Her stiff beige-coloured face stayed stiff and beige-coloured.

'If only you will listen to me, you will understand, Lady Forbes. For just a little while of your time. I beg!' A sudden movement made it look as if he was going to go down on his knees to her.

If he actually had gone down on his knees, I think Doris would have sent for the porters to haul him away. But he kept upright, beseeching.

Doris looked him up and down. She said: 'I will listen to you. And *no* funny accents! . . . *I* know you!'

'Thank you so much.' He took off his gloves — his hands were small and slim-fingered. And he undid his overcoat, showing a nearly black suit and tie. I was expecting him to smell of scent, but he didn't.

'What is it you want to explain to me?' said Doris.

'That I'm being *kept from my work!*'

It says much for the hypnotic effect he was able to make even on me that it was only afterwards that I put a ribald interpretation on the speech.

'What work?' said Doris.

'My work for Dr. Challoner. I'm his assistant.' He forestalled Doris's next question. 'He doesn't pay me. We regard it as an apprenticeship. I don't need the money. I have money.' He was looking at her without wavering all the time.

'If you have money,' said Doris, 'what do you want?'

'My career. My future! I shall be his assistant. I shall study for a degree as a sociologist. He says I've got it in me to be a success. If I can work with *him!*'

He paused.

'*He* doesn't want me to be kept out of the College. He depends on me. He told me so.'

'Really?' said Doris. 'And who does want to keep you out of the College?'

It sounded like a psychologist's question, but, coming from Doris, it was not.

Minelli looked at her, his dark-eyed glance sharpening. 'People who don't like me — people who are jealous of me, and jealous of Dr. Challoner. . . . They spread lies about me.'

Doris's unseeing eyes widened.

'Yes,' he said. 'And I think you believe them. And tell the College porters I'm forbidden to enter the College, to go to my work. Yes, I think you believe them, and Lord Forbes believes them.' He looked from Doris to Stanley and back. 'That's why I had to come and tell you the truth. People can't help believing lies when they're prevented from hearing the truth. Tell me, isn't that so?'

Actually I thought he'd got a point there.

'Then what,' said Doris, her glare returning in full force as she thought about her own sufferings, 'about the telephone calls?'

'Yes, Lady Forbes,' Minelli replied instantly. 'I know about the telephone calls because Brian, Dr. Challoner, thinks it's me who's making them. But *it isn't*! . . . It must be somebody else. Dr. Challoner's asked me to stop them. How can I, when it's somebody else?' His eyes seemed to flicker and tears came into them.

Stanley and I looked at him in momentary stupefaction.

'I hope you're not going to cry!' said Doris.

'I don't think so. . . . Though . . . it gets me very worked up.'

None of us commented on that.

He looked at us. 'You think I'm beginning to be a nuisance, and that it's going to be hard to make me go away.' He stood up, buttoning his overcoat. He seemed to hold back a sob and he smiled politely. 'I will go now. Please, which is the way?'

Doris said: 'You don't need to go till you've said all you want to say.'

Stanley made a deprecating gesture which she missed.

'Oh, thank you, Lady Forbes!'

Doris stood up beside him.

'Thank you, Lady Forbes.' He moved closer to her, waiting to be shown out. 'There's only one more thing I want to say, one very small thing. But it means everything to me!'

'What?' said Doris.

'Don't believe what people say! Please look into it yourself!' Tears came into his eyes again. 'Will you only do that? *Please look into it yourself!*'

Doris said: 'All right.'

At that he finally wept. Doris, standing beside him — the two of them were about the same height — happened to be touching her string of pearls with the hand that was nearer to him. He suddenly made an uncontrolled movement towards her. (I jumped up from my chair.) The movement was to rest his forehead while he wept in the crook of Doris's elbow.

'Stand up!' she cried. Turning a glare of consternation at Stanley and me — 'What am I to do?'

With her volition paralysed she began to pat him on the head.

Stanley and I, saying 'Come along,' disengaged him. Stanley led him from the room and showed him out of the house.

We all sat down again.

'I'd better close that door,' said Doris.

After the horse had gone, I thought.

'Are you sure you're all right, Dear?' said Stanley. 'Do you think you should have a little brandy?'

'Of course I'm all right.' Doris came back from closing the door and drawing the curtains: she sat down and said: '*I think that boy's speaking the truth!*'

Stanley said: 'As he sees it, you mean, Dear.'

'Yes.' She was sitting with her back straight, her substantial behind on the edge of her chair.

Stanley said: 'He *is* making the telephone calls.'

'I shall wait for the police to find out.'

The police. We were all silent, Stanley and I for reasons that differed from Doris's. After a while I said to Stanley:

'Shan't we be in a better position to decide what steps

to take if we know exactly where we stand? Brian's relationship with the boy . . .' I glanced at Doris.

'If you mean,' she said, 'whether Dr. Challoner has had that mad boy in bed with him, you can say so, Sir Jack. It doesn't interest me, but I know what it is.'

'I did mean precisely that, Lady Forbes.'

Stanley thought about it. To my astonishment he decided to do something. He said: 'Yes.'

I said: 'Why don't we ask Brian, directly?'

Stanley thought again. 'I wonder if he's in now? We might ask him to come across.' He got up to telephone.

'I,' said Doris, 'will leave you when he comes.'

I had a fleeting suspicion that she paused — in order to be pressed to stay? She was an uncomprehending woman, and in a coarse-fibred way she was pretty hearty. I doubted if she'd had a specially hearty time with Stanley, but that was no cause for believing her when she gave us to understand that what happened in other people's beds did not interest her.

Stanley returned from the telephone.

'Challoner's coming over, my dear.' He didn't press her to stay.

While we were waiting Stanley brought in a decanter of whisky and some glasses. (As Doris thought it was bad for Stanley to drink alcohol at night she had left him to get it for himself.)

In due course the doorbell rang and Doris showed in Brian. He came across the room looking exceptionally tall and thin. He was wearing a narrow pair of slacks and a turtle-necked sweater. The sweater was black, and it made the silver flecks in his hair seem to shine. He looked pale and furtive-eyed; but this time the furtiveness did not seem superficial to an underlying toughness and stability. I thought he was simply dithering with anxiety — as any other man in Brian's predicament might explicably be dithering too.

We told him what had happened.

He listened, one long thin leg folded over the other, his body leaning forward. He was drinking his whisky pretty fast. Short-nosed, narrow-eyed, crew-cut. A little of his colour came back.

'We thought you ought to know,' Stanley finished up.

Brian pulled himself together. 'Yes.'

'We want to plan some tactics.'

Brian glanced at me — we were agreed over the generally academic nature of Stanley's so-called tactics.

'Yes,' he said. 'Where do I come into it?'

There was a pause. Stanley said to me: 'Jack, I shouldn't feel at any disadvantage in questioning Brian, but I feel that as you're on more intimate terms with him, you might prefer . . .'

Brian gave one of his sharpest, most furtive glances at both of us, exactly the sort of glance that made Alice feel he was going to run up the curtains. And then he smiled.

'I see.'

I knew the smile at once as a sign that he was in control of the situation.

'You want to ask me,' he said, 'if I'm having a homosexual affair?'

Stanley said urbanely: 'Yes, Brian.'

Brian said:

'I'm not. And I never have.'

We looked at him closely, I, I'm sorry to confess, with some surprise.

'I know it makes an obvious interpretation of recent events,' Brian said. 'Only too obvious to some people. For instance, Alec Benda.'

I recalled Alec's looking at me with his big, malicious, half-moon lidded eyes and saying: 'What *else*?'

'Alec,' said Brian, 'is not an impartial interpreter of certain categories of event.'

Stanley and I smiled ruefully. I said:

'Well, what *is* the interpretation of these events? The boy's presumably homosexual, and mad into the bargain.'

'Right,' said Brian. 'But actually I'm neither. I'm not mad. Nobody has ever thought I was. And I'm not queer.' He paused. 'I'm just not, repeat not, queer.'

He drank some whisky. We waited.

'I suppose in the present state of the game,' he said, 'that's not enough of an explanation.'

Stanley and I didn't shake our heads in disagreement. Brian was framing what he was going to say.

'The boy doesn't excite me. If he did I might think about sleeping with him. In fact I might think about it more readily than you might imagine. . . . You see, boys don't excite me, and — to put it frankly — women don't, either.' For a moment he looked down at his whisky-glass in embarrassment. Then he went on. 'To put it frankly again — I don't seem to be excitable, period. That's the story.' He paused. 'I haven't had to tell the story to anyone for a long time. Not since I told it to a psychiatrist some fifteen years ago.' He managed to give us a wry, darting smile. 'Fifteen years haven't made the telling much easier.'

Brian drank some more whisky, while Stanley and I looked at each other. I suppose I must have said 'Oh dear. . . .' I was feeling the sort of inexplicable apology for oneself, and I'm sure Stanley was, too, that one feels when one goes healthy into the room of somebody in hospital.

Brian said:

'Any more questions.'

Stanley said: 'No, Brian. I think you can take it we've gone as far as we need.' He gave him a steady look.

Suddenly something — perhaps it was the rare revelation of him in a moment of unalloyed sincerity — made me realise Stanley was an old man.

'And Brian,' he added, 'we think a lot of you.'

There was a long pause. We all drank some more whisky. Then Stanley said to me:

'Jack, I should be glad of your first thoughts about our tactics.'

CHAPTER FOUR

The Young are Independent

We didn't make much headway that evening, or any subsequent evening, for that matter, in working out tactics for suppressing Minelli without a court case and headlines in the local newspapers. We found ourselves at a peculiar loss in dealing with the situation. It's all very well to say the borderline between sanity and insanity is very fuzzy; that the sane merge imperceptibly into the insane; that we all, who consider ourselves sane, have our streaks of insanity. All I can say is that Stanley, Brian and I, in dealing with Minelli, felt we were dealing with someone who differed from us in kind.

We might have found it easier if we hadn't been inhibited by fear of the damage he could do to Brian Challoner, to Brian's friends, to the College. Also I thought there was a deeper and more subtle inhibition, that I had noticed in both Alice and myself when the telephoning started. It stemmed from being forced into direct contact with bizarre sexuality. Reading about it in a textbook was one thing; having it on the other end of your telephone line at 2 a.m. was quite another. There was something creepy about it, paralysingly creepy.

One of the consequences of the evening, though very surprising, was in my opinion entirely to the good. Lord Forbes pledged himself publicly to use any influence he had to get Challoner on to the Royal Commission. Ridiculous though I privately thought the end in view was — I didn't see the Commission having any effect whatsoever — I was nothing but glad for Brian's sake. If he really wanted to get on to the Commission, I was glad for him to succeed. I was in favour of all my friends who wanted to get somewhere getting there. To everybody on the cucumber-tree, I wished a happy, happy time!

I didn't see the Commission having any effect; because few human beings, let alone just teenagers, are totally un-susceptible to the pornography of sex and the pornography of violence, while the discovery of the age on the part of the movies, the advertising industry, television — and lately *soi-disant* highbrow writers of plays and books — is that many human beings can be roused to part directly or in-directly with *money* for them. There's the rub, as it were.

And as if the rub weren't hard enough to bear, the subject is given a touch of egregious absurdity by our being solemnly exhorted to subscribe to a psychological theory, of all things, in *favour* of the pornographies of sex and violence — you know, the corny old Safety-Valve Theory. A bit thick, I thought it was. When we could all see that most people went in for pornography to inflame themselves when they weren't inflamed already, everybody was coming solemnly to think of it as the reverse. I must say it seemed to me a shade ironical that society, having ceased in the biggest possible way to be mealy-mouthed, was becoming in the biggest possible way mealy-minded.

But I couldn't help looking forward to the sociologically fascinating day — which surely couldn't be far off now — when one saw on the walls of the best people's sitting-rooms very high-priced Beat-up-and-Rape pictures, their presence being explained by their possessors with enormous psycho-logical gravity: 'If we didn't have those on the *walls*, that's what Ethel and I would be *doing*! . . .'

Heigh-ho, what a world! And if Brian Challoner wanted to help give it the cachet of a Royal Commission's enquiry into it, who was I to stop him?

For a spell nobody received any telephone calls, and that

was a dispensation. Perhaps Minelli was allowing an interval — as any sane person would allow — for his case to be looked into personally by Lady Forbes. When the interval was over, however, he was seen all day long hurrying ghost-like up and down the street outside the private entrance to the President's Lodgings.

Doris Forbes refused to go out through the main gateway of the college when she wanted to do her shopping.

'I shall confront him,' she announced. 'I shall tell him that I am looking into his case personally. That must be sufficient for him.'

Two or three confrontations of this kind appeared to do the trick. He was not seen again.

Afterwards Stanley Forbes's characteristic tactics of not doing anything were practised, in lieu of anyone having any better tactics to suggest, by all of us.

Alice was the only person to dissent. 'How *can* it blow over?' she asked.

I said: 'I think these things ebb and flow.'

'Then won't they *flow* again?'

A very good question. I said that if they did we should have to take a different line, but perhaps by then Brian Challoner's appointment would be made. Then suddenly I felt inspired.

'On the other hand,' I said, 'the boy may focus temporarily on somebody else. *I* know! . . .' — and this was where the inspiration really came in — 'On Doris Forbes!'

Alice rejected my inspiration. So we left it at that.

I had other things to occupy me. Mike Bowen and I really had got going on some exciting work. Having to think about anything else at all seemed a tiresome interruption, in fact a destructive interruption. I got out of attending committee meetings in London. I even lost touch, for the time being, with Bill Taylor. He was doing all right, I thought.

Bowen and I sometimes met in the evenings for more work at my house or occasionally at his. He was living in

lodgings. My supposition that I should be expected thank-
lessly to bestir myself to get him rooms in College was
wrong. He didn't want them. I was familiar with the general
principle of living in digs instead of in college — that
although one's landlady was more likely than not to be a
voyeur, fewer people in total saw what was going on.

Roz was allowed to have tea with Bowen in his rooms.
Somehow tea, in Oxford, is associated with propriety; rather
as, in the U.S.A., the convention is that impropriety between
young people can't be going on, whatever the meal, if the
door is open.

'Darling, you are only eighteen,' Alice said to Roz.

'Nearly nineteen,' said Roz. 'But it's immaterial.'

On another occasion I said to Alice: 'I know I'm going
to wait outside the house at night with a shotgun. I know
what young men are out for. After all, I was one . . .'

'Darling, were you a *menace?*'

(Those four remarks should tune you into our domestic
life at the time.)

One evening I had been working with Mike at his house.
Alice was entertaining some interior-decoration clients
whom I didn't propose to spend time on. When we came
to the end of the work, Bowen said he would like to walk
back to my house with me.

I was surprised. I knew that he couldn't be expecting to
see Roz because she was elsewhere. It was a beautiful night,
so I presumed he must be wanting some air and exercise —
while we were working we had been fortifying ourselves
steadily with beer.

We went out into the street, still talking about work.
Actually we were arguing about the holes that the mathematicians might try to shoot through some rather intuitive
assumptions we were currently making. The problem was
of the kind that Mike described in his up-to-date slang as
'hairy', meaning complex in surface detail and involving
more parameters than anybody would want to cope with
simultaneously. In a word, messy.

He walked along beside me looking tall and athletic, and seemingly in high spirits. His friendship with the College's young pure mathematician was providing a bonus of usefulness, in the feel that he was getting for how mathematicians' minds work.

The time was well past dusk, yet, although the street lamps were shining, there was still a dark-blue light in the sky.

After a few minutes we stopped arguing and just walked. We came to where a flight of steps led down to a promenade through public gardens beside a canal.

'Let's go this way,' he said.

It made a detour, but I had no objection because the walk was more picturesque, especially at night. It was a small patch of Oxford I was particularly fond of. Let other people have the dreaming spires and the houseboats on the Isis — the stretch of canal, with its ineffable evocation of my lower-class boyhood, was more 'me'.

Our feet scrunched on the gravel path. We heard a scuffle, as we passed, from a little summerhouse in the bushes. Otherwise there seemed to be no one about. The water was still and black beside us.

After a while I said idly: 'Do you like Oxford? Are you happy here?' We were coming to a pretty little terrace of Victorian houses overlooking the canal, where I'd once thought I should like to live.

'Oxford's a lovely place,' he said.

The Americanism, 'lovely', pulled me up. I wondered which word he would have used before he left Australia.

'And I'm very happy. I told you, the first day I came into your lab, I was going to be happy, do you remember?'

'You don't regret Berkeley? California?' We stopped at Quaking Bridge while a car went by. Then we crossed the road and went on beside the canal. High above us, on the other side of the water, the old walls of the Castle rose into the night sky. Paradise Street!

Bowen laughed. 'I regret the climate. You don't know

how much we Aussies miss the sunshine when we're in England.' His voice was light-toned and I suspected he was making fun of me. Then he said: 'I envy Roz going out to Stanford, from the point of view of climate.'

I thought his introduction of Roz's name into the conversation was pretty *voulu*. Oh well, I'd done that sort of thing myself when I was his age. I said:

'Stanford has the edge over Oxford for climate.' I recalled my first sight of Stanford, its tree-lined roads and impermanent-looking buildings glowing in brilliant Californian sunlight. With its thousands of comely young persons, a size larger, a size healthier, a size maturer than their English counterparts, strolling about the campus flashing bare arms and bare legs, it made me think of a gigantic, idealised holiday-camp.

Between us and the canal there had been some highish railings which now gave way to lower ones, low enough to rest one's elbows on. Bowen had been walking more slowly, and now he stopped to lean on the railings and look at the water. Just in front of us there was a sluice gate from which water poured, white and foaming, through a narrow channel and thence away under a low bridge. On the far side of the channel was a patch of grass, and then the soaring perpendicular grey walls of the castle tower.

Bowen said: 'You know why I'm happy here.'

I didn't get the cue. I said. 'You've made a hit with most of the people in the College. And your work's going like a bomb!'

He turned away. The light of a street-lamp made his face look paler and longer — in profile it showed the slight concavity I'd noticed when I first saw him. Concave, but handsome all the same.

'It's more than that,' he said, turning back to me. '*You* are an observant person.' He made it sound as if my being observant made me a man in a thousand.

I got my cue — but I refused to take it. He said:

'It's Roz.'

'H'm,' said I.

'I'm in love with your daughter, sir.' In a humorous, embarrassed way he stood to attention.

Now I was taken back once again to the first day he came into the lab, to my premonitions of exactly this, and to my desolating fall in spirits. 'He's come to take her away from me! . . .'

'Sorry I made such a Victorian speech,' he said.

I shrugged my shoulders.

'That's the way it is.' He paused. Even in the dim light I could see that he meant it.

I turned away from him, and looked at the scene, at the rushing flow of water — why did it maintain the constant wavy profile against the wall of the channel? Against the dark stones of the tower a glimmering silver birch caught my eye. . . . Suddenly I realised how long it was since I was a young man falling in love. Listening to the timbre of a voice on the telephone, seeing the sheen on someone's cheek, noticing the sweetness of her breath, wanting in some indescribable way to get nearer, closer. . . . Oh, oh, oh!

I said to myself: 'Good God!'

'What?' said Michael Bowen.

'I was only expressing surprise. At myself. Not at you.'

He was puzzled. I wondered if he would be more puzzled or less if I actually told him what had gone through my mind. Probably, I thought, if I knew anything about the censoriousness of the young, slightly shocked. I said:

'Why on earth are you telling this to me?'

As soon as I'd spoken I realised that my spirits, now it had come to the point, were nothing like as desolatingly low as I'd imagined that other day. I suppose I must have got used to the idea in the meantime. If Roz was in love with him and wanted to marry him, that was it. She might have chosen a much worse man, in fact she'd have had a job to choose a better. His future was taken care of through his being very clever and very talented; her future as his wife through his being considerate and good-natured.

He made a movement with his shoulders and half turned to lean over the railings again. I glanced again at the silver birch, glimmering like a girl. . . .

He went on with his own preoccupations. 'I thought you ought to know.' He altered his tone. 'No. I mean, really, I want to know what your attitude is.'

I had to turn towards him again. 'My attitude?'

'I want to marry her.'

'Have you asked her?' With incredulity I thought he might be asking my permission first. With incredulity and error, as it turned out. He said:

'We've discussed it. I gather she isn't very keen on it.'

I said: 'She's too young, of course.'

'It isn't that. I don't think she is too young. People grow up more quickly than they did in your day. . . . The thing is — she's not keen on marrying. On marriage. She says she wants other things. To do other things.'

'Good Lord!' I said. 'Well, really! . . .'

He grinned. 'Glad to hear your surprise.'

I realised that if I didn't watch out, I was going to find myself on *his* side.

'She wants to do other things,' I said. 'That's laudable enough.' I thought about her writing a novel. She could write novels as a married woman. Despite my feeling that some young man was going to take her away from me, I most of all wanted her to marry, to marry happily. And here I supposed my vanity came into it: I wanted her to marry a young man whom *I* could think something of.

He said: 'I don't think she understands herself.'

I was afraid that having spent some years in the U.S.A. he might be going to maunder on into saying she was 'confused' or 'insecure' — neither of which, if I knew anything about her, he'd find she was.

'We'll see about it,' I said very quickly. 'I'll have a chat with her.' I shuffled my feet to indicate that I was ready to move on.

'Thanks a lot!' He peered at me more closely in the feeble

light of the street lamp, and presumably guessed what I was thinking. 'It's an ironical situation, isn't it?'

I didn't reply. I somehow felt the word 'irony' had to be kept for great occasions, not chucked about, as people nowadays seemed to chuck it, at every turn.

We moved on, down Paradise Street. I thought how little I knew about Roz in adult independence. I tried to recall things she'd said that might give me clues. About her novel, for instance. I hadn't seen it yet. Did she mean to become a novelist? I admit it seemed to me extraordinary. Roz, aged eighteen — nearly nineteen, but that was immaterial! Soon to leave for Stanford, into the blue.

'I hope you're not feeling cold, sir.'

I had tried to get him to drop the American habit of 'sirring' me. (I couldn't believe Australians did it.)

'As a matter of fact, I am.'

We continued our walk.

When we got to Carfax Bowen said goodnight to me and turned back. I invited him to come home with me but he refused. He'd said all he wanted to say. And when I came to think of it, when I came to think that he'd mobilised me to support his suit, it struck me that he'd done pretty well for himself.

And I had said all I wanted to say to him. It was Alice I wanted to talk to now.

The lights were all shining through the sitting-room windows when I let myself into the house. I went upstairs and found Alice's clients just on the point of leaving. When they saw me they decided to stay.

'Has Roz come home yet?' I asked Alice.

'She decided not to go out after all. She went up to her room to do some typing, and' — Alice read my intention to go and talk to Roz — 'she asked us not to disturb her.'

I sat down and talked to Alice's clients. They politely admired all over again for my benefit our sitting-room. Actually it did look charming in spite of being cluttered, with its white lamps, golden-coloured fruitwoods, and clear blues in the covers. The pieces of furniture were mostly early nineteenth century, and the clutter rose from their being a bit too big for the room. I didn't object: a slightly over-large Biedermeier armchair was reserved for me, and it was a good deal more comfortable than what Alice called 'a pretty little early Georgian number' would have been.

One of the guests admired the possible Gainsborough over the fireplace: he happened to be sitting in my armchair.

At last they went.

'Darling, you were so good with them,' said Alice, 'I mean, you really were. Do you think they'll give me a contract? I think they will, don't you?'

I said Yes, but it was my private opinion that over anything to do with houses people were at their least reliable. They seemed to abandon their minds, their will, even their manners. As for giving contracts . . .

We sat down together on a sofa and I told her about Mike Bowen. Alice liked him, but I'm bound to admit that she didn't seem him as such a golden boy as I did. Nor, for that matter, did she see Roz as such a golden girl. She said:

'They couldn't possibly get married before Roz goes to Stanford. And then they'll only see each other off and on for years. Actually, mainly *off*.'

The thought crossed my mind that Bowen might go back again to Berkeley to be near her, or even join the lab in Stanford. A disaster for our lab!

I pointed out that as I understood it, Roz was not keen on marrying Bowen or anyone else for the time being.

'Yes,' said Alice. 'I suppose that *is* interesting . . . I dare say a lot of girls of her age say that because they don't know their own minds, but Roz does know her own mind. I mean, doesn't she?'

'I think we shall have to ask her.'

Alice gave me a smile I didn't especially care for: 'I think that's for *you*, isn't it, darling?'

'One or the other of us,' I said, as if I hadn't noticed.

'Or both of us. Why not? . . .' I realised that I should have increased, rather than diminished, my moral disadvantage by retorting that when we'd been perturbed about George it had been she, etc.

We were silent.

There were sounds from upstairs. Roz was moving about: she must have finished her typing. I wondered if she would come down to see us. The opportunity to ask her might arise tonight.

'She usually goes in to see if Julie's all right,' said Alice, 'before she goes to bed.'

We heard Roz coming downstairs. Alice and I glanced at each other.

The door opened and Roz came in. The first thing we noticed was the colour in her cheeks. We scarcely noticed the quarto sheets of typing paper in her hand. I was thinking: Goodness, she looks pretty!

Roz held out the sheets of paper. 'I said I'd show it you when I'd written a third of it.'

We stared at her.

'Here it is!' she said. She put down the sheets of paper on the table just behind us. 'Goodnight, darlings.' And she went out of the room again.

Alice and I now stared at each other. Then we simultaneously reached for the typescript. Alice turned over the outer sheets and we looked at the first page. As my eye glanced over it, I felt a quite startling intimation that it was the first page of a real novel.

Alice and I stayed where we were, sitting on the sofa, till we'd read the hundred pages through. Alice reads more quickly than I do, so she finished twenty pages ahead of me and waited for me. She watched me read the last paragraph.

Then we looked at each other.

'Extraordinary,' Alice said. 'Isn't it?' She glanced at the door, as if to make sure Roz was not standing there. 'It's about George and Katie, really, isn't it?'

I nodded.

'How does she *know* these things?'

'Don't ask me!' I simply felt that I'd had one of the biggest surprises of my life. '*You* are an observant person,' Michael Bowen had told me. Little did *he* know!

I recalled my conversation with Alice when Roz told us she was going to write a novel. Alice had said something about what Roz could write about at eighteen, and I'd replied: 'What it's like to be seventeen or sixteen.' I should have been surprised if Roz had produced either a 'sensitive childhood' novel, or a novel about what it was like to be a sharp-eyed, not-yet-quite-knowing little girl of twelve. Roz didn't seem to me that sort of girl. But I hadn't bargained for her writing about what it was like to be twenty-eight and married. Like Alice, I wanted to know how she knew about these things.

The answer was of course that she didn't know all about these things. Some of them she got wrong. But she was sufficiently interested in people, and got enough of the things right, for the book to be identifiable, even when only a third of it had been written, as a real novel. My intimations had been right.

'I suppose,' said Alice, 'it isn't very well *written . . .*'

'Christ!' I said impatiently. 'If she knows how to *make* a novel, she can *learn* to write.'

On the strength of these hundred pages, written fast and carelessly, it appeared to me that Roz could be a novelist. It was staggering. I experienced joy.

Alice could see what I was feeling. 'You don't think we think it's better than it is—'

'Because she's our child? I'm trying to compensate for that.'

'That wasn't what I was going to say. I was going to say because of . . . the subject.' Alice suddenly looked down at the pages of typescript strewn around us. She looked down in such a way that I should not have been surprised if tears had come into her eyes. I put my hand out to her.

She looked up, dry-eyed. 'It *is* moving . . .'

Roz's novel was really about George and his wife, Katie, transposed with changed physical appearance from being on the stage to being painters. They were married and geographically separated — George was an artist in mosaic murals, who had been commissioned to decorate a building in Mexico City: Katie was a fabric designer for a firm that sounded rather like Sekers. They had a young child — Julie, beautifully described.

'You mean,' I said, 'Roz thinks the marriage could break up?'

'That's what this' — she pointed to the novel — 'is leading to, isn't it?'

I was certain it was.

My joy was suddenly dispersed. Julie, poor darling little Julie! . . .

Alice said: 'I expect you're thinking about Julia . . .' I knew that she, on the other hand, was thinking about George.

I couldn't meet her reproach. It was all very well to say George was a mature man, leading a life totally independent of mine. The fact was that when he went on to the stage I had lost patience with him more profoundly and irrevocably than I ought. His was an offence by association. You may have noticed already that I am unable to mention the theatre and the people in it without slighting them. All I can say is that in my experience they included a higher proportion than did any comparable group of people I'd come across, who were lacking a stable core of judgement or taste, liable to think any fashion of the moment was the greatest thing ever — 'What's In must be Art.' George was quite a clever man, not quite as clever as Roz, perhaps, but that didn't affect the issue when he said he wanted to spend the money he had inherited on going to R.A.D.A. He had also inherited from the same side of the family aristocratic good looks. I'm afraid I pointed out to him that for stardom at the moment a young actor was apparently required, so that mass-audiences could identify themselves with him, to have plebeian good looks.

So I couldn't meet Alice's reproach. Yet, although I'd thought first of Julie I was pretty distressed on behalf of George and Katie.

'Perhaps Roz is wrong,' I said. 'She *can't* know about these things.'

'But you thought the same thing, didn't you? . . .'

I said stubbornly: 'We may be wrong.'

The conversation ended. Alice collected the pages of typescript and put them in order. Her mood changed. She said with a reflective smile:

'Now you'll have *two* things to ask Roz about in the morning.'

I said: 'Good God! I'd forgotten all about Mike Bowen.'

'Were you putting first things first, perhaps?'

I grinned at her. 'The order in which they're to be put is Roz's business.'

'Then I should ask her, if I were you. I really should. Do ask her, darling!'

I said I would.

And in the morning I did.

Roz always got up first in the morning in order to keep Julia quiet. She made early-morning tea and carried it up to Alice's room. When I heard movements in the house I went down to the kitchen.

Roz was sitting on the edge of the table waiting for the kettle to boil. Her hair, not yet done up into its doughnut, was combed down over her shoulders. She was looking thoughtful, and she jumped when I came quietly through the door. She said:

'Have you read it?'

'Of course.'

I told her what Alice and I thought about it.

'Do you think I can write a novel? That's the question.'

I said I thought she could, but that she ought to ask a professional writer. 'You might ask Alec Benda,' I suggested.

I

Roz considered. 'I shall ask Alec Benda to help me improve it,' she said. 'I shan't ask him if I can write it.'

'Oh,' I said. That appeared to be that.

'If you and Alice think it's the beginning of a novel,' she said in explanation, 'it's the beginning of a novel. Period.'

That, I thought, seemed to be even more than that. I went to the cupboard and got out cups and saucers.

'Are you thinking of becoming a novelist?' I said diffidently, over my shoulder.

'For a time,' said Roz.

I turned, and found that she had got off the table to stand facing me.

'Shall we talk about this? I'd like to — I mean, I want to . . .' Her cheeks had gone pinker.

'Of course.' I now sat down on the edge of the table. The kettle was beginning to sing. 'Where's Julie, by the way?'

Roz crossed her fingers. 'She must have gone off to sleep again.' She took some teaspoons out of a drawer and put them with the cups and saucers.

'I know it sounded off-hand when I said for a time. I didn't mean it that way. You see, writing novels is part of a plan.'

'Yes?'

'To make money.'

There was a noticeable break in the flow of empathy between us. 'Oh,' I said. Roz said quickly:

'We've talked about money before. Going after the £.s.d. I know you won't like it. Not just like that. But it isn't just like that. It depends on what you use money *for* . . .' She paused.

I said: 'What do you propose to use it for?'

She said more slowly: 'I think I want to make films in the end.' She looked at me. 'That must be the way to influence the biggest number of people.'

I found myself unable to say anything at all.

Roz suddenly smiled. 'At least you didn't laugh at me.'

'My darling child!' I had a job to prevent tears coming into my eyes.

The kettle had begun to boil. I handed her the teapot and she poured some boiling water into it to heat it.

'It's a long time ahead,' she said. 'But whatever you want to do, you can't do it without some money to start with.' She put the teapot down on the stove and turned towards me again.

'Do you think you can make enough?' I said.

'How do you know if you don't try?'

She emptied the hot water away and put tea in the pot. 'From Stanford I could go to Hollywood,' she said, 'if I had some money and the right contacts.' She paused. 'George must have got to know some people who'd be useful. And I know Joan knows some quite important film people there . . .'

Joan! I thought.

Roz interrupted herself: 'But the thing to do now is to concentrate on the first steps.'

I found myself without words again. It all sounded like fantasy to me. And yet — for one thing I couldn't be certain she wouldn't carry it off; and for another thing I knew above all I mustn't scorn her plan. One has to try and get used to what one's children mean to do. I'd taught myself that lesson over George.

Roz waited for the tea to infuse.

'That's why I think talking about getting married is a bit of a waste of time. You know . . .'

I said: 'What about Mike Bowen?'

'I like him a lot. I like him more than any other men I've met — he's a bit older than they were.' She smiled with a diffidence that suddenly reminded me of Alice's. 'If I were thinking of getting married, I could happily marry Mike.' Her diffidence disappeared. 'I suppose he's talked to you about it?'

'Well, yes. . . . Only last night, though.'

'He said he was going to. But he's the sort of person who would. 'He's very "open".'

'I like "open" people.'

'So do I!' She looked away, and frowned for a moment. 'But they're sometimes a bit less *interesting* than . . .'

She didn't finish the sentence. As her voice trailed away I thought I was hearing Mike Bowen's chances trailing away too. But perhaps not. Though supposedly 'open', he had manoeuvred me pretty well. Also he was strong-willed. And of course powered by sexual attraction. Roz might not find herself staying so neutral about it all.

Roz said: 'Tea's ready.' She poured it. 'I'll take Alice's up to her.'

I remained in the kitchen to drink mine in solitude. From a confusion of thoughts, one suddenly stuck out — the extraordinary idea of anyone, not a scientist, who was able to write novels, doing it as an incidental activity in life. Writing novels wasn't like doing scientific research; but it *was* on the same list, so to speak.

I listened to Rosalind's footsteps climbing the stairs, one flight after another, gradually out of my hearing.

My daughter. Aged eighteen. 'Good lord!'

I couldn't help hearing an echo: 'Actually nearly nineteen. But it's immaterial . . .'

CHAPTER FIVE

Meet the Acting Chairman

Before I heard from Bill Taylor again it was about three
weeks after his telephone call when he'd said he would ring
me back tomorrow. 'Perhaps tomorrow' — I recalled the
actual words which I hadn't precisely taken in at the time.
He asked me to meet him in London.

I arrived at Power Centre just before noon and went up
to Bill's office.

'He's got Sir Amos Wilson with him,' his private secretary,
a ladylike girl, told me when I went into the outer room.

'That's O.K.,' I said, while she took my hat from me and
hung it up. She was quite intelligent, presentable, lively.
I wondered why she had never got married.

Sunlight was shining brilliantly through the window. On
the sill there was a large growing plant, small-leaved, with
little pink flowers dotted all over it — 'Busy Lizzie' it had
always been called when I was a boy.

I was shown into Bill Taylor's room.

Bill was sitting at his desk and he jumped up springily.
'Jack!'

He came across to me, holding out his hand. 'Thank you
for coming!' We shook hands.

'I hope you don't mind Amos joining us.' He made a
gesture with his hand towards Amos Wilson, who was standing by the window.

The gesture was something new. Of course I may have
been wrong in thinking so, but that was the way it struck

me. There was something new about the gesture which can be described in one word. 'Grandeur'.

I wanted to smile. Not at Bill, in his new position, making slightly grander gestures, but at his being so caught up in making them that he didn't notice he was making them at his old friends. Maliciously delighted, I hoped to see him make some more.

At the same time, malice apart, I felt relieved and glad, especially glad. Somehow, though I didn't yet know any of the circumstances, I felt he was going to become Chairman. He *looked* as if he were going to be Chairman. Without any doubt.

I went and shook hands with Amos. 'Of course not,' I said, answering Bill.

Bill's office was L-shaped — he had always been rather pleased with it — and we moved from the desk-cum-conference-table part to the other part, where there were some easy chairs upholstered with dark-blue leather, bookshelves and a coffee-table. More sunlight, more windows, more view over London. I remembered his saying, years ago when he became Deputy Chairman: 'I think, when I become Chairman, I shall throw the machine by insisting on keeping this office.' (Norman's office was a huge, long room.)

'We wanted,' said Bill, 'to ask your advice.'

I have to admit I was not entirely certain whether he was referring to himself and Amos or using the royal 'we'.

He grinned; small, strong, bright-eyed, slick-moustached. 'Actually I'm asking everybody's advice.'

We sat down in the leather-covered chairs, and he handed round cigarettes. On the coffee-table there was a big Ronson lighter, which had been presented to Bill by Nuclear Division when he became Deputy Chairman. We lit our cigarettes with it. Amos Wilson read the inscription on it — his fingers were nicotine-stained — before he put it down. He puffed his cigarette as he glanced at Bill and me without saying anything.

'The position is this,' said Bill. 'The Minister hasn't

finally committed himself to reorganising R. & D. Norman told us he had. But he hasn't.'

Amos Wilson gave me a leer.

'He's a pretty decent sort of chap, you know,' Bill went on. 'And the civil servants could be worse.'

I was amused.

'He's prepared,' Bill said, 'to listen to reason.'

'This means,' said Amos to me, 'he's prepared to listen to W. R. Taylor.'

'This amounts,' said Bill, not to be scored off, 'to the same thing.'

I leaned back in my chair. I had a feeling of well-being. Bill, I thought, had established himself in control of whatever was going on.

I considered Amos Wilson's presence. Bill and Amos were clearly in alliance. That was a marvel, for one thing; and very useful, for another. A thought struck me — if Bill got the Chairmanship, was Amos going to get the Deputy Chairmanship?

I considered the absence of Herbert Hobbs.

Bill said: 'What's your view, Jack? Do we reorganise R. & D.?' He paused. 'Or don't we?'

I thought.

'Is it all change?' said Amos. 'Or as you were?'

I looked firmly at Bill. 'All change,' I said.

There was a pause.

I don't know what the other two were thinking, but I guess it was not what I was thinking — which was that Herbert Hobbs had proposed a major change merely to extricate himself from a private impasse to which he'd brought himself through uninhibited personal imperialism; that because Hobbs had proposed it, Bill and I had opposed it; that it seemed from any detached point of view likely to give no more than marginal gain to the N.P.B.; and that now, given a free choice, I said straight off: 'Do it!'

To what, I thought, had the whirligig of Time brought us.

'Would you care to give us your reasons?' said Bill. A month ago he would have said 'Why?'

I paused a moment. The real fact of the matter was that Time, whether it was circling in a whirligig or making a bee-line, was just a vector that went one way only. We simply couldn't, I thought, go into reverse.

I gave Bill some reasons for going forward.

'Of course if you do carve out an R. & D. Division,' I said, 'it's essential that Darwin gets it.'

I was thinking of all the troops at Courtenay Bagpuize, for instance, threatening to emigrate to the U.S.A. if Bert Hobbs's man got the job. (A tiresome lot, they seemed to me at this particular moment, who needed to be sharply smacked and told to stay where they were.)

'This I agree with, in principle,' said Bill, 'and so does Amos.'

I picked up the 'in principle' and waited. Amos Wilson lifted the lighter and read the inscription again.

'The Minister is prepared to listen to reason,' said Bill. 'He's a pretty good chap. The one thing that's been sold him, by Standsfield and Hobbs, is Beckett.'

'Oh Christ!' I said.

Amos Wilson put the lighter back.

I said: 'You'll have to un-sell him, that's all.' I thought it served Bill right. If, in his new role, he had the additional weight to throw about that he'd made some play with when I came into the room, he could jolly well throw it to some purpose. I think Amos Wilson had the same idea.

'This seems to be the assignment,' said Amos. For the time being he didn't look as if he were going to touch any-one for a fiver or offer a hot tip for the 3.21. He merely looked as if he thought it was Bill's line and he had less confidence in Bill than he had in himself.

'Right,' said Bill.

'Right,' said Amos.

If they were in for a penny, I thought, they might as well get a pound — so I too said:

'Right.' (Saying 'right' one after another was an American-ism that had come in.)

The main business of the meeting, so far as I could see, was over.

There was another quarter of an hour's discussion, after which Amos Wilson went away.

I said to Bill: 'What's the news of Norman?'

Bill said: 'The coronary doesn't appear to have been a very serious one.'

'Oh,' I said.

We had walked back to the other part of the room, and Bill sat down behind his desk.

'Does he,' I asked, 'have an estimated time of return?'

'To work, do you mean?' Bill was looking down at some papers, without reading them.

'Yes,' I said.

Suddenly he lifted his head and sat back in his chair. He looked at me.

'I've been to see him, of course. There were bits and pieces I had to show him from here.' He tapped his pile of papers. 'He still *is* Chairman.'

I waited.

Bill looked at me steadily. 'The coronary wasn't a very serious one. But *he's* in a state about it.'

'He was always in a state about his health.' I was thinking that hypochrondriacs usually lived on and on and on.

'He wants to come back to put *me* down again.' Bill laughed harshly. 'But he sounds as if he's terrified of doing it.' His eyes looked unusually light and clear and question-ing. 'What do you think?'

I thought I'd rarely known of hypochondria stopping a hypochondriac from doing something he really meant to do. All I could find to say was:

'With Norman you simply never know.'

'It's generally known that what Norman decides to do is what makes the biggest hell for everybody else.'

In that case, I thought with gloom, he would come back to the National Power Board. I checked myself.

'No. Look, Bill, we're being silly. . . . You've just got to get on with it.'

Suddenly his chagrin disappeared and he grinned.

'This is true. This, as a matter of fact, is what I'm doing, Jack.' He paused shortly. 'As a matter of fact, I'm working on it *pretty hard!*'

Looking at the papers again, he pushed them all away from him.

'Somebody else can have these. Those that aren't too difficult for me are too easy.' He stood up. 'Where do you want to go for lunch?'

I had no ideas. I didn't really think about it. I was thinking that I would go and see Norman myself.

After lunch I went back with Bill to Power Centre and, without telling him, rang up Norman's house.

I was answered by Lady Standsfield.

And I was politely refused.

I was somewhat taken aback, even though I was new to the idea that with Norman anything could happen. I knew that everybody got snubbed by Norman — I'd been snubbed by him in the past. 'Sir Norman has decided to see no one connected with the Power Board, other than Sir William Taylor when there are some papers to be signed.' That message could only have come from Norman, personally.

I returned to Oxford in a state of wry amusement and exasperation.

Alice said: 'What did you expect?'

I regarded it as an unhelpful remark. I said I'd expected Lady S. to tell me when I could go and see Norman.

Alice said nothing.

I speculated on whether Norman's heart attack had been worse than we'd been led to believe.

'It *may* be . . . I mean, it's always possible, isn't it. But . . .'

'But what?'

'It may be that he doesn't want to see you, darling.'

'Or anyone connected with the N.P.B.'

'Exactly.'

I said I didn't see why she found it so easy to comprehend.

Alice said: 'Hasn't it occurred to you that he doesn't like any of you? That he doesn't like being at the National Power Board? I mean he's, well, a *fish out of water*, or something like that. . . . A non-fish *in* water. . . . You know. Everybody else is technological, as you call it, and he *isn't*. He must feel it.'

'Feel it, my foot!'

'I thought you all made him feel it. I thought that was part of your tactics.'

Actually it was.

'So,' said Alice.

I repeated: 'So.' And I thought it over. A non-fish *in* water. Well then, the thing for him to do was to get out of the water, and leave it to the fish. I said to Alice:

'It's a touching idea but I can't really believe there's anything in it.'

'But there must be *something*, mustn't there?'

I saw no end to the argument if I replied. As a matter of fact I supposed, when pressed, that there actually might be something in it. Poor old Norman . . . he gave us a hell of a time but, in a different way, I supposed we gave him one in return. He was reported as saying, when he got into his office in the mornings: 'What are they trying to keep from me, today?' I couldn't believe it. Not Norman.

Alice said: 'I think I shall send him some flowers or books or something. As a sympathiser . . .'

The following day she sent him a parcel of books. And for her pains she got a characteristic acknowledgement.

'*It is kind of you to think that I may be in need of novels to read for relaxation.*'

Even Alice was daunted.

I made no comment, but I felt a strange kind of regret.

It must be awful, I thought, never to be free from that kind of sensitivity.

I made no further attempt to see Norman, and in Oxford we had no news of him.

One evening Bill Taylor rang me up just before dinner.

'I'm speaking from home,' he said. 'I've got to tell you the news — you're going to like it!'

'Oh!' I cried. I could hear the excitement in his voice.

'Official confirmation has been sent me. Of the next stage in my . . . Escalation!'

'You've been promised the Chairmanship — in writing!' I cried, knowing it hadn't anything to do with the next irrevocable stage in a war leading to Armageddon. I was gasping with relief, delight, satisfaction. 'Thank God for that!'

I heard Bill laugh.

'I couldn't congratulate you more,' I said. 'It's simply wonderful!'

'I've got,' said Bill, 'the Green Light!'

What an escalation! What a light! The only thing I wanted to know was when it was going to be. I said:

'Is Norman going to come back?'

'This is not known.'

'Norman knows you're going to get it?'

'The Minister went to see him first.'

'Well,' I said, reverting to delight and satisfaction. 'That's that!'

'Right,' said Bill.

'Right,' said I.

There was a pause. I was surprised that he didn't ring off.

'By the way,' he said. 'This will amuse you. I saw some correspondence between Norman and Charles Quain, about part-time members. About whether the Power Board has too many of them.' He paused. 'They were divided into two categories: those whose contracts should be renewed automatically; and those whose contracts should be reconsidered, with a view to termination. The Chairman had put *you* in the second category.'

Whether I was speaking on the telephone or not, I said: 'Well, f—!'

'This I thought would amuse you.'

'Amuse!' I said. 'That's your idea of amusing, is it?'

Much as I'd always admired him, I'd always thought he was deficient in humour.

A new idea struck me. 'When you're Chairman of the N.P.B. are you going to turn sadist, too?'

Bill thought for a moment.

'No harm is done by cracking the whip now and then.' He laughed. 'Meg says I try to do it at home. But she stops me.' He paused. 'At the Power Board, *you* must stop me, Jack. If you can.'

I said: 'At the present moment you sound as if nobody could stop you doing anything, anywhere.'

'This is how I feel.'

'Alice and I shall get drunk tonight.'

He didn't reply. I guessed Meg would not get drunk with him.

In the telephone the pips went.

'That's all for now,' he said. 'See you Thursday.'

'See you then.'

We rang off.

I can tell you that Alice and I celebrated.

On the following Thursday I went up to a meeting at Power Centre. It was to be in Bill's office and I got there a few minutes early. I'd forgotten to ask Bill on the telephone if Amos Wilson was going to get the Deputy Chairmanship, and whether the Minister had been brought round from seeing Hobbs's nominee as the new Member for Research and Development.

Bill's secretary showed me into his room. Bill was out. I was faintly irritated, because Trevor Darwin was going to be at the meeting and I couldn't ask Bill in his presence about the R. & D. job. I went over to the window.

Outside it was pouring with rain. I reflected on how new buildings with lots of windows made one more observant of changes in the weather. I looked out at a grey sky from which dark veils of rain slowly drifted across the roof-tops. Water splattered and ran on the window-panes. There was a wind blowing.

Bill came in, Amos Wilson with him. I glanced from one to the other. Bill noticed, and, for once, guessed my thoughts.

He nodded his head, grinning, and said:

'Yes. You can presume on the next obvious stage in *his*' — he glanced at Amos — 'escalation.'

I laughed and held out my hand to Amos.

'The Treasury came up with the case,' said Bill, 'that with the Chairman being a Scientist cum Engineer, the Deputy Chairman ought to be an Administrator.'

'Aw s—!' I said, for some unknown reason coming out with America's favourite expletive.

'This,' said Bill, 'I wasn't going to wear.'

So all was well.

Amos looked at me with a wolfish leer, and said:

'What odds will you give me on Standsfield's coming back?'

Bill interrupted us peremptorily. 'Where's Darwin? Where's that sod Hobbs?' He looked at his watch.

'It isn't time, yet,' said Amos. He turned back to me. 'Come on, Jack, I didn't hear what you said.'

I didn't have time to reply. The door opened, and in came Herbert Hobbs.

Tall and heavy, his *embonpoint* swaying and his double chins aquiver, Uncle Bert padded into the room with short steps, his arms standing out at the sides. I hadn't seen him since the day, three months ago, when the visit of Norman's three-man working-party to Courtenay Bagpuize had co-incided with one of my trips there.

'Good morning, Hobbs,' said Bill provocatively, in view of the fact that they were privately not on speaking terms.

Hobbs lifted his hand. 'Just a minute, just a minute . . .' His voice sounded very breathy. I looked at him again. His high rectangular forehead was paler than usual. His eyes had a neurotic look.

Bill stared at him with surprise.

'Let's sit down here for a minute, friends, before we start our meeting,' Hobbs said. He made for the nearest chair at the conference table. 'I've just had a shock.' He shook his big, fat head from side to side.

'Quarter of an hour ago,' he said, 'Bill Beckett came in to see me . . .'

We waited.

'To tell me he's leaving us, leaving the Board.'

'What!' shouted Bill. If the volcano had exploded altogether I should have thought it was completely explicable.

I hope you see the final turn of events in all its ageless force and beauty. With no Beckett to whom Herbert Hobbs's double promise of his own Membership of the Board had to be redeemed, there was no need to have carved out a new Division.

So the gross upheaval in the National Power Board during the last six months *need never have taken place at all.*

'Tell us more,' said Amos Wilson, sitting down opposite Hobbs and watching him with eyes wide-open, if too close together. It had obviously occurred to him that Hobbs might not be telling the truth.

'He's leaving the Board,' said Hobbs. 'It's a great loss to us. He's been offered a place on the board of ——.' (He named a large firm that was rival to Matthewson's.) 'And he tells me he's accepted it.'

Bert Hobbs looked at us accusingly. 'It's all this anxiety. If only we'd been able to tell him definitely that we were going to take him on to the Board here, he'd never have done it. But the strain was too much!' He paused. 'The blame lies fair and square on *our* shoulders! . . .' He took out his pocket handkerchief, just in time to mop up two large tears.

'What I can't get over,' he went on, 'is that he didn't take me into his confidence. I've practically been a father to him. Yes, a *father*! . . . Ever since I picked him out of all the other lads in C. & O. to be one of my two right-hand men.'

I caught Amos Wilson's eye, and he blinked at me. He must have decided that Hobbs was speaking something near to the truth. I looked at Bill. He was still standing up, erect with fury.

A squall of rain rustled across the windows.

Herbert Hobbs lifted his hand again. 'Now I begin to wonder,' he said lugubriously, 'if I was wrong to pick him out. My friends, what do you think?'

None of us, it appeared, was prepared to give an opinion on Bert Hobbs's rightness or wrongness. So far as Beckett's action was concerned, it seemed to me that the man might well have been showing common sense. I had no reason to believe that he was either so vain or so ambitious as to think he was a better choice than Darwin for the new Division. But — and this sounded even more probable — he might well have decided he'd finally had as much as he could take of being mucked about by Herbert Hobbs.

Bill Taylor began loudly: 'I can tell you what I —'

'Don't!' Hobbs interrupted him. 'Let's talk it over quietly, first. We're all disillusioned by Beckett. And I'm the most disillusioned man of us all. You see, I'm asking myself, now, if he hasn't shown us, perhaps just in the nick of time, that he's not the sort of man we want to join us on the Board.'

Uncle Bert looked at us in turn, solemnly and wilily. 'Remember,' he said, 'we're not short of good material on the Board already. I've been having second thoughts. And I won't say they mayn't turn out wiser than the first. . . . It's my belief, now, that we couldn't find a better man for the new R. & D. Division, even if we looked outside the Board, than Trevor Darwin.'

If you can't believe your ears, what you *thought* you heard has certainly been said. That is one of my most convinced beliefs — and I had to call upon it to sustain me now.

I looked at Bert Hobbs, nodding his head gravely, as if he were genuinely under the impression that he was getting away with it. Or was he? *Could* he be? You'd have to be a child, I thought, to think you could get away with something like this.

Bert Hobbs *was* childlike. About every fat man, come to that, there was something almost babylike, I thought; something babylike, along with adult cunning and subtlety. At the moment Bert Hobbs had lost his adult cunning and subtlety.

I looked at Bill and Amos to see how they were taking it. Not well. They were not taking it at all well.

If I'd had any doubts about whether Bert Hobbs had lost his adult cunning and subtlety, they'd have been settled by his next speech. He said:

'And we can fill Trevor Darwin's place as Member for Nuclear Division by that very fine scientist from Courtenay Bagpuize.'

The mesomorphic, unblinking faces of Bill Taylor and Amos Wilson finally expressed something. Contempt.

I looked at Hobbs again. If I hadn't thought he was a most dangerous, and formidable, if childlike man, I should have felt sorry for him. His failure was grotesque — his failure at this particular moment.

'Right,' said Amos to him.

I waited for Bill to say 'right'. He said nothing at all, and in doing that I concurred with him. Feeling contempt for Herbert Hobbs was an indulgence. For the time being Uncle Bert had lost his touch. For the time being only. . . .

Bill sat down at the head of the table, his short military crop of hair catching a grey light from the windows.

'Gentlemen,' he said. 'Let's get on with the job!'

CHAPTER SIX

The President's Portrait

The dining-tables and benches had all been removed from the Swedish-looking dining-hall at Clarendon. In their places were neat rows of numbered chairs. The atmosphere was humid and warm, and the afternoon light, reflected to and fro between the smooth white walls, was radiant. The College's two huge pictures, on the one hand the brilliant hard-edged abstract, on the other the luminous populated seashore, simply shone. At the top end of the room, above the High Table, hung a picture still shrouded. It was the portrait of Lord Forbes, the first President of the College. It was now finished, and its unveiling was imminent.

Midsummer Day. The Oxford season of garden parties was at its height. The undergraduates had gone down; and in gardens, on lawns, dons and clergymen and visitors from the Commonwealth (usually appearing to come from Pakistan or Nigeria) foregathered to eat strawberries and cream and drink tea.

For the unveiling of Stanley's portrait we were going to eat strawberries and cream and drink champagne. The ceremony was to be performed by a very distinguished elderly Cabinet Minister, and many of the participants came from London, from the National Power Board, Whitehall and suchlike.

Alice and I arrived in the College early. Already a lot of people were there, standing about in the quadrangle of sunshine, moving in and out of the open doorway of the

President's Lodgings. They all had glasses of champagne.

'Isn't it a marvellous idea!' said Alice. 'Doris Forbes told me she was going to give everybody a drink first of all. Even she realises unveiling ceremonies are *dire*. . . . I mean, she didn't actually say that. She worked it out that everybody would enjoy the ceremony more if they'd already had a glass of champagne. . . . That's what she *said*.'

Doris Forbes liked her drink, and also, in her coarse-fibred way, had a feeling for the physical well-being of other people. I said:

'It's a marvellous idea, provided that when they've already had a glass of champagne she can get them into the ceremony at all.'

'She's instructed the servants not to serve anybody with more than one glass.'

'Ho, ho, ho . . .' I said. We were going towards the Lodgings. One of the college servants, dressed as a waiter, came up to us and handed us our ration.

Doris came out of the doorway and down the steps. She and Alice exchanged regal kisses. Doris was wearing a hat composed of flower petals, some blue like her eyes, others beige like her complexion.

'I'm afraid He's a bit tired,' she said. 'The excitement, you know.'

I thought that was fine nonsense for a start. Since term was over Stanley had done no work, and so far as health was concerned he appeared nowadays to be in eternal bloom, silvery, pink and ever bland.

'He's in His study at the moment' — she lowered her voice reverently — 'with Dr. —.' The elderly Cabinet Minister was always called Mr. I could only suppose his having been the recipient of twenty-six or more honorary degrees in a distinguished lifetime qualified him for Doris's reverent mode of appellation.

'Oh, good! . . .' said Alice, in what sounded to me like idiotic gush.

'I came down,' said Doris, 'to have a look round.' She

swivelled her opaque glare across the quad. 'I just wanted to make sure they hadn't let that poor boy in.'

That poor boy? I realised she meant Brian Challoner's case of Don's Dread.

'Have you had any more telephone calls?' Doris asked. We shook our heads.

'Good,' she said. 'I've seen him several times in the street. And I've told him I'm looking into his case personally. That keeps his mania down, you know.' She nodded her head with sapient authority. 'Just play them along.' She went on nodding. 'That's the way to treat them.'

'I think it's absolutely noble of you,' said Alice.

Doris glared round the quad once more, and then, with her bottom sticking out, she satisfiedly stumped back into the Lodgings.

Alice and I drank some champagne and turned to find someone else to talk to. Immediately behind us I saw to my astonishment Norman Standsfield and his wife.

Alice and I shook hands with them, glad as well as astonished to see Norman out again. I could not prevent myself from searching in his appearance for traces of illness. He looked much the same, tall and giraffe-like in his civil servant's morning suit, his fine watch-chain looped across the waistcoat, a pearl tiepin in his tie. His grey hair was freshly clipped. His wife stood beside him looking quiet. Neither had a glass of champagne. Were there unusual red spots in his cheeks? . . .

Norman said dramatically:

'It may interest you to know that this afternoon is my *last* public appearance as Chairman of the National Power Board.'

He was watching my expression. Of course I felt relief for Bill Taylor, even triumph. And yet inexplicably I felt regret.

'I can't ignore what my doctor says.' He glanced away, suddenly anxious. 'I've just got to take care of myself.'

Alice said something sympathetic.

Norman turned to her, his expression transformed again. 'Not at all, Lady Alice,' he said. 'There are still some things they appear to want me to do!' He bowed to her swoopingly from the waist. And he gave me a sidelong glance. 'I'm retiring from a full-time appointment only to take up several part-time appointments.'

He knew I must be wondering what they were. Directorships of firms? *Who* could have made him offers? I thought it was typical of him not to allow himself to seem to have been put at a disadvantage even by illness.

'But of course,' said Alice. 'That always happens.'

'I can give you plenty of examples, Lady Alice,' — he smiled brilliantly — 'when it hasn't.'

Alice said: '*How* interesting! . . .'

I wondered if he really would find something to do where the free play of his talents was not marred by the exigencies of his temperament. At this time in his life? It seemed hardly likely. Somehow one felt the pattern must be fixed. And yet? . . . Anyway there must be something in the wind, some job he really had his eye on.

Norman glanced over Alice's shoulder. 'I think I see some more friends whom I haven't seen since my illness. Would you excuse us?'

He had seen, coming into the quadrangle, Herbert Hobbs and his wife. We excused him readily. After he'd gone I told Alice nothing would induce me to go and talk to Hobbs. I felt the effects of the champagne and the sunshine.

'In fact I'm not going to talk to anybody today whom I don't like. And that' — I had noticed a foolish bald head flashing in the distance — 'goes especially for Alec Benda, scribe-in-chief to the Luddite group.'

The Luddites, I have to tell you, were doing well, as anyone knowing Stanley Forbes might expect. I still found it impossible to make Stanley understand that the *only* means of preventing a man like John Farrow from getting his way was to slap him down at the start. Right down to the ground. Nothing else would do. The implacable cannot be placated. Every step you take to placate someone who's implacable is a step only of surrender to him.

The doctrine is harsh, but it happens to be realistic. Stanley recoiled from the harshness. And so it seemed to me only a matter of time, prolonged to the maximum by myself and the other scientist Fellows, before Clarendon turned down prospective students of physics and engineering to make room for students of Eng. Lit. (I didn't imagine Farrow would see the need for more than a token force of undergraduates doing philosophy, sociology, political science and Creative Writing.)

In the beginning I'd thought it very important that Clarendon's students of physics and engineering should be taught something of the Other Culture. How was I to know they'd be eliminated in favour of men who were not only going to study The Other Culture alone, but were going to be stirred by their teachers to hatred of the scientific culture into the bargain. How was I to know? . . . Another of my harsh doctrines was that the answer to that particular question was normally: By the gumption you appear to be lacking.

'Jack! . . . Jack! . . .' Our making our way across the grass towards the alley that led to the Hall was interrupted.

It was Brian Challoner.

He looked as skinny as ever, with his crew-cut. But his expression was furtively bright with happiness.

'I thought you'd like to know. I've just heard . . .' He glanced round to see if anyone in the crowd was listening. 'I've got what I wanted. I'm going to be on this Circus!'

I was delighted. We shook hands. Alice waited to be told exactly what he meant. Meanwhile a servant went by with a trayful of glasses. I said: 'We simply must have another drink.'

'I shan't be around here so much,' Brian said. Fleetingly he gave me a straight, firm look. 'And by the way, I've decided not to join in the move for undergraduate students of my own. And I'm definitely *against* undergraduate students for Farrow.' He broke off. 'I must be getting along.'

He walked a step or two away and then came back.

'In case you haven't heard,' he said: 'Farrow thinks he ought to have a number of students equal to the maximum in any of the scientific subjects. He calls it Parity.'

In spite of the fact that we were all getting more crowded together, he managed to slip away from us.

I'd heard all I wanted to hear. 'Parity!' The affront was particularly egregious because 'parity' happened to be one of the most revered terms in theoretical physics. I could have taken a hatchet to Farrow right now.

'What a lot of people,' I heard Alice saying. And then, above the hubbub, came the trumpet voice of Doris Forbes.

'Come along now, everyone. Come along!'

My doubts about how she would get us into the ceremony were settled. She was much too short to be seen at the back of the crowd, but one felt that she might well be using a lathi or a nightstick.

'Come along now!'

In the hot, humid sunshine some scores of us crowded towards the entrance of the Hall, and in a patient leisurely way, relaxed by the champagne, waited to get in. In the distance we heard the sound of a fire-engine. It seemed to come nearer and then stop.

Everybody went on chattering. Not far away from me I saw Reg Popper and his wife; he gave me the V-sign, presumably expressing approval, on behalf of himself and his friends at Courtenay Bagpuize, of the way affairs had been settled at the N.P.B. They were no doubt satisfied with the Leadership.

We heard the sound of another fire-engine. It seemed unusually loud. Everybody stopped chattering for a moment. Another fire-engine. The sounds came from the direction of the college gateway.

Suddenly the head porter came tearing from his office in the gate-house —

'Where's the fire?'

Behind came a string of firemen in full fighting-kit.

For the next few minutes there was a farcical uproar.

Somebody, we learnt, had dialled 999 and said the College Hall was on fire.

Somebody! On the telephone. . . .

Of course there was no fire.

In the uproar Doris Forbes, I scarcely need to say, gave the display of generalship we would all have expected of her.

'This is how to play *us* along, isn't it, darling?' Alice whispered to me in the crowd as we finally passed through the doorway into the Hall.

I glanced at her.

'I'm not surprised to see you think what *I* think,' I said.

'But what else? *Somebody* dialled 999. . . . I mean it couldn't be anyone else, could it?'

'Sh! . . .'

We found our way to our gilt chairs.

All around us we heard people saying to each other sapiently and happily — after all, they'd been drinking champagne — that it had been a hoax!

Alice and I exchanged peculiarly meaningful glances at that.

'What will Doris do about him?' Alice said.

I shrugged my shoulders.

'She can't ignore it, can she?' Alice persisted.

'No.'

'But you must admit it was a *funny* idea. . . . *Much* funnier than ringing us up at 2 a.m.'

'Sh! . . .'

At that moment applause began, as the main performers in the ceremony made their appearance on the dais under the portrait. I wondered if Minelli had jumped on his bicycle and hared from his telephone box to the college in time to make a dramatic appearance at Doris's side.

He had not; and the ceremony, nearly half an hour delayed, and not commanding quite the degree of attention it might have, began the stately course that Doris Forbes had planned for it.

The distinguished elderly Cabinet Minister pronounced his eulogy of Lord Forbes. Only Doris could have thought he didn't go far enough. He turned out to be a great one — even greater than most speakers of Power Board language — for the American habit of pronouncing the indefinite article as 'ay'. For example: 'Lord Forbes is ay great scientist, ay great President of the College, in short . . . ay great man!'

I spent my time between counting how often he did it, and speculating why everybody did it. Were they afraid that if it was pronounced 'a' the indefinite article might be missed? (There was no need to worry — the Russian language, for instance, had got on perfectly well without an indefinite article, or a definite one, come to that, for donkey's years.) Or did they fear, in excessive refinement of manners, that if they pronounced it 'a' it might be mistaken each time for a tiny burp?

I could scarcely contain my delight when he got to 'ay-gain' and 'ay-nother'.

The portrait was unveiled, predictably signalling the start of a controversy about its merits that was likely to split the college for the next decade. And then we all swarmed out for strawberries and cream in the sunshine, which was by now becoming slightly overcast.

I must have been silent for a little while. I heard Alice ask me: 'What's the matter, darling? You're looking sad. Are you sad?'

'No. Just thoughtful.'

'I suppose thoughts make one sad.'

'No — just the need for more champagne.'

We ate our strawberries and cream, watching the familiar people all around us.

I said: 'It's just the combination of circumstances. Norman Standsfield disappearing from the scene. Stanley Forbes commemorated in oils. You know, end of an era . . .'

'But eras are *always* ending. That's how you know we're having *eras*. Anyway, darling, Bill Taylor's era is just beginning. You must admit *that*.'

I wondered why she'd suddenly brought in Bill.

She said: 'Look at him!'

I followed her glance. There was Bill, standing alertly balanced with his feet apart, one hand thrust into his trouser pocket, the other holding a glass of champagne. His solid, square head, though placed several inches lower than that of the men he was talking to, somehow rose from his shoulders in the epitome of confidence; and whatever he was saying to them must certainly have been brash.

'Oh Gawd . . .' I said, laughing.

From beside us came the sweet voice of Roz. 'I've been looking for you two.' Behind her stood Mike Bowen. They were both looking happy.

'Just after you'd left there was a cable from George,' Rosalind said. 'His film's finished and he's flying back from L.A. straight away. Katie rang up — she'd had a cable, too. She's coming tonight after her show's over. . . . Julie's wild with excitement.'

Alice and I glanced at each other. We knew each other's thoughts. George and Katie — Roz's novel. Could Roz be wrong? In fact at this moment, when Roz was thinking about George and Katie, rather than the characters in her novel, she seemed absolutely unworried.

Then Alice said to Roz: 'Didn't you bring the cable?'

'Oh darling Alice, can't you be satisfied with my telling you?'

We all laughed at Alice.

Alice looked Roz up and down. 'That's a pretty dress.'

Roz blushed. I thought what a pretty girl she was. (I didn't ask if, and how, she had won the money to buy it with.) In a couple of months she would be going away to California.

And George and Katie would be taking away Julia.

I found it impossible for the moment to say anything.

Mike Bowen said: 'Let me get you some more strawberries and cream, sir!'

Roz said: 'It's champagne he wants.'

I said: 'You can get me both.'

They went away. I could understand why Roz looked so bright-eyed and happy, but not why Bowen did — she had told him quite clearly that she would not marry him.

And then I remembered that at his age the presence of one's beloved is strong enough to obliterate all thoughts of when she is gone. I thought: I wonder what's going to become of *them*. . . .

Alice said: 'Bill's coming to talk to you.'

I saw Bill making his way through the crowd.

'Jack.' He looked up at me, grinning. 'You've heard the news.' He meant the news of Norman's not coming back to the Power Board.

'I have.'

We stared at each other.

'He's decided not to come back. This is something I don't understand.' He laughed. 'Effort will not be employed by me to persuade him to change his mind.' He looked away momentarily. 'Now we can all get cracking.'

'When the dust has settled,' I said idly.

Bill glanced quickly at me. His slickly trimmed little moustache changed its line. 'There's some more dust to be raised first, Jack.'

'What do you mean?'

'We'll let Hobbs get his K. And then the next stage in *his* escalation has to be arranged.'

'What's that?' I felt dismay.

'The High Jump.'

I stared at him again, this time quite separated in feeling from him. He went on.

'You always told me he was my — what was your phrase? — my most formidable enemy. Well, this was true. I'm now able to see it.' He paused. 'He's for OUT.'

'Is this feuding never going to end?' I cried.

Bill said curtly: 'This isn't possible as long as Hobbs is in the Power Board.'

I might have said: This also is true. All the same my spirits had been curiously dashed. I said:

'Where will he go to? How can you get him out?'

Bill said: 'Remember it's agreed by everybody that the National Power Board is too big.' He grinned, as if he felt he were getting the better of my dismay. 'I'm getting out a few scenarios.'

I couldn't believe he meant to get rid of Coal & Oil Division. Just the idea of that made me quail too much to go on with the conversation. Was he being vindictive? Was he only doing what men in his position always did? Was he even talking straight common sense?

Bill looked up at me, and his light eyes shone as if he were trying to set right my feelings by offering pure friendliness.

'You were right, Jack. You know you were right. This is true.'

I hadn't the faintest idea what he meant I was right about, but I smiled.

'That's for you to say,' I said. 'And I don't know that it makes any difference — I scarcely expect you to take my advice . . .'

'You ought to, Jack.' He looked at me, tilting his head to one side. 'You ought to.'

'Oh?' I laughed now.

He went on looking at me in the same way. 'You're a man,' he said, 'you know, of . . . many Expertises.'

I burst into laughter frankly.

Bill smiled out of friendliness — he didn't see anything funny. Then he said:

'I've got to get back to London now, but I want to see you soon.'

He got out his diary and we made a date.

Then he went away. I said to Alice:

'How about leaving?'

Alice said: 'It's time you left, isn't it?'

I said suspiciously: 'What do you mean?'

She said: 'You're looking terribly . . . not sad, you said you weren't sad. I can see that. But . . . elegaic.'

'Good God!' I laughed. 'Anyway — Midsummer Day and you're aged fifty-five: wouldn't you feel elegaic?'

'My dear.' She slipped her arm through mine.

We made our way to the college gateway. When we got there I disentangled her arm. I said:

'Will you go home by yourself?' I paused. 'I think I'll go back to the lab for an hour.' I saw her surprise. 'Actually while we were listening to the eulogy of Stanley Forbes I had an idea.' I paused again. 'I think I'll just go to the lab and *try* something.' I laughed at her. 'You know, on the back of an envelope.'

Alice said: '*I*'ve had an idea! For your next birthday I'm going to buy you some envelopes with *backs* on both *sides* . . .' Her brow looked clear, her eyes sparkling hazel.

'I won't be long. It'll either work or it won't.' I kissed her cheek. 'See you later!'

With a laugh Alice turned to go home.

PRINTED IN GREAT BRITAIN BY
NORTHUMBERLAND PRESS LIMITED
GATESHEAD